Praise for Terry Spear's
Deadly Liaisons

"Ms. Spear has a way with words, creating a paranormal mystery sure to hold you spellbound as the twist and turns of the tale unfold. A must read!"
~ *Karen Michelle Nutt, PNR Paranormal Reviews*

"Terry Spear writes a gripping story that holds this reader spellbound."
~ *Cherokee, Coffee Time Romance & More*

"There were some get-the-ice cubes love scenes between the two, but the mystery and the twists about all the killings and the investigation kept my interest throughout."
~ *Amazon Nymph, Literary Nymphs*

"Daemon made me fall in love with vampires. He was so real and sexy I wanted to say, 'Bite me, baby. Bite me!'"
~ *Nicole North, author of Devil in a Kilt and Red Sage Secrets Vol. 27 Untamed Pleasures*

"Readers will be quickly engrossed in Daemon and Tezra's emotionally charged story. Terry Spear's world of vampires will have the readers begging for the series to continue."
~ *Rhonda Valverde, VampireRomanceBooks.com*

Look for these titles by
Terry Spear

Now Available:

Writing as Terry Lee Wilde
The Vampire...In My Dreams (YA Vampire)

Deadly Liaisons

Terry Spear

A Samhain Publishing, Ltd. publication.

Samhain Publishing, Ltd.
577 Mulberry Street, Suite 1520
Macon, GA 31201
www.samhainpublishing.com

Deadly Liaisons
Copyright © 2010 by Terry Spear
Print ISBN: 978-1-60504-332-6
Digital ISBN: 978-1-60504-240-4

Editing by Jennifer Miller
Cover by Scott Carpenter

First Samhain Publishing, Ltd. electronic publication: March 2009
First Samhain Publishing, Ltd. print publication: January 2010

Dedication

I dedicate *Deadly Liaisons* to my mother, who introduced me to my first vampire story, a play at Brevard Community College opening night, where everything that could malfunction did. From the actors repeatedly tripping over a rug onstage, to the mist disappearing before Dracula slipped down through the trapdoor, we loved it! And years later, I enjoyed seeing Dracula on Broadway, which again made a wonderful impression. I thank my daughter for all the help she gives, and my family for all their encouragement. To my Rebel Romance critique partners who weren't "into" vampires until they read mine and now several write their own versions. To my editor who helped to make this the best it can be. And especially to my fans who make writing the stories all worthwhile.

A final note: My mother died of breast cancer the night of the ebook release of Deadly Liaisons. So I wish to further dedicate Deadly Liaisons to those stricken with the disease of cancer and to the families and friends who comfort them in their time of need. My thoughts and prayers go out to you.

Chapter One

Streetlamps poked scant fingers of light into the gray fog coating the warehouse district, deserted at the ungodly hour. *Perfect conditions for another murder.*

Unable to slow her racing heart, she feared the renegade vampire would hear the blood whooshing through her veins, begging him to take her life also.

Not far from where she stood, the dried blood of the three policemen murdered last week—their jugulars ripped out—stained the pavement. *Too close for comfort.* She wanted to move away from the spot, to distance herself from the recent killings, to be anywhere but here.

She peered into the murkiness, straining to see any sign of movement, listening for any human sound. Where the hell was the police officer she was to meet?

Come alone, Officer Stevens had warned. And she'd obeyed. Had to, if she was to learn the bloodsucker's name. Yet, she couldn't shake free of the feeling she'd been set up. Though she'd risk anything to learn who had murdered her parents.

Drawing in a deep breath, she felt like she'd stuck her head in a freezer and taken a good strong whiff. Even the turtleneck, leather jacket, matching pants and knee-high boots she wore couldn't keep out the chill—typical Oregon autumn.

She poked her wristwatch again. Stevens said he would be here—ten minutes ago.

Dread bunched in the pit of her stomach. It was eerily like ten years before when three police officers had been murdered, except she was a sixteen-year-old huntress-in-training then, not yet an investigator with the Special Crimes Unit. She stared into the mist, half expecting Patrico to meet her like he'd promised ten years ago. A senior member of the League Council, he was the only one who'd believed in her theory that a vampire had murdered the police officers. That the same vampire had killed her parents. But Patrico never showed up and later was found dead—here—as if this was the vampire's favorite killing ground.

The mist thickened, enveloping her, sending a shiver up her spine. Was it him? The bloodsucker she vowed to destroy? Would he kill *her* this time?

Dammit, get a grip!

Unnaturally, the air warmed around her. The mist caressed her hair, leaving the strands wet down her back, her cheeks moist and her jacket dimpled with speckles of water. The faint fragrance of Green Irish Tweed—the same cologne her father had worn a decade ago—haunted her.

It was *him*. The vampire spawned from hell, wearing the cologne he'd stolen from her parents' home so long ago. Her skin crawled with dread. She concentrated on his emotions—cool, collected, amused. The mist thickened around her, like all the other times he'd plagued her when she was out in the open during the evening hours or on a gray day. *Him*, not the usual weather-induced vapor.

Muscles tensed, she touched her wrist blades to ensure they were in place. Instinctively, she grasped for the sword sheathed at her waist, the silver blade capable of destroying a rogue vampire with just a nick to his heart. Though while he was in the form of mist, she couldn't harm him. Not until he shape-shifted into something that had a heart. She *hmpfd* under her breath. Heart? He had none—in any manifestation.

"Show yourself, you bastard, let's end this now." With a whoosh, she unsheathed the sword. If only she'd killed him long ago, but it was too late now for regrets. Too late, yet she kept rehashing her mistake. If she hadn't taunted the bastard with her telepathic ability...

"Tezra." The serial-killer vampire whispered her name telepathically, intimately, as if they were lovers.

Before her emotions could unravel any further, a man called out, "Tezra Campbell!"

Her heart jumped. Officer Stevens! His footsteps stalked in her direction.

Before she could shout back and let him know her location,

the footsteps and their echo died.

"Officer Stevens?" She hastened toward the last sound of him, her sword readied, her skin prickling with apprehension. She knew when he didn't respond, when his footfalls died...

Tears pricked her eyes, and she slowed her pace.

Her breath caught, and she froze. Crumpled on the ground, Officer Stevens appeared like the other three police officers had a week ago, nothing more than discarded refuse.

With a hesitant step, she drew closer. "Officer Stevens?"

A different fragrance lingered in the air—sandalwood. The officer's? Or someone else's?

She paused and attempted to sense another vampire's presence. To see if the emotions nearby were different from those exhibited by the one who had murdered her parents. A barrage of rage from the vampire hit her. She'd never felt that kind of blind anger from the killer who'd murdered her family. No, he was cool and always composed, as if he played a game. Not so with Stevens's attacker. He seemed bent on revenge. She tightened her hand on her sword, but she had to see to Stevens.

Sword still readied, she crouched beside the police officer. Her free hand trembled as she felt his wrist. Warm, barely any pulse. Then his heartbeat stopped. Her head pounding, she reached up and jostled his shoulder. Part of her brain knew it was already too late, but the other half couldn't assimilate the truth. Stevens fell back against the asphalt. A strangled cry escaped her lips.

The man's blue eyes stared vacantly, his mouth gaping. Blood spilled from his torn jugular onto the pavement and touched the tips of her boots. As if the bloodsucker had been rabid, angered beyond reason, the monster had ripped Stevens's throat open, dug his fangs all the way to the spine, breaking it and leaving a shower of blood on the asphalt and nearby warehouse brick wall.

Nausea swamped her. She bolted away from the body and emptied the contents of her stomach. At the same instant, she sensed the vampire who'd murdered her parents changing into a solid form, his aura ancient, one of those turned by the Black Death that swept through Europe in 1347.

Staring into the mist, she gripped her sword tighter. Wolf? Bird? Maniacal man? What form would he take to terrorize her this time?

This was how she'd learn the bloodsucker's name tonight. He'd give it to her before he killed her.

"You wish my name, sweet Tezra." The air rippled with his calming presence, different from the other murdering vampire, whose antagonism she still sensed close by. *"You shall soon know it."* A hint of dark promise coated his telepathic communication, then the atmosphere of tranquility vanished and she knew he was gone.

Ten years ago, she thought she could unsettle him by showing off her telepathic ability, taunting him with the knowledge she knew he'd killed the police officers, hoping he'd make a mistake and she'd learn his name. Then she could have turned him over to the Council of Hunters and they would have terminated him for the murders he'd committed.

Until he showed her just how powerful he could be. By murdering her parents and then Patrico, he proved how naïve and stupid she had been as a gullible sixteen-year-old huntress-in-training. If she could only turn back time...cloak her abilities like she had always done...

But it was too late now. The terror of the night her parents died could never be reversed.

The remaining vampire still lurked nearby. As angry as he was, she was certain he murdered Officer Stevens and the officers a week ago, based on how identical the killings were. Now she had to investigate two serial killers who used different methods of operation—one who'd killed police officers recently and the other a decade ago. Yet the fact both were here at the same time indicated they were in collusion.

Focus, she commanded herself. She stared into the misty dark and attempted to sense anything further about the vampire. He remained silent, motionless. She reached out her empathic abilities and sensed anger still seething in the being hidden from her sight—close enough to make her skin crawl.

Jerking her cell phone off her belt, Tezra called her best friend. "Mandy," she choked out.

"What's wrong, Tezra?" the police dispatcher asked, her voice ripe with concern.

"Let Chief O'Malley know there's another police officer down. Dead." Her hand shook, and she fought to gain control of her emotions. "Warehouse district."

"I-I'll tell the boss," Mandy said. "Who was it?"

"Officer Stevens."

"Oh, God."

"Don't let the Special Crimes Unit get wind there's been another murder or that I'm here or there'll be hell to pay."

"Yes, all right. Can you hold?"

"Yeah, but hurry the guys out here, will you?" It didn't matter Tezra was a highly skilled investigator or trained in self-defense by the Special Crimes Unit. The fog, the cold, the sight of Officer Stevens's body and the dreadful sensation that the murderer of the police officers lurked nearby put her on edge. If only he'd show himself, she'd prove to the SCU she had what it took to be a huntress.

Tezra paced to warm her chilled blood, the cell phone pressed against her ear while she waited for further word. Her gaze focused on the area she sensed the vampire loitered.

"Tezra?" Mandy said, breaking into her concentration. "Chief O'Malley wants to talk to you."

Tezra waited for the questions he was bound to ask. Why had Stevens planned to meet her here? Had she seen who'd killed him?

"Investigator Campbell, a couple of units are on their way," he said, his voice strangely gruff.

"If the SCU learns about this, they'll be all over the case. You know I'm not allowed to work any high profile cases right now." *Again.*

She was not a rogue, dammit. Yet, that's what the powers-that-be at the SCU always tossed in her face—"borderline renegade". If she didn't get a grip, she'd be eliminated from the SCU forever. So what was she supposed to do? Review small-time cases—a vampire biting a woman without her express permission, a case of a vampire changing an underage human. Sure, the vampire crimes weren't acceptable. And sure, they needed investigators handling cases such as these. But she had a calling to right the bigger wrongs. Some investigators were more geared to handling the mundane stuff and were happy to do it. Not her. She really wanted to be a huntress—terminating vampires who murdered in cold blood.

Hunters of vampires had been affected by the same plague vampires were centuries earlier. The hunters' blood had resisted the virus to a greater extent, but had also mutated to a certain degree. The increased strength and ability to hear like vampires set them apart from humans unaffected by the plague. Unlike vampires, hunters didn't have the thirst for blood, couldn't shape-shift, exist as semi-immortals, or see in the dark—though that aspect would be really handy right about now—and rarely had telepathic abilities.

It was as if balance had to be brought back to the world. The hunters were capable of dealing with vampires who chose to murder helpless victims when most mere humans didn't have the strength to fight them.

So technically, she was a huntress from birth, only due to SCU politics her job was investigating crimes instead of serving as a huntress who terminated the evil vampires.

"Yeah, but I want *you* to handle the investigation," the chief said.

Tezra shoved a wet curl off her cheek. "You know how the higher-ups are. When it comes to cases like this, they choose their own investigators with no direction from any other law enforcement agency. Hell, they're like the FBI when it comes to dealing with local policing agencies."

She was still waiting for the chief to question her as to why she was here in the first place. Her typically overactive imagination was already dredging up all kinds of murderous scenarios, one involving the chief. She really had to get a hold on reality.

He was mute for so long, she thought her phone had disconnected. "Chief?"

"I know who killed your parents."

Feeling like she'd been kicked in the chest, she could barely breathe. Then for an instant, she thought something moved closer to her.

She readied her sword to swing it in case the vampire changed to solid form and encroached on her space. There were no sounds in the warehouse district—no traffic noises or birds chirping at this time of night, and because of the cold—no bugs, nothing but the rapid beat of her heart sending the blood rushing like Niagara Falls into her ears.

But there was no warmth like she'd felt before either. She saw nothing but the unrelenting fog, the dead officer, the blood puddled on the pavement, the red contrasting with the gray. She took another deep breath and could smell no odor but the wet, chilly air.

Maybe the vampire had left. She couldn't sense his anger any longer.

"Who was it?" she asked, her voice rushed, certain before the chief could tell her, the murdering vampire would silence him too.

"Krustalus."

She let out a breath. She considered hundreds of leads she'd had, but the name didn't mean anything to her. "How—?"

"I've sent the units and want you to take charge."

She parted her lips to speak, but the phone clicked dead, the name "Krustalus" lingering like an open lesion in her mind.

But that didn't matter. If Krustalus killed her parents, he was hers to terminate.

She pocketed her phone, tightened her hand over the grip of her sword and listened for the arrival of police vehicles bringing more city cops to aid her. She stretched out her ability to sense other beings, searching for any sign of the evil that might still lurk nearby. Then the distant wailing of police sirens pierced the fog.

She cursed under her breath. She'd warned both Mandy and the chief to maintain this under wraps until she had time to investigate! So much for keeping the murders quiet for a little while.

She had to get tissue samples from the dead policeman before the SCU learned she was working on the case without their permission. She had to confirm that the same vampire who killed Stevens had murdered the officers of the week before and ensure he wasn't Krustalus.

The whining sirens jangled her already raw nerves. *Can you make it any more obvious?* she wanted to scream. Maybe if the police stayed off the radios—now monitored closely by the SCU after the police had botched another case and eliminated an innocent vampire—she'd get away with her investigation one more time.

❧

Tezra's skin prickled while the ten city police officers aiding her investigation studied her every move. At least she no longer sensed the vampire who had most likely murdered Stevens in

15

the area.

Attempting to ignore the uneasiness growing in the pit of her stomach, she turned Officer Stevens's head and considered the way the vampire's fangs had dug all the way to the spine, breaking it.

But then something else seized her attention, held her hostage.

"A dark huntress." The words hissed in her mind, his threatening telepathic communication forcing a chill into the marrow of her bones. Not Krustalus. Not the angry vampire either. Someone else.

Involved in the crimes also? Or just curious?

Having the rare gift of being able to read anyone's mind in the vicinity, she knew the policemen's thoughts, and none triggered her concern like whoever this was. The police already knew she was SCU. Hidden from her sight—watching her like a predator waiting for the right moment to proceed with the kill— he recognized she was not just another city police officer.

And not just a huntress by birth, but a borderline rogue. She frowned. How had he known?

With the skill of an ancient telepath and empath, she sent mental tendrils into the mist, trying to sense his emotions, listening for any further telepathic communication, dangerously drawn to the creature. But what was it that made him different from the rest? A hint of sexual fascination—he desired her, to a degree. And the notion intrigued her, when it shouldn't.

She shook loose of the perilous feelings sucking her in and realized six of them—not just the one—silently watched, sitting on warehouse rooftops across the street, all newly arrived.

She sensed curiosity from the unseen beings in the fog. They must have turned up while she was concentrating on her investigation. Which was the problem with being an empath. Like listening to several conversations at once and not hearing any, she couldn't concentrate on multiple tasks at the same time. She had to focus—and now, that's just what she was doing. Trying to sense if any of these newcomers were in complicity with the murdering bloodsuckers.

Unique as a voice, their telepathic messages reached out to one another, communicating freely amongst themselves— assuming no human could hear them.

"Bad news," one said. There was no malice in his tone, only

soft regret.

Another grunted. *"Knew it would come to this."*

From farther away in the old warehouse district, one hissed. *"Like hell you did."*

"It'll get much worse before it gets better." This one sounded like the seer of doom. *"She won't be able to deter him any more than..."*

The vampire seer of doom quit speaking when the one who'd tagged her as a dark huntress growled his disapproval and again communicated to the others. *"A huntress from the Special Crimes Unit."*

The others instantly grew silent as if he warned them this investigation was now in the hands of a different kind of predator. One who could more readily seek out the rogue vampire and have him terminated.

Another glided in on the fickle breeze in raven's form, swooping too close to her for a normal bird, too late at night to be anything but a shape-shifting vampire. Checking her out? Taunting her?

He flew to one of the flat warehouse rooftops. Like a flock of birds of prey, they stood on top of the two-story brick buildings observing, their communications silenced. Like an invisible energy field full of electrical activity, the ancient vampires' auras radiated more power than the others'. Three had lived many centuries.

Tezra prayed with fervor they knew who murdered the police officers, would spill their secret, and tonight she would have the identity of the beast.

Boots tromped toward her at a hurried pace. Illumination from the police flashlights reflected off the fog, casting an eerie glow over the few visible feet.

Before the body belonging to the heavy footsteps came into view, she knew who it was. Bernard, her hunter watchdog, short, squat, mean and determined, like a well-trained Rottweiler. His broad nose had been broken in a barroom brawl. A raised welt across one cheek—where a vampire's extended canine had dragged across it before Bernard killed him—had left a permanent white scar on Bernard's otherwise tanned face, adding to his roguish appearance. His stifling sweet cologne and the heavy odor of onions on his breath reached her when he drew close.

She ignored him, knowing he'd question her reason for being here even if Chief O'Malley failed to. If it meant locating her parents' murderer, she wouldn't give up the investigation, not even for the head honchos at the SCU.

Bernard crouched beside her. His black hair, normally neatly bound, dangled loose about his shoulders, which meant someone had roused him from his bed, most likely yanked him from the arms of a sleeping woman. He leaned even closer and spoke in a hushed, harsh voice. "The SCU didn't approve your taking this job."

She offered him as straight a face as she could muster. "The City asked me to check into it and the SCU agreed to the arrangement."

Bernard stared at her, his blue eyes widening. The bushy black brows that bridged his nose elevated. "Your name isn't on the active investigators list," he said, his voice wary.

Nope, the SCU had removed her name from the list of officers credentialed to investigate high-profile renegade vampires. And definitely wouldn't have approved it. But if she could bamboozle Bernard...

"Special assignment," she prevaricated.

He gave her a look like he didn't believe her, then considered the dead officer. "So what do you think is going on?"

Thank heavens he was going to let her get away with it. He was probably as concerned as she was about the killings—the SCU be damned for not allowing her to search for the truth. "I'm wondering what madness propelled him to murder these officers." She couldn't shake loose the images of the ones she'd examined years earlier. "Remember those cop murders from ten years ago? The three officers slain by a hunter's sword?"

"Yeah, so what has that got to do with this case?"

"I think the recent killings are connected to the earlier ones somehow, but that two different vampires committed the atrocities. Although a more farfetched theory is that only one bloodsucker is involved and after all these years he changed his MO. In that case, he could be trying to cloak the older killings. Or is his mind teetering on the brink of madness, like a human serial killer who has to murder for the compulsion and thrill?"

Thankfully, Bernard voiced no opinion while she tried to work out the scenario aloud.

"No, too implausible. Two vampires were here tonight.

Krustalus—the vampire who murdered my parents—taunted me, but I'm sure he didn't kill Officer Stevens. Speaking with me, then eliminating the officer isn't his way. Too easy to assume he did the killing. Besides, the sandalwood cologne I smelled was someone else's. Or was that his ploy? Confuse the issue? But no, another was there who seemed angry with the world and continued to loiter a while longer. Gloating over the killing, probably. Maybe wanting to see what I'd do next."

She paused, afraid she'd let her empathic secret slip. Bernard's expression darkened, but thankfully he didn't ask how she knew another vampire was there.

"Krustalus? You have a name now for the one you claim killed your parents?"

"Chief O'Malley gave it to me."

His frown deepening, Bernard considered the dead officer again. "Your guess is as good as mine."

Grinding her teeth, she vowed to catch them both.

She motioned to a policeman. "Measure how deeply the teeth sank into the officer's throat, and have the medical examiner send the tissue samples to me. Oh, and find out what cologne he wore."

The officer raised a brow quizzically. "Yes, ma'am."

"You come from a long line of investigators and hunters with the SCU," Bernard said to Tezra. "Hell, I think you're the only current member who has ties to some of the first who settled in America prior to the Revolutionary War. You don't want to be the first one in your family to be kicked out."

"Second, but who's counting?" She was proud of her heritage, but the SCU would *not* dictate to her when it came to proving the vampire—Krustalus—murdered her parents!

"The situation with your Grandmother Irving isn't the same. Becoming the rogue vampire's lover when she was supposed to eliminate him—"

"I still can't fathom why she did it." The thought any huntress would set aside her convictions to fool around with a renegade vampire curdled Tezra's blood.

She rose to her feet and studied the surrounding warehouse district. Except for the brick building poking out of the mist six feet from where she stood, she couldn't see a blamed thing.

"You're setting yourself up on this one," Bernard growled.

19

"Why?"

"The SCU doesn't feel this job warrants one of their more prominent Special Crime investigators, so they gave it to me as a special assignment. Just to get me off their backs for a while." She hoped she wouldn't be struck dead for lying, but it was the only way to continue her work to determine the truth behind all the killings. Under her breath she added, "The targeted victims are eerily similar to the ones murdered ten years ago—same occupation, precinct, approximate age, and all male." And the fact that Krustalus was here when Stevens was murdered? He had to be connected somehow to the recent ones too.

She faced the police officer in charge of the site. "I'll give a report to your chief by midday tomorrow."

"Yes, ma'am."

"That police dispatcher, Mandy Salazar, hooked you into this job, didn't she?" Bernard asked.

Heading for her car, Tezra didn't answer him.

"She's bound to be the death of you."

"*True,*" the seer-of-doom vampire said.

Tezra fought looking in the direction where he stood and said to Bernard instead, "Listen, despite the SCU frowning on my relationship with Mandy, she's been my friend for the past four years." She gave Bernard a scathing look. "When I needed someone, you were there for me, and so was she. I don't care that members of the elite vampire investigative and elimination unit don't normally socialize with regular police. Since when have you known me to live strictly by SCU rules?"

She shoved her ice-cold fingers into her pockets. "But no, Mandy didn't solicit my help in solving the crimes this time."

And neither had the police chief. Just Officer Stevens's urgent communication sent privately to her: *Come alone and I'll tell you the name of the vampire who murdered your parents. Warehouse district. An hour from now.*

Had the bloodsucker forced Stevens to lure Tezra here, using his vampiric abilities to persuade his victim? So that she would witness Stevens's death firsthand? Yet, the vampire didn't show himself, wouldn't give her the chance to fight or identify him. *Bastard.*

Bernard growled. "Hell, you know Mandy likes women better than men, and a lot of guys are beginning to infer things about your relationship with her."

One of the vampires snickered. *"That negates my interest in the dark huntress."*

"Wouldn't stop me," another said.

"Silence!" the one who'd originally called her a dark huntress said.

He was the one who intrigued her the most. Since he seemed to be in charge of the others, did he know anything concerning the murders?

Trying to ignore the vampires' telepathic communication, but not about to take Bernard's bait, Tezra raised a brow. "Aren't you supposed to be sleeping or something?"

"Senior Member Ingrid alerted me you were here without anyone to watch your back."

Tezra let out her breath, exasperated that the senior staff already knew of her involvement, but surprised Senior Member Ingrid hadn't told Bernard to stop her. She'd hoped Bernard had gotten wind of it on his own, the way he often did in matters concerning her, playing his bodyguard role to the hilt.

"If you aren't careful, Bernard, the renegade vampires will want to eliminate you too." If he'd kill Patrico and her parents, why not Bernard also, since he was her bodyguard? She didn't want the bastard vampires to murder anyone else, and Bernard would be a prime target.

Ignoring her warning, he asked, "How do you know it's a he?"

No vampiric communication now. Everyone waited for her response. Wouldn't they be surprised to learn their own words confirmed the murderer was a he?

"Deeper bite marks. Severely crushed windpipe. The vampire who did this appears to have an uncontrollable rage." No way could she tell Bernard she'd heard the vampires' communications. Keeping her telepathic and empathic abilities secret was the only way to get along in this crazy, mixed-up world.

"I'll give the senior staff a report on your actions tomorrow morning. They won't let you continue to conduct the investigation."

Unruffled, she poked the buttons to the keypad of her Ford Taurus. "It won't matter now, will it? I'm already involved in all of this mess, and Krustalus will continue to come after me. I won't have a choice *but* to terminate him." The other also, since

21

she was certain he wouldn't want her to learn his identity and he'd target her for termination next. She didn't have the legal right to eliminate bloodsuckers except in self-defense, but if she ever confronted either of them face to face, she imagined legalities wouldn't be an issue. She yanked her door open.

Before she could slip into her car, Bernard seized her arm. "You need a hunter mate to keep you in line."

"What? You think I belong to that all-exclusive members-only club? Just because a lot of you feel the female investigators and huntresses should marry only within their ranks, don't include me, buster."

Tezra sensed one of the vampires' anger. Internally, he bit back a hiss.

The others merely watched, intrigued. Would her hunter bodyguard force her to obey? That's what crossed their egotistical minds. Except for the one. He was different from the rest, his feelings darker, sometimes hidden, sometimes worn across his chest like a banner for all to see. For now, he barely contained his rage, which totally threw her. Why would he care how Bernard treated her?

She jerked her arm free from him. Hunters could be as arrogant as vampires. "Go home to your concubine."

The murdering vampire wasn't watching her any longer. But what if the ones who observed them were in league with the murderers? All they'd have to do was relay everything she said or did to the others. Faking agitation, she poked her finger at Bernard's chest and raised her voice, willing to do anything to keep the killer vampire from targeting him next. "You're *not* an investigator! Leave this to the professionals!"

"Dammit, I know what you're attempting to do." His words were couched in anger, and he spoke low for her benefit only. Bernard growled at her. "You think he's watching us, and you're trying to keep me safe. But the SCU cannot afford to lose a brilliant investigator."

"Brilliant investigator? Why, Bernard, I think you might be interested in me."

"What's the use?" He shrugged. "You shun any hunter's attempt to make you his own."

"I'm not ready to settle down. Besides, SCU hunters have to keep a squeaky clean profile. None would be interested in a woman who tests the rules so much. Even borderline hunter rogues probably figure I'd get them into even deeper water if they had anything to do with me."

"You wouldn't have to settle down completely. Don't you ever desire something more than this?" He motioned in the direction of the crime scene. Then his callused fingers touched her cheek, and he leaned down to kiss her lips, his onion breath repulsing her.

"Sorry." She placed a hand on his chest and stepped back. For now, she was more concerned with how the vampires might see her relationship with him. "Besides, you're all talk when it comes to settling down. Hell, several women keep your bed warm on alternate nights." She cocked a brow and his lips curved up. He'd never do as a marital prospect. "Got to go."

He folded his arms, a frown digging into his temple. "Why the SCU ever selected me to watch over you is beyond my comprehension."

"They know we get along so well. Talk to you later."

He shook his head. "You'll be the death of us both."

Yeah, if he didn't keep his nose out of her affairs, she feared one of the murderers would attempt to kill them both. Unfortunately, the stern look on Bernard's face indicated he wasn't about to let her do this on her own. She would have to use some stronger tactics of persuasion to convince him to leave well enough alone, or go underground with this like she'd done concerning the other group of unsolved murders. The SCU definitely wouldn't approve. Which meant more trouble was bound to head her way.

Glancing in the direction of the buildings where some of the most ancient vampires still stood, she sensed they represented far more difficulty for her than the Unit could ever dish out.

"Another killing, Atreides?" Daemon turned away from his twin brother and again studied the SCU investigator, Tezra Campbell. He'd gained her name from the police officers' discussion of her when she was far enough away not to hear their crude comments. Not a few of them wondered what it would be like to peel the leather from her skin and expose the beauty beneath, to roll with her under the sheets, to find out if she was as hot in bed as she looked crouching at a crime scene.

The petite brunette tucked her hip-length hair behind her ear, the leather pants molding to her curvaceous legs and the short-waisted jacket showing off one hell of a sumptuous ass. The black turtleneck wrapped around her throat like protective armor. Daemon found himself wanting to pull it aside and feel the blood pulsing rapidly through her neck, to taste her tender skin, lap up her warm, sweet blood and sense her tremble beneath his fingertips, drawn to his power.

He clenched his teeth, trying to ignore the feelings she stirred in him. Lust, nothing else, he chided himself. Yet, there *was* something about the woman that drew him in, more than her enticing form or resolute determination to take on a case that would earn her the death penalty from the vampire who had killed the police officers. Even more than the way she tried to ensure the hunter's safety should the rogue vampire target him next.

Daemon could have sworn she touched his mind, though normally humans couldn't do such a thing. Yet, the gentle stroke he had felt hadn't come from a vampiress seeking intimacy. If it had, she would have pursued him and attempted to solicit his response. The touch he had felt had been different, like the mist brushing his skin, softly, almost imperceptibly, there. No quest for sexual fulfillment, no personal communications meant solely for him. Something secretive, elusive and intimately seductive.

She closed her car door, and the engine roared to life.

"Such is the way of this violent world," Atreides finally said, as if he'd been caught up in the woman's mesmerizing qualities too.

Daemon's twin looked nearly identical to him except for being a tad shorter, his sable hair slightly less dark, and his eyes more of a chestnut brown, paler than Daemon's. Tonight Atreides wore a black leather trench coat, like he always did when he was on the prowl for a new blood bond. He appeared to be in one of his stranger, unfathomable moods. Something was percolating, but despite Daemon's attempts to catch glimpses of his thoughts, Atreides kept them shielded. Which meant Atreides was up to something. How many times would he have to get his brother out of some misadventure that might get them both killed?

"You had nothing to do with this police killing either, Atreides?" Daemon asked.

"Why do you always think so ill of me?" Atreides pointed to another warehouse. "More of our kind watch, as curious as we are about who's killing the police officers. So what do you think about the new investigator?"

"She's *not* a regular police officer, but an investigator with the SCU—worse, a borderline rogue, a dark huntress, who is bound to cause even more trouble."

Atreides's lips turned up so slightly, only someone who knew him as well as Daemon did would have noticed. "Ups the stakes a bit for the killer, don't you think?"

The muscle in Daemon's jaw tightened. "If he kills her, there'll be an outcry from the SCU. No doubt we'll have another bloodbath on our hands."

The woman's car disappeared into the fog.

"Many of us liked the good old days," Atreides said.

"Back to the slaughtering, back to a time when vampires preyed on humans and SCU hunters eliminated any vampire to even the score. An inhumane period of darkness for humans and vampires." Daemon shook his head. "You're not still angry over Uncle Solomon's death, are you?"

He knew his brother was. Knew the wound still festered from losing the last of their natural kin to overzealous cops investigating murders committed by a killer vampire they had *assumed* their uncle had been involved in.

"If you want to help the investigator, look elsewhere for the killer. You know he'll target her next."

"She's offered herself like a sacrificial meal." Daemon grunted. "A foolishly arrogant notion. Though the murderer will have a more difficult time of it—she'll be easier to kill than a hunter, but infinitely more of an...interesting challenge for the rogue than the city police officers."

"Will you aid her?" His brother's lips turned up, his eyes sparkling.

"What do you think?" Daemon couldn't help the sharpness edging his words.

Atreides hesitated to respond, wearing an odd expression that Daemon couldn't read.

"You respect their work to a degree, but have no more love

for them than they have for us," Atreides finally said.

"Despite your preference for the good old days, Atreides, I want peace for everyone's sake."

If Daemon was forced to, he'd help the woman with her investigation to keep that peace. But only if there were no other alternatives.

A strange sense of foreboding washed over him. No matter how much he wanted to stay uninvolved, he couldn't fight feeling Tezra Campbell would soon need his protection. Nothing worse than tangling with a member of the SCU who viewed vampires with disdain.

"Don't do anything to get yourself into trouble, Atreides," Daemon warned, then headed to the police station to find out more details concerning the killings. He'd locate the murderer *without* involving himself with the woman.

At least that was the plan.

Except for the second bedroom she'd converted into an office and lab, Tezra's apartment was cloaked in darkness. Perched on her leather chair, studying samples from two previous killings on slides under the microscope, she rubbed her temple to massage the headache brewing there. Too many late-night hours investigating the murders. She took another sip of her coffee and grimaced to find it cold. The phone jangled, shattering the peace and her nerves.

Lifting the receiver she said, "Yes?"

"You...you needed to know about my husband, Officer Stevens?"

"Cynthia Stevens?" Tezra hadn't thought the bereaved woman would call her but that someone from the police force would. The sound of the woman's barely controlled emotions didn't help Tezra keep her own feelings out of it.

"He...he didn't wear cologne. My...my husband. He was allergic to stuff like that. I couldn't even wear perfume or he'd..." Cynthia broke into fitful sobbing.

"I'm...I'm so sorry, Cynthia. I...I wish I could have saved him."

"You? What could you have done against the demon?

He'll...he'll kill them all." The phone clicked dead in Tezra's ear.

He'll kill them all, echoed in Tezra's tired brain. He'll kill who all? All the men at the precinct? She slowly let out her breath. Hell, now what? She needed to know what Cynthia knew, but she figured the widow was too distraught to question at the moment.

But the business about the cologne...didn't it prove that two vampires were present tonight? One wearing her father's cologne, the other wearing sandalwood? And Krustalus had attempted seductive solicitation while the other vampire was filled with rage?

She glanced at her watch. Where the hell were the new tissue samples?

As if in answer to her unspoken query, her front door opened. She knew damn well she had locked it. It shut with an ominous click. She sat frozen, listening for footsteps. There was no sound save the central heater rumbling as hot air spilled through the overhead vent.

Slowly, she slid her chair away from the desk toward her sword. A rush of adrenaline flooded her system, readying her for the perceived danger.

Before she could reach her sword, a man appeared in the doorway of her office and silently observed her. An ancient vampire. Since she had not invited him in, who the hell had? And why had he come through the front door? A game, maybe. To give her warning he was on his way, taunting her. Or perhaps to ensure she was all alone in the apartment, to avoid complications should there be a hunter here to protect her back, lounging in bed, waiting for her to finish her work.

The vampire's dark brown eyes watched her with unblinking severity. His sinister look and the size of him—six-feet, broad-shouldered—chilled her to the bone. Dressed in black slacks, shoes and a satin shirt, large-collared with full sleeves, he reminded her of a well-clothed pirate. The buttons opened halfway down his chest revealed a smidgeon of dark brown hair, triggering the notion he was marketing his goods— to conquer, to will her to him, to sate his hunger. He looked starved while he devoured every inch of her with his sexist glare.

Bolting from the chair, Tezra yanked her sword out of its stand next to the desk. Her heart thundered, and she knew the blood pulsing rapidly through her veins would trigger his bloodlust. Yet, he watched, no reaction at all.

"How did you get in?" she snapped. She spread her feet apart, giving herself better balance, preparing herself for his attack.

"What have you learned about the killer?" His voice, dark and deep, could seduce a female human easily into offering her throat to him before he bit into her jugular.

"Why? Are you afraid I've told the police who you are?"

His lips twitched.

She didn't waver in her stance. She couldn't kill him unless she was certain he was a rogue. Then again, if he advanced on her, she'd assume the worst.

"If that were so, what name did you give?" He walked over to her microscope, leaned down and peered into it as if he owned the place.

Her ire grew.

Since the distance between them remained the same, she shifted to ensure she still would meet him head-on if he attacked. Her hands clammy, her sword grew heavy while she kept it raised and ready for a fight.

The name *Daemon* flittered across his mind...and hers.

Daemon looked up from the slides when she didn't respond.

"Your name's Daemon." She would have enjoyed the fleeting look of surprise that crossed his face if it wasn't for the danger he represented.

He opened his mouth to speak, then shut it again. He rose to his full height. "How do you know my name?"

She wasn't afraid of him. Being killed by a vampire in the line of duty was an honorable way to die, though she wasn't really contemplating defeat. "I've been investigating you," she lied.

He studied her, trying to break through her mental barriers to find the truth. The gentle probes stretched out to her, attempting to locate a weakness in her resolve, but her telepathic shield to keep him from penetrating her thoughts remained in place. His face grew shadowed in darkness. "When you wish to be honest, you can do some work for me."

She raised her brows. *Conceited bastard.* "Why have you

killed the policemen?"

"*Dark huntress,*" he telepathically said, his gaze willing her to surrender to his superiority, his charm.

Pursing her lips, she fought showing her surprise. He was the one who'd tagged her as a dark huntress while she was investigating Stevens's murder. The same vampire who'd seemed sexually fascinated with her. The one who appeared to be in charge. Her skin tingled with fresh awareness, though she tried to keep her reaction neutral.

Then with a noble air, he cocked his head slightly as if dismissing her question. "You'll get nothing from me until you tell me how you know my name and have connected me with these crimes."

No one knew of her telepathic abilities except Krustalus. Not even what was left of her family. And she aimed to keep it that way. No way did she want the SCU to use her like they had her Aunt Jessica and her aunt's lover, Camilla. The organization had manipulated them to find out information—even going so far as to pry into areas the SCU shouldn't.

"How did you get into my apartment?" she asked again, her voice razor sharp.

Daemon appeared only mildly annoyed, as if she were an insignificant pest. "If you won't cooperate, so be it." He waved his hand and vanished, transporting in the way of the vampire, their movement so fast, the eye couldn't follow.

A chill trickled down her skin. She couldn't help feeling he was the invisible man, watching her. She knew he wasn't here since vampires could not hang about in a completely invisible state, but that didn't dilute the unnerving feeling that a part of him lingered in her office—maybe because she still detected the faint aroma of his spicy cologne. Nor could she wipe out the tingling in her brain where he tried to penetrate her defenses.

A knock on her door sounded, making her jump half out of her skin. Certain it was finally the police officers with the tissue samples from the crime scene, she strode down the hall to the front door, ready to give them a tongue lashing for arriving so late. She couldn't crush the anger swirling in her blood that someone—probably her apartment manager—had let the vampire into her place, either. Now, Daemon could return anytime he wanted. She peeked out the peephole and was only vaguely surprised to see her faithful hunter watchdog, Bernard, standing on the porch. Icy blue eyes and his haggard face warned her of trouble.

She opened the door, but before he even spoke, a hint of red caught her eye, and her gaze shifted to the parking lot.

A police officer lay deathly still next to her car, the blood pooling from his throat onto the gray concrete slab.

Chapter Two

After carefully examining the officer's body, Tezra discovered he wasn't carrying any tissue samples—*if* he had been the one bringing them to her. A gold wedding band encircling his finger looked brand new, and her heart sank deeper. She examined his I.D. *Alex Mitchell.*

Hating she had to make another call like this tonight, she contacted Mandy, explained the details of the murder, then repocketed her phone. She considered the way he'd been killed, the same MO as the others. Why hadn't the police taken more precautions? Cynthia's words came back to haunt her. *He'll kill them all.*

"Pack your things. You're coming home with me," Bernard said, his words spoken as an order but in a monotone fashion, not gruffly, not braced with a hint of fight as she expected.

"It'll take me a minute." She touched the policeman's hand. He looked much younger than the others, a rookie? Not the same as the other killings. The killer's way of telling her to leave the case alone? She swallowed hard, but her throat was dusty dry.

When Bernard didn't say anything, she glanced up at him. He appeared confused, not bargaining for her to sweetly agree? No smart-ass reply? Man, he had to be awfully tired if he was going to give her the silent treatment.

She surveyed the mist, but didn't sense anyone in the area. "Did you kick your bed guest out already? Where am I supposed to sleep?"

Bernard motioned to the apartment. "Get packed. I'll watch for the police."

She hesitated, not used to giving up a crime scene before

the officials arrived, but it was looking bad for her always to be the first one at the scene of the crime. He stared at her as if annoyed she wouldn't do as he asked.

"All right." She returned to her apartment and looked around at the chintz-covered sofas, the light wood furniture, the first she'd had since she'd been on her own. As soon as she could, she had to move her belongings to a new secure place. Somewhere the vampire, Daemon, couldn't enter at will. *Damn him.*

She stalked into her bedroom. Covered in a pale blue comforter, her bed waited for her like a lover with open arms. She realized then how exhausted she truly was. Tired of the killings, of chasing the vampire but not cornering him, of worrying about another murderer who might kill more, tired of getting nowhere fast. She filled her leather bag with clothes, personal items and two hunter's swords.

Bernard's couch made into a double bed in his studio apartment. She *really* didn't want to sleep with him. But the SCU senior staff must have sent him for her, and with Daemon gaining access to her place and another police killing—this one too close to home—it was just as well she stayed somewhere else for the night.

She returned to the living room where Bernard stared back at her, his eyes tired.

"Why aren't you waiting for the police?" she asked, her voice rising an octave.

"They're here."

No sirens this time? She shook her head and handed her suitcase to Bernard.

Would the SCU put a real stop to her investigation? She pulled the door open, planning to go to Bernard's pad. As soon as he fell sound asleep, she'd leave and find a place where she could investigate undisturbed.

When she and Bernard left her apartment, she glanced in the direction of her car. No body. "Where's the crime scene? The tape? The police?"

"The SCU's handling it."

Bernard tossed her bag into the backseat of his pickup. His blue eyes seemed to hide some deep-seated sorrow. When she tried to read his mind, it was void of any thoughts, just like her mind would blank out when she was really tired.

She glanced back at the spot where the officer had lain. *Damn the Special Crimes Unit.* As fast as they'd handled the site, they must have brought an army. "Which officer is handling it now?"

Bernard didn't reply.

With the lateness of the hour, she figured he was as exhausted as she was. Or maybe he was more exasperated with her than usual.

That something more was amiss didn't register—not until they were on their way across town to his place, and it finally dawned on her they were going in the wrong direction. As if dipped into a half-frozen lake, her skin chilled, fear taking root at once. Had the SCU ordered she be put into protective custody for her own safety?

Tension filled every fiber of her being. She wouldn't be incarcerated ever again if she could prevent it. She'd go mad if they confined her.

"Where are we going, Bernard?" When he didn't respond, a dreadful feeling of claustrophobia forced her heart to speed up. "Bernard, where are you driving me?"

"You shouldn't have taken this job," he said, his voice emotionless, not like him at all. He should have growled at her, scowled at her.

Her thoughts swirled with renewed worry, and she rubbed her temple, trying to get her concerns under control.

"I know, I know, Bernard. You're so right," she said, pretending to go along with the charade. "I'm not going to do any more investigating into the matter. Isn't that what the SCU has decreed?"

He glanced at her, his look detached.

Twice now, she'd said something totally out of character for her. And twice he'd responded in the same way: uncharacteristically. What the hell was wrong with him?

"Bernard, tell me where you're taking me."

He didn't reply.

"The SCU thinks I'll what? Jump out of a moving truck if I discover you're taking me somewhere safe? Hell, I know that's what you're doing." She crossed her arms with false bravado. "I'm glad you came when you did. What with the visit I had from the murderer…"

Bernard glanced at her but didn't say a word. Now she *really* knew something was wrong. If she'd told him that earlier tonight when he was acting more himself, he'd have thrown a fit.

"Anyway, then the police officer with the tissue samples was killed before he reached me and the samples stolen..."

Again, Bernard looked at her, but his gaze shifted to the road once more.

She attempted to read his mind again, hoping for some inkling of what was the matter. *Nothing.* She reached out to touch his arm. This time he looked sharply at her. Gladdened to see a more typical reaction from him, she patted his shoulder and concentrated on his thoughts.

Nothing on Bernard's mind—a completely blank slate. Though there never was any guarantee her abilities would perform under sleep-deprived conditions.

Taking a deep, calming breath to placate her raw nerves and focus her energy on planning her escape, she leaned into the soft leather seat. She listened to everything around her while the pickup sped down the dark two-lane road, trying to determine where he was taking her.

She turned her attention to the scenery. They'd slipped out of the suburbs into the countryside, but nothing seemed familiar.

"Listen, I know that sometimes the SCU resorts to using strongarm tactics to put rebel investigators and hunters in line, which I am *not*, Bernard!"

She still vividly remembered the time when two of the hunters confined her to a chair, got into her face and tried to coerce her into giving up the notion that a vampire had killed her parents. The way they had treated her like she was some kind of a criminal made her believe they were all in on a conspiracy. Which was making her feel horribly delusional right now, and she had to keep her mind straight on the matter. A vampire killed her parents. That's what she knew.

"Are...are you taking me to SCU headquarters?" She tried to sound sweet and innocent, and not hotter than a boiling kettle of water. The place the headquarters personnel met was kept secret since the vampires threatened annihilation of the SCU two years earlier. So it would make sense that she wouldn't know the location, but—

Then a vampire communicated close by. Her skin immediately crawled, and her senses went on higher alert. She wanted to warn Bernard, but she couldn't without alerting him that she had telepathy.

"Where are you?" a dark voice telepathically asked, one of the voices Tezra had "heard" in the warehouse district after the police officer was murdered.

Who the hell was he speaking to?

"I'm nearly there." Bernard sounded relieved he was getting rid of his passenger soon.

Bernard? Her heart nearly stopped. Somehow he must have lost the battle with a couple of vampires despite how strong and capable he was.

She touched her wrist blades, giving herself a slight sense of security. Out of reach, her swords were in her bag in the backseat. Though she couldn't kill Bernard just because he'd been turned, not unless he threatened to harm her.

"You've done well, Bernard," the vampire communicated, his voice clipped.

"She asked me where I was taking her."

"You didn't tell her." A hint of alarm edged the vampire's words.

"No."

"That's good. Not too much of a struggle, I gather?"

Tezra detected a bit of humor, hopeful maybe that she hadn't come so willingly?

"She came without questioning."

Yeah, dammit, and if she'd been thinking more clearly, she would have definitely been more on guard. Trying to keep her temper in check, Tezra shielded her mind from the vampires, hoping they'd slip and tell her something useful. Like which of them had killed the police officers.

In a flash, a vampire appeared in the backseat. His smell was different from Bernard's—a slightly spicy cologne, new leather coat and a hint of blood, indicating he'd probably recently fed. The nape of her neck tingled with anxiety. In such an awkward setting, she couldn't maneuver to get at him. To her horror, he reached over the seat, grabbed her wrists and rested his cheek against hers.

She ground her teeth in frustration and twisted to wrench

herself free from the ancient vampire's strong grasp. If she could reach the goodness in Bernard, she still had hope.

The blood rushed from her arms and hands while the vampire held them up high, effectively keeping her from opening her wrist blades. He chuckled darkly when she struggled—amused to bring her to her knees? She wasn't on her knees yet, damn him.

When the truck pulled to a stop, she renewed her struggles, though she felt the uselessness of it.

Bernard opened her door, and his heavy cologne and familiar onion breath greeted her. The traitor leaned over and removed her wrist blades while the vampire in charge continued to hold her still.

"Remove her boots and cell phone," he commanded.

Bernard bowed slightly, and she wanted to slap him hard. *Break free from his spell, Bernard. You can do it! Don't let them own you.* Her silent prayers could be only that. Her heart felt as if a ton of lead suddenly encased it when he yanked off her other boot, where her last concealed weapon, one of her favorite daggers, remained.

After Bernard finished disarming her, the other held on tight. To show his absolute power over her? Without her weapons, merely a plaything of a vampire?

Gloat for now, you bastard, but you'll get yours, she wanted to scream.

Bernard removed her cell phone, caught her wrist when the vampire let go and tugged her out of the truck.

"Here I'd seriously considered marrying you, Bernard. The deal is off," she growled.

He stared at her, and she wondered if the message had filtered to his vampire-controlled brain. Hustling her up the walk, he moved her quickly into the house. Once inside, she couldn't tell how many vampires were in the house, their minds shouting with a mixture of thoughts—confusion, anxiety and anger that the vampire had brought her here.

Bernard pulled her down a long, narrow hall and into a dark room. Not a hint of light illuminated the place. She couldn't see a thing, only felt the vampires lurking in a semicircle around her, watching her like the ones had done while she had crouched at the scene of the dead policeman. Electricity vibrated between them, thick with white-hot heat.

Were any of these vampires from her previous run-ins, borderline rogues, not bad enough to terminate but definitely standing on the edge between civility and chaos? Tilting her nose up and smelling, she tried to identify any of them. Masking the vampires' unique scents, a pungently fragrant shampoo had recently been used to clean the carpeting.

"You shouldn't have brought her here," one of the vampires communicated.

"Take her to the room I prepared for her," the one who had ridden partway in the pickup ordered. *"She's mine, and no one will disobey me in this."*

Tezra sensed he was the only ancient in the room. For now, he didn't seem to want her dead, but she figured it was only a matter of time.

"We have gone along with you thus far, but you have—" The vampire suddenly quit his communication, and every one of them remained silent.

The one in charge would have no disrespect from his rabble rebels, she figured, though she missed the cue because of the darkness of her surroundings. He must have given a look that silenced them, or conveyed the message privately.

Bernard led her into another dark room and sat her on a mattress. "Sleep," he said with tenderness and handed her a blanket.

The strong scent of vanilla wafted to her. Triggered by the sweet fragrance, she fought the bile that rose to her throat. It was the same smell that had assaulted her in the kitchen where her parents had lain dead, the bottle of vanilla extract shattered in a million glass fragments. Chocolate chips, flour, sugar—all scattered on the tile floor, mixed in a pool of her parents' blood.

She shook loose from the painful memories and attempted to determine who stood nearby. Listening for a sign that any of them were with Bernard, she sensed the leader's presence— darkly contemplative, the heat of his body too close, his scent the same she'd smelled in her apartment—way too appealing.

"Go, join the others, Bernard. You have done well tonight and have earned my respect."

Tezra wished she could touch Bernard's thoughts, to free him from the vampire's control, but she had no way to reverse what the vampires had done to him. She prayed they'd leave her alone so she could concentrate on finding a way to escape.

She shielded her mind, which came as naturally to her as taking a breath. She hid her thoughts always as a habit to keep herself safe, but she'd learned to do it only after she'd put her family's lives in jeopardy. She mentally squashed the feeling of hopelessness deep into a pocket, closed her eyes and pretended to sleep.

"*I feel you are much more dangerous than you appear,*" the vampire said. "*My brother is too concerned about you, too drawn to you. What are you contemplating?*"

The idea he knew she could communicate telepathically sent a shard of ice hurdling down her spine. Then she realized he was only speaking to himself and couldn't break through her impenetrable shield.

"*Daemon is here,*" a panicked vampiric voice said from the other room.

Her heart raced, her mind a fog, but any lure of sleep instantly faded. The vampire who had gained access to her apartment was involved in taking her hostage? Hell, why should that surprise her?

The vampire near her bed cursed under his breath. "*I'll be right there.*" The door shut and the lock clicked.

Hoping none of the vampires had been left behind to guard her, Tezra sat up on the squishy mattress and listened. Shrouded in darkness, she couldn't see a blamed thing, yet she sensed no vampire nearby.

The vampires communicated with each other in the other room.

"*Daemon, what a pleasure.*"

"*You mean, 'what a surprise', Atreides. What are you up to now, my brother?*"

The one who had kidnapped her was Daemon's brother?

Not wanting to miss a word, Tezra barely breathed.

"*Why do you always fault me?*"

"*Don't play coy with me. You have turned Tezra's bodyguard. Why? When the SCU learns he has disappeared, there will be an uproar, and I won't have it.*"

So Daemon wasn't in on changing Bernard, nor had he anything to do with taking her hostage. Still, he could have murdered the policeman at her apartment and planned to kill her too.

"He isn't totally turned. He hasn't fed."

"And he won't. You'll wipe his mind of the night's activities and free him," Daemon warned.

She sighed, a bit relieved he'd let Bernard go. She sensed the hostility growing between the two brothers. Would Daemon aid her too?

Not wanting to chance it, she made her way to the door and groped around the wall until her fingers touched a light switch. With the utmost care, she flipped it up. No illumination. The blood rushed in her ears, her adrenaline surging. Feeling her way past the bed to the window, she touched the top of the frame and flipped the lock open with a metallic click that she was certain the vampires could hear all the way to the California border. Moonlight glistened off steel bars caging her in just like the home for troubled teens where she'd been incarcerated. She swore under her breath.

She closed her eyes and tried to reason a way out.

Struggling to make the right choice, she thought to reach out to Daemon. She'd let him think it was another vampire telling him the truth about her captivity, only she'd channel the message to Daemon and only Daemon.

Her head pounded with a mixture of exhaustion and frustration. She wasn't certain she'd be successful, and she was afraid she'd let Atreides or the others know she had the telepathic gift.

She intended to copy one of the younger men's thoughts to disguise her own telepathic voice. She was certain Daemon wouldn't recognize it as hers, because she'd never shared her telepathic voice with him, but maybe he'd believe her, or the man she pretended to be, and come to her aid.

"The others seem to be hiding some news from me. What has happened, Atreides?" Daemon asked before she could attempt her ruse.

"You already know about the other police killing. You got the tissue samples from him. So what else do you want to know?"

Daemon took the samples? Her heart thumped even harder. Then Daemon must have killed the officer before he came to see her, or maybe right afterwards and before Bernard came for her. Or had Bernard been there too, and witnessed the whole affair? *Damn Bernard!* The SCU hadn't removed the body. The vampires must have.

"What's wrong, Daemon?" Atreides asked.

Dead silence.

"Daemon?" Atreides sounded like he was in big trouble, and she was in even bigger trouble if Daemon had killed the officer and found her here.

Holding her head in her hands, Tezra kept her mind shielded and quiet, wishing she could slow her racing heart.

The wooden floor creaked while one of the vampires paced. The pacing abruptly stopped.

"Is someone in the house? Someone not of our blood?" Daemon was trying to locate her, to hear her blood rushing pell-mell through her veins.

"No. No one. Why do you ask?"

"Damn, Atreides, who have you got locked up in the house this time? It's...a woman."

Atreides didn't respond.

Daemon stormed down the hall until he reached her room. She dashed across the floor, but before she could make it to the bed, he appeared inside. Though she couldn't see him, she recognized his spicy scent. Backing up, she bumped into the bed's unforgiving, hard oak footboard, instantly trapped. She raised her hands to defend herself, hating to feel so vulnerable without her weapons.

"Dammit to hell, Atreides," Daemon growled, moving toward her, the hair on her arms standing at attention.

Atreides appeared next to him. *"Sorry, Daemon. I only meant to keep her safe."*

For a minute, silence ensued, then Daemon laughed out loud, a heartfelt, gut-wrenching laugh from the belly.

Tezra couldn't figure out the joke. Atreides seemed sincere in wanting to keep her alive. So why did Daemon think it was so funny? Because he didn't want to keep her that way?

Trying to calm herself, Tezra took a deep breath.

"What should I do with you, huntress?" Daemon asked.

She wasn't a huntress by occupation, though if the SCU had allowed it, she would take on the role in a heartbeat and eliminate every renegade vampire there was.

She glowered in Daemon's direction, unable to do anything more, and felt the heat of his body so close her own skin grew feverish.

"She will vanish and you will tell no one I have taken her," Daemon said.

Vanish as in they meant to kill her?

"The others know I brought her here. They'll notice she's gone."

"Tell them she slipped away, but you won't tell them she's with me."

Atreides spoke again, this time with a mixture of regret and accommodation. *"I will do as you ask."*

Nearly giving Tezra a stroke, Daemon wrapped his arm securely around her waist and pulled her hard against his body. Before she could cry out, or pull away, or scream in protest, he yanked her into a black void of space, transporting her the way of the vampire. Her head and stomach swirled as she teleported with such speed. The air wooshed past her in a rush as if she were on a wild carnival ride in total darkness.

She closed her eyes, hoping she didn't perish during teleportation.

Chapter Three

Daemon deposited Tezra on the guest bed in the dark cellar, the perfect place for SCU troublemakers. Normally he used the windowless room for visiting vampire friends desiring a deeper sleep and to store his favorite bottles of cabernet sauvignon, pinot noir and chardonnay racked against the concrete block walls. Stark otherwise, but perfect for his needs.

Particularly at the moment.

For some time, he considered the woman, her posture rigid, attempting not to show her fear. Tezra glowered at him, her heart still racing exasperatingly fast.

Daemon flipped on a light in the cellar with a wave of his hand. The unsettling woman squinted under the glare of the exposed 150-watt bulb overhead.

"Why do you think I'm the murderer?" he asked.

Her mutinous expression didn't falter as she crossed her arms under her breasts, her chin tilted up in obstinacy. He couldn't help staring at her rounded breasts in the form-fitting black turtleneck. The way her nipples began to harden intrigued him. What would it be like to touch them, to hold her breasts, weighing each fleshy mound in the palm of his hand?

His gaze shifted to her defiant green eyes, the gold star that shot out from the pupil entrancing him. *Entrancing him!* An ancient vampire who in six hundred and fifty years had only been enchanted once before by a huntress of the elite Special Crimes Unit.

He hardened his resolve to keep his interest in her strictly business. He wouldn't permit the killer vampire to terminate her and create a war between his people and the hunters. Simple as that. "You *won't* ignore my questions. When I ask one of you, I expect to be answered, civilly."

"You killed the police officer and stole the tissue samples," she accused, her tone icy.

"The officer was already dead. You're tired. I venture you wouldn't stay awake for more than an hour if I shut off the light and allowed you to sleep." He attempted to read her mind, but a wall surrounded her thoughts, deterring him, irritating him. "But I won't afford you the opportunity if you don't answer my questions."

"Barbarian." She spoke the insult with hatred. She hadn't a clue what barbaric really meant. Not like what he'd seen during the wars before he was changed. "Let me see the tissue samples," she ordered.

"What evidence do you have that suggests I'm the killer?"

Her full pink lips pursed.

"Well? I'm not a patient man. In fact, lack of patience is one of my greatest faults."

"Try arrogance."

He smiled, not meaning to, but he couldn't help it when the woman, petite of stature, deprived of sleep, imprisoned against her will, could still make a sarcastic comeback.

"What would it be like to lie with you? Full of vinegar, sparring with me at every turn?"

Her eyes darkened and widened at the same time.

In his mind, he quickly readdressed the situation in the warehouse district. Had she been the one who touched his mind with a gentle probe like a sensual caress? A huntress telepath?

He had to know if she was the one who'd touched him so intimately. *"You smell like roses, springtime fresh. Your warm, sweet blood streaming through your veins, begs me to satisfy my growing bloodlust."*

Speaking the truth at every turn, he studied her reaction to his mental taunt. He hadn't fed for two days because of the police killings, because it sickened him that one of his kind could stoop so low. For the time being, he couldn't force himself to take a human's blood, even though he wouldn't hurt the donor.

Her blood pounded wildly in her veins like an aphrodisiac, luring him to take his fill. She tried to remain emotionless, but her cheeks blossomed with color, the tinge of pink spreading to her neck. Her breasts rose with her quickened breath.

"No woman is immune to me. We're alone. Why don't you admit you find me...irresistible?"

"Arrogance is the only thing that becomes you," she snapped.

Hell, she *was* telepathic. That certainly shed a different light on the situation. "Sleep, well, huntress."

After shutting off the light, he left her alone in the room to contemplate her situation further. Maybe after she slept she'd be more cooperative.

Shaking his head, he seriously doubted it.

Upstairs, Daemon poured himself a glass of wine at his bar and stared at the high-ceilinged greatroom, full of antique mahogany furniture covered in dark brown brocades and velvets that had been in his family for centuries. He contemplated his next move concerning the murdering vampire when the woman screamed from her cellar prison, interrupting his thoughts.

"Let me out of here, you...you—"

"Sleep, Tezra." He considered forcing her to sleep, but—

"Don't tell me what to do! Daemon, let me out of here!"

Before he could respond, his longtime friend and confidant, Maison, asked from outside his home, *"May I enter?"*

Tezra grew quiet as death.

"Come in," Daemon replied, slightly perturbed by the intrusion, but suspecting word concerning the huntress would soon spread, and several of his kind, even the killer, might attempt to see him.

His blue eyes wide with curiosity, Maison appeared next to him. He wore his golden hair tied back in a leather strap. Jeans and a buttondown collared royal blue shirt was his typical attire despite his being the regional director of the vampire clans in Oregon. "I've heard disturbing news."

Daemon motioned to Maison to silence his words. He poured a glass of Chablis for him, then led his friend to the couches in the greatroom. "We have a guest."

Maison listened for several moments to detect Tezra's presence. Her blood pulsed rapidly through her veins, enticing any vampire within range. "She's not one of us."

"No, but she has telepathic abilities."

Maison's facial expression changed from curiosity to concern. "Why have you...you do not think she will make a superior blood-bonded mate, do you?"

Daemon choked on his wine and sputtered, "No."

Maison rubbed his square chin and concentrated again. "Then why is she imprisoned in your cellar, if I may be so bold as to ask, my prince?"

"Atreides took her hostage."

"Damn, Daemon. You know how many already think he's involved in these killings."

Irritation flowed through Daemon's blood. His brother couldn't be the murderer, though even he had some doubts as to the state of Atreides's mind since the police officers had killed their uncle. "It isn't him."

"Every time another city police officer dies, he's glad. Even though we know he isn't involved, his actions make him suspect."

"He tried to protect the woman."

Maison's blond brows arched. "The one in your cellar? I hear her rapid breath, her pounding pulse, even the gnashing of her teeth. Who is she?"

"The one the murderer will target next."

"The woman from the Special Crimes Unit who's investigating the murders?" At first Maison frowned, then his face lit up. "The bait. Very clever of you. I feared you had fallen for another one of them."

Daemon scowled at him.

Maison quickly said, "I understand your reasoning for taking the woman into custody."

"We can't afford an all-out war between the SCU and the vampire clans. That's where this is headed if this maniac recruits copycats, especially since some already admire him for his brashness, feeling humans aren't of consequence anyway. But those of the SCU are a different matter. Because of their training and cunning, and since they were affected by the plague like us, some rogues feel they're much more of a match and want to target them. The rogues' actions are folly."

"I agree." Maison took a seat and drank some of his wine. "What's the plan?"

"We find the renegade and terminate him."

In many ways, Maison and Daemon were a lot alike. They had both been through so many wars the images of blood and broken bodies blurred. They wanted the best for their people and everyone else concerned.

"Let me out of here, Daemon!" Tezra screamed.

Daemon's jaw ticked as he fought smiling at the woman's tenacity. "I'd assumed she'd fallen asleep."

Leaning forward, Maison set his half full glass on the coffee table. "When will you let the others know you have her?"

Daemon glanced in the direction of the cellar. "When the trap is set." He turned to face Maison. "In any event, I don't want her harmed. If she remains on her own, whoever the killer is will most likely eliminate her. When the word goes out that I have her in protective custody, I'll need you, my brother and three of our most loyal friends to help safeguard her. Until then, have an additional security detail provide perimeter protection."

"When do you want the word sent that she's here?"

"I need to learn what she knows about the killer. The more we understand about who he is and what he's become, the better chance we'll have to fight him. Give me two days at the most."

"If she doesn't know anything?"

"We'll have to take our chances."

Maison finished his wine and rose from the couch. "I'm on it." He turned his head in the direction of the cellar. "She is crying."

"A woman's ploy to soften me. It will not work."

Maison nodded. "I'll send the security force at once."

When Maison vanished, Daemon poured himself another glass of wine. But Tezra's sobs grew. Sighing, he set the glass aside, then appeared next to the bed where she sat.

"Go to sleep, huntress."

"I'm an investigator by trade, not a huntress!"

Though he was well aware her job description stated she was an investigator with the SCU, the way she'd protected her bodyguard and doggedly pursued the killer vampire, she seemed more suited to being a huntress. Which made him wonder why they hadn't trained her in that field instead.

Even as tired as she looked, she was beautiful, her pink

glossy lips pouting, her green eyes sparkling. The image of freeing her from the leather she wore instantly came to mind again. "You're exhausted. Sleep."

"I can't sleep like this. I can't stand being in a room without windows, buried beneath the ground. It...it gives me claustrophobia."

Suspecting she had ulterior motives, he held firm. "It's the safest place for you...for now."

She rubbed her temple. "No. I'll go mad down here."

Folding his arms, he said, "If I take you from this room, you'll have to sleep in my bed with *me*." Which triggered unbidden images of tangling in a carnal embrace with the enchantress.

"Why don't you just lock me in another bedroom?"

Darkly amused at her suggestion, he gave her a wry smile. "You'd find a way to escape. You'll stay here."

"Why do you think your brother didn't murder the policemen when others believe he did?"

"He didn't kill *you*."

She studied him, then took a deep breath. "Please, let me out of here. You can use me as bait upstairs, aboveground. Please don't make me stay in this tomb."

"You won't like it in my room any more than you do here." He was certain of it, and he was sure she'd try to worm her way out of his bed if she could too.

She was petite like Lynetta, the huntress who'd stolen his heart, but the similarity ended there. Tezra's hair was longer, darker, more striking, her eyes emerald, hiding a history he sensed would reveal a hell of a lot about her if he could dig into her psyche and discover it. He was certain she had no intention of being used as bait, not by him or anyone else. Some SCU officers lived on the edge, notoriously lying when it suited their purpose. He couldn't trust her.

Yet, he tried to sense if she were telling the truth about her dislike for the cellar. A light sheen of perspiration covered her skin. Her breathing was too fast. It appeared she really *was* claustrophobic.

Cursing, he grabbed her wrist. He heard her sudden intake of breath, felt her maddeningly enticing rapid pulse beneath his fingertips, begging him to drink of her nectar. Trying to ignore the feelings she stirred in him, he growled inwardly, transported her to his room and deposited her on the bed.

Coffee-colored curls cascaded over her shoulders in a windswept mass, giving her a wild, untamed look. Her expressive eyes showed her every emotion, from earlier when he entered her office and she'd been so startled, to now, pleading for compassion.

If he gave in to her this time, what would he do next? He was determined not to lose his soul to her like he'd nearly done with Lynetta.

"Can you turn on the light?" she asked.

Waving his hand, he switched the crystal bed lamp on, illuminating the room in a sultry pale glow.

She surveyed the room and simply said, "Big...and dark."

"It has windows and is on the *second* floor." He motioned to the bed. "Tuck yourself in."

"Are you certain you can't lock me in and sleep somewhere else?"

Unwilling to play games any longer, he advanced on her.

Her eyes widened.

"In bed, or I will ignore your wishes and return you to the cellar."

Frowning, she proceeded to remove her leather jacket. "If you were a gentleman, you would leave." She gave him an annoyed look, her eyes challenging him.

He raised a brow.

"Forget it." Dropping her jacket on a chair, she climbed under the velvet comforter, still fully dressed. She watched him with narrowed eyes. "Well?"

"Well, what?"

"Aren't you going to turn off the light?"

His lips twitched, betraying a smile. After extinguishing the light, she still looked in his direction, though as black as the room was he knew she couldn't see him.

She sighed deeply. "Well? Aren't you coming to bed?"

He reiterated, "Sleep. And do not aggravate me further. You won't be able to leave this room, so don't contemplate—"

Before he could say anything more, he sensed his brother outside, of all the damned things.

"Daemon, will you let me in?" his brother implored.

Her eyes widened.

"He won't take you from here. Sleep, Tezra."

Scowling, she closed her eyes.

He waited until her breathing softened, then he locked the door to his bedroom. Furious with himself for letting her manipulate him so, he left her to meet with his brother. If he wasn't worried she'd try to escape or someone might attempt to reach her, he'd sleep in the cellar himself.

Daemon reappeared at the bar, grabbed his glass of wine and took a couple of healthy swallows. Biting back a curse, he said, *"Freely, I open my house to you, my brother."*

Atreides appeared next to him, but turned his attention toward Daemon's bedroom upstairs. "Why is the huntress in your room? Not confined to the cellar? Hell, even you said she was a dark huntress—they're the worst kind."

"Not that it's any concern of yours, she's frightened of the cellar." He poured his brother a drink. "And technically she works as an investigator, not a huntress. My mistake. So why are you here?"

"You can't fall for the woman, Daemon. You know what happened last time. For sixty, no seventy years, you wore the blackest mood." Atreides took a swig of his drink. "Besides, you have the worst luck when it comes to turning women you intend to be your mates."

Daemon studied him, still relieved that his brother had tried to protect the woman and hadn't planned to terminate her. "Dammit, Atreides, I'm only interested in ending the serial killers' reign of terror. If he murders her, the SCU will come down hard on all of us. You and I know it. But worse, the killer knows it."

"All right," Atreides conceded, but Daemon sensed his brother's unease. "Did you discover anything from the saliva samples of the latest victim?"

"Only that it is *not* one of our closest friends. Unfortunately, we don't have a databank for vampire DNA."

"Maison said you plan to use her as bait." Atreides paced, his long stride eating up the carpeted floor. "You haven't had a woman companion in many years. Just a quick fix here and there. I don't think it's safe for you to share the same room with her."

"You're suggesting?"

Atreides stopped and faced Daemon, his look serious, like

their uncle's had been when he laid down the law. Atreides's resemblance to their murdered relation was uncanny—same sturdy jaw, same raw edges, no rounded flesh to soften the harsh look, same dark furrowed brows and narrowed brown eyes.

Atreides cleared his throat. "I'm suggesting that she sleep in the cellar. Alone."

"I'm not as needy as you seem to think, and I have more control than that. Why did you really come?"

"What if I stayed with her? I have no affection for those serving the SCU, especially after what you put me through for the past several decades. *I'll* guard her."

For all Atreides's denying he cared anything for SCU personnel, Daemon wondered if his brother had more interest in the woman than he was letting on, which could prove disastrous. "I wouldn't wish to sacrifice you. Return home to your blood bonds. Keep your ears tuned in case someone mentions something that will aid us. Also, she's a telepath. If we need to share something private, channel your telepathic communication directly to me."

"She's a telepath? Dammit, Daemon, now you really can't stay with her."

Daemon wasn't used to his brother's interference, and he wouldn't tolerate it from him or anyone else. "She hasn't any control over me. Go, and remain alert."

Atreides hesitated, then reluctantly bowed his head and left.

Daemon ensured all of his safeguards were in place, the spells that would keep any vampire from entering his home who'd been invited in before. Though normally his brother and others could pop in anytime they liked when his house wasn't safeguarded, it would be rude to do so. Everyone asked permission to cross the threshold into a vampire's abode, unless the one who gained entrance did so with malicious intent.

When Daemon walked into the bedroom, he sensed Tezra's light breathing, her slower pulse. *Asleep. Thank God.* In a flash, he removed his clothes, having no intention of remaining clothed when he normally didn't sleep that way. The bed was his after all, and he hadn't wanted her in it in the first place. If she didn't like it, she could return to the cellar.

"Hmmm, yes," she murmured in her mind.

He stared at the brunette, her long hair draped over her damnable skin-tight turtleneck, but she appeared sound asleep.

"Yes, yes," she said again.

He raised his brows. She talked telepathically in her sleep? Taking a deep breath, he slid under the covers on his side of the bed, though technically both sides were his.

"Tell me, what are you thinking?" he asked, slipping into her thoughts.

She lay very still, and her mind seemed to shut down. Her subtle jasmine fragrance lingered in his sheets. He took a deep breath, his blood stirring. Her heart rate had increased, and she whimpered, clutching at the pillow beneath her cheek. She shook her head back and forth slowly as if her reflexes were dulled. A sob escaped her lips.

Reaching out, he ran his fingers over her hair, the strands soft beneath his fingertips. He meant only to calm her. Touching her cheek, he found tears. He pulled his hand away as if she'd burned him. She was only having a nightmare. It would go away, but if he began to have feelings for her, his nightmares would only begin.

"Katie...Katie, oh no, dear God, Katie." She spoke the words breathlessly in her mind, hesitant, frightened.

Was it some jumbled, made-up nightmare, or a past recollection? She wept more, and he fisted his hands. If he returned her to the cellar, he could sleep. No, he couldn't. He'd still hear her thoughts.

"Oh dear God, oh dear God." She bit her lip until he smelled blood.

Dear God was right. The pulsing, burning need to taste her blood filled him with a sense of urgency.

What now, dammit? He could lick her wound, memorize the taste of her blood for all eternity and stop the bleeding, or he could agonize over the smell of it, listen to her rapid pulse, and try to keep his canines under control.

"Mom, Dad, oh, what have I done?" she cried.

As much as he didn't want to care, or know anything about her, he couldn't help himself. He never ignored someone who was in pain.

He leaned over and touched his tongue to her lip, licking

her sweet, warm blood. With his heart hammering, his canines extended. For too long he hadn't fed, and her blood imprinted on his tastebuds, urging him to take more.

Worse, she quieted under his touch, which served to further his craving.

He pulled the collar of her turtleneck down, ran his tongue over her neck, sensing the delicate pulsing of her blood beneath the skin, and grazed his teeth over her sensitive flesh without nicking her.

Already he was way too aroused, both sexually and bloodlust-wise. Atreides was right. Daemon hadn't been with a woman recently enough to quench his thirst for someone as enticing as the woman lying beside him.

He moved away from her, but her heart sped up, and she seemed caught in the nightmare again.

"Tezra, everything's all right now," he said in a soothing voice. He shouldn't get any deeper with her than he already was, but he wanted to discover what disturbed her. Taking her hand, he held it firmly and concentrated on her thoughts. The wall normally surrounding them had disintegrated in her sleep-filled state.

He reached out to see her nightmare, to discover whether it was a vivid, mixed-up dream, or a true memory from her past.

A voice reached out to him, an ancient vampiric voice Daemon thought he'd heard before but couldn't recollect. It had to be someone he'd known in the distant past, but he couldn't make any connection, only a vague familiarity.

"I punish you, the child, for complicating my work. Now you see that I am more powerful than you will ever be. Both you and your sister, Katie, will live a hell for the rest of your mortal days. See what your meddling in my affairs has brought you?" a male voice said to her, the words only a distant memory in Tezra's thoughts.

Her reply showed the same vehemence and determination. *"To the end of my days, I'll hunt you down. I vow this on the blood of my parents. With my huntress's blade I will carve out your heart and end your semi-immortal life. I swear it, you bastard!"*

"Who is he?" Daemon asked, forgetting for the moment he was not her leader, that she didn't have to tell him a thing, and if she were conscious, probably wouldn't.

She tugged at his hand to pull him closer. *"Katie, we'll get through this. I promise."*

Hell, he had to find out where her sister was staying or she'd be in just as much danger, he was certain. Unless...unless she was already dead.

Taking a deep breath, Daemon pulled Tezra into his arms to stop her heart from racing, her body from trembling on the frosty autumn night. But he knew he shouldn't tempt his soul with her soft body resting against his hard chest, that he shouldn't allow her leg to press against his arousal, already agonizing for release.

Thrusting those thoughts aside, he held her tight.

She stirred and nestled her head against his chest, her silken hair tickling his skin. Inhaling deeply, he filled himself with the pure fragrance of her, the springtime freshness and floral scent that was all Tezra.

He tried to clear his mind of how dangerously enticing she was. Yet it didn't work, not with her warm breath stirring the light hair on his chest, or the way her leg hooked over his excruciating arousal. Not the way her heart pounded, the blood whooshing through her veins in a steady rush, cajoling him to feed.

No doubt she would think him the devil when she woke, only he felt *she* was the one with the black magic spells, corrupting him, and not the other way around.

Holding her close, he finally managed to sleep for several hours. Until Tezra's shrill cry jarred him from his peaceful slumber.

Chapter Four

Awareness reaching her groggy mind, Tezra realized she rested in the arms of a naked, very aroused, warm-bodied vampire, while the sunlight filtered around the edges of black velvet curtains. She jerked free and fell off the mattress, landing on her butt next to Daemon's high four-poster bed.

Unable to slow her rapid heartbeat, she jumped up, cursing him. "You arrogant bastard! Who the hell said you could sleep with me? Well, hold me like that?" she amended, recognizing the bed *was* his and the night before he'd told her in no uncertain terms he was sharing it with her no matter how she tried to talk him out of it.

Unmoved, Daemon looked contemptibly smug and didn't say a word. His darkened eyes watched her, his sable hair fanned across the pillow. Annoyingly full of himself, his well-sculpted chest exposed, he propped his head against his arms. The black satin sheet caressed the hard muscles of his lower body. His prominent arousal snagged her attention for a second glance, though she chided herself for looking...twice. She stormed to the bedroom door barefoot.

"I need my boots. Your brother took them from me," she ground out. She grabbed the handle of the door to the hallway and twisted. *Locked.*

"Couldn't we at least start this late wakeup with an agreeable good morning? It's a shame not to enjoy morning pleasantries, is it not?" Dark honeyed words spoken like a lure to draw his prey in, but his bedroom charms wouldn't work on her. Much.

"Let...me...out...of...here," she snarled, every word laced with fire.

"You said the cellar gave you claustrophobia." He waved his hand, and the curtains parted to reveal French patio doors opening onto a balcony.

"Being with *you* gives me claustrophobia."

He pulled the covers aside and stood. Her mouth dropped when she saw the beautiful length of him, er, rather, the tallness and hardness of his whole body. The shirt he had worn the night before must have been from an earlier wardrobe of his because he definitely had the build of a well-muscled pirate who hoisted sails for a living. And, no doubt, he'd raped, pillaged and plundered along the way.

She waved at the bed. "You said you'd protect me. Is this what you call protection?"

A slow smile gave him a predatory look, his nearly black eyes sparkling while he tied his hair back in a tail with a black leather strap, but he didn't make any attempt to dress.

She knew the look of madness in his eyes, the lust and the overwhelming urge to feed, to satisfy his hunger.

"You haven't fed in a while," she guessed, moving toward the patio door, keeping him in her sights as she backed up, wishing she was armed.

He advanced with the sleekness of a panther, his muscles rippling as he flexed them, his lips still curved up at the corners. "I have many questions I wish answered, Tezra."

The way he said her name sounded like he was attempting to draw her to him—to feed—hypnotic, willing the victim with words cloaked in black velvet.

"I didn't think you were the killer *until* you walked into my apartment. Why else would you have been there?"

"How did you know my name?"

"You told me."

He cocked a dark brow and stopped.

"You thought it. I read your mind."

He lifted his chin.

A lightbulb moment?

"Listen, you protected me in your way last night," she said, frowning, "and I want to—" she nearly choked on the words after being held against her will, "—thank you, but I have work to do, so just—" she bumped into the patio door with her backside and reached for the doorknob, "—get my boots back for me, and we'll call it even."

"What are you afraid of?"

His voice held no animosity toward her, only craving, desire and bloodlust raging through his system. She swallowed hard, and her skin tingled with anxiousness. Itching to have a sword in her hand, or the retractable knives fastened at her wrists, she mentally cursed Bernard for disarming her.

"I'm afraid of nothing," she lied and hoped Daemon couldn't tell. She tried the patio doorknob. *Locked.*

"Your voice trembles."

Here she thought she had her traitorous voice under control.

He skirted the bed, taking his time to reach her, showing off his wares that she attempted not to take account of...too much.

He tilted his chin down, the look in his eyes seductive, dark and dangerous.

He twisted his head toward the patio door, and she sensed the aura of a vampire outside, paralyzing her. *Krustaluṣ.* Her skin chilled and her nape crawled as if he wrapped his icy fingers around her neck.

Breaking free from the paralysis, she turned and stared out the window, but didn't see any sign of the beast in the gloomy, mist-laden morning.

"Who is he?" Daemon asked.

"Krustalus," she said with venom in her voice.

Daemon rested his hands on her shoulders, caressed them, sending a blanket of warmth through her, but she fought the sensual feelings, the heat, the strength, the allure.

"Don't, Daemon. Are you in league with the devil vampire?" If he were trying to placate her concerning Krustalus, it wouldn't work. Yet on another level, she felt Daemon's motives to soothe her were instinctual, protective. But she couldn't take him touching her while the murderer was so close by.

Daemon withdrew his hands from her shoulders. "What has Krustalus done?" he asked, his tone edged with suspicion.

Turning her gaze from Daemon's stern look, she glanced back out the window. "Nobody believes me."

"I'm not just anybody."

That was for sure. And she'd certainly never spoken to one

of his kind about it. Her fingers itched for a weapon.

"Tezra?"

"He...he killed my parents and terrified my sister so that she has not spoken for ten years." She wished she could strike the vampire down this instant. Staring into the mist, she vowed she wouldn't allow him to shake her up like he always did when he stole into her life.

She clenched her teeth and bit back the hopelessness that he would ever be brought to justice, that her sister would be freed from her silent prison. Tears threatened to spill, but she willed them back, not wanting to shed another drop, not while the menace lived. Rage burned in her soul, and if left to fester long enough, it would leave her bereft of feeling anything but hate until she died.

Silently she cursed Daemon for bringing up the painful subject, yet she assumed he only meant to help. The floodgates threatened to open, her head hammering with gusto as she tried to keep her emotions under control. *Show the vampire your emotions, and you've lost the game,* her teachers would warn her. *Always control your feelings.*

"No record of this crime exists, or I would have been made aware of it. Why hasn't the SCU taken him down?" Daemon asked, his voice shadowed with annoyance and concern.

Tezra lost it. She whipped around, tears blurring her vision, her heart in her throat. "Because they don't believe he did it, dammit. They don't believe *any* vampire did it. But I know! *I know,* because I made him do it. Because I forced him." She choked back a sob.

Daemon stared at her in disbelief. She stood so close to him her breasts nearly touched his chest. Her green eyes filled with tears. He wanted nothing more than to touch her, to hold her tight, but his heart warred with his mind to keep his distance. He tried to ignore the way her blood beckoned to him, the way she looked so damned vulnerable.

Taking a deep breath to break the spell the enchantress held over him, he said, "Talk to me, Tezra. Tell me what you know."

"You'll be like all the rest who don't believe me." Pain reflected in her words, and he wanted to crush the life out of any who had caused her anguish.

"What happened?" He pulled her toward the bed, and she

balked.

"You *are* going to put some clothes on, aren't you?"

Daemon lifted a brow. "You are sure you want this?"

She frowned, and he gave her a small smile then let go of her hand. In a flash, he threw on a pair of black denims.

"Enough. Tell me what happened." He lifted her onto the high bed, then sat next to her.

"Can he come inside?" She seemed filled with emotions, wavering between fear of the vampire and red-hot anger.

Her teachers would have taught her to control such feelings, especially in front of a vampire. Which made him believe she could cross the line and become a renegade. But he wasn't about to let her go there. Not when it could cause further difficulties between her people and his.

"I've never invited Krustalus inside my home. I only vaguely recall meeting him once in Scotland in the early years after my change. A brief encounter in a tavern, as I recall. Nothing remarkable about the man captured my attention."

She clasped and unclasped her fingers. "If I had my sword, I'd ask him in."

This was a dangerous notion, and he couldn't fathom why she would wish to put herself at such risk. "If the SCU hasn't condemned him..."

She growled her response. "*I* condemn him for the murder of my parents."

She didn't have the authority. "What proof do you have, Tezra?"

Turning her glare from him, she stared at the floor. "He didn't take their blood, just slashed their throats and left them to die in front of my sister when she was twelve. I was training at Portland SCU's elite school, learning how to use my wrist daggers, learning how to be a huntress, but when I came home..." She looked at the patio door. "My sister's in a world of her own, doesn't speak or seem to understand most of what I say to her. It's all my fault she's the way she is."

Daemon *knew* Tezra had trained to be a huntress. He sensed it in her actions, in her thoughts when they weren't guarded. A dark huntress. Reaching down he took her hands, forcing her to unclench them. Her long nails had dug into the skin, but hadn't cut it yet. He didn't need to be exposed to any more of her blood.

He doubted the crime was Tezra's fault, but she seemed to think the burden of guilt rested on her shoulders, and he was bound and determined to find out why.

Before he could question her further, Krustalus spoke to him privately. *"It is I, Krustalus. Will you invite me in? I have important issues to discuss with you."*

Daemon had ruled the vampires of America since the time of the American Revolution. Krustalus had never pledged his allegiance to Daemon's rule before, not that it was required as long as the vampire did nothing to stir up trouble. So why all the interest to see him now? To get at Tezra? Or did he have some larger just as equally dark purpose in mind?

Daemon sensed a smugness emanating from him. *"I'll meet with you in an hour at Popia's Wharfside Restaurant."*

"Ahh, you are busy with sweet Tezra. Give her my love, will you, Prince Daemon? 'Til then, milord," Krustalus communicated in a mocking tone, then left.

Now suspecting what Tezra had said about Krustalus was true, Daemon tightened his hold on her hands. Why else would the vampire know her well enough to recognize she was in the house with him? Why use an endearing term in connection with her name?

She relaxed as if a ton of bricks had been lifted from her shoulders. "He's gone," she whispered. "He spoke privately to you, didn't he?"

"Yes, he said he knew you were here."

"Of course he knows." She yanked her hands free. "He always knows where I am, and I sense his close proximity, but he won't come near enough when he's in human form for me to catch sight of his face. I only know the demonic tone of his thoughts. He was there, taunting me before Officer Stevens died." She rubbed her neck.

Daemon glanced at the ribbed material of the turtleneck she wore and a new concern flickered across his mind. "Has he bitten you?"

Her eyes widened, but she shook her head.

But something about her action, the way she'd touched her neck when she thought of Krustalus taunting her, drawing close, made Daemon think there was something more to the situation than a vampire out for revenge.

"I thought you'd been called to investigate the murder. That others were with you at the time. What the hell were you doing alone in the warehouse district beforehand?" he snapped, not meaning to. But dammit, didn't the woman know how dangerous her actions were?

Her spine tensed. "Stevens said he knew my parents' killer's name."

"And he said to come alone?" Daemon asked, his voice hard. "You didn't see it as a setup? Hell, woman."

"Of course I considered it." She narrowed her eyes. "But I had to know the vampire's name."

Daemon shook his head in disbelief. "He couldn't tell you over the phone? You had to meet him in the middle of the night in an isolated place...the same place the other officers were murdered?"

She didn't say anything in response, just glowered at him.

"So Stevens gave you Krustalus's name, then the vampire murdered him. You witnessed it."

"*No*, I didn't see him kill Stevens. If I had, I would be an eyewitness and have the proof I needed, now wouldn't I? He's too clever for that. Besides, I think there are two of them. Stevens never had a chance. The chief gave me Krustalus's name over the phone when I reported the murder."

Daemon took an exasperated breath. "Why did Stevens say for you to come alone as if he were the only one who knew Krustalus's name, but the chief gave it to you without even meeting you there?"

"I don't know!"

"Did you see Krustalus kill your parents?"

"No." She shook her head and sniffled, her teeth gritted as if she were trying to fight back the tears.

"Then how do you know it was him?" It wasn't that Daemon didn't believe her, only that she had to have proof. If she attempted to kill Krustalus without provocation, she would be no better than what she assumed Krustalus was. "Why wouldn't he have taken their blood? I don't know of any vampire who would kill like that and not drink his victims' blood."

"I don't know."

Puzzling over her parents' deaths, Daemon rubbed his chin. "Vampires often fight each other using swords, usually over territorial disputes, but serial killers use their fangs to murder. Why are you so sure a vampire murdered your parents?"

She jumped off the bed and paced across the Turkish rug. "Don't you see? He did it that way to throw the SCU off! He did it that way to get back at me!"

"Why you?" Daemon didn't attempt to conceal his skepticism. Why would a vampire kill her parents in an atypical fashion *for her sake*? Had the trauma of her parents' deaths affected her mind too?

Tezra stopped pacing and glowered at him. "I knew he'd begun killing humans, but I didn't know his name. After reading his mind, I taunted him with the knowledge I gleaned. Young and stupid, I never thought he would discover my identity, because I couldn't determine his. Hoping I could goad him into making a mistake, I planned to turn him in to the SCU. I thought I'd become famous like Michael Tarantos, who at sixteen discovered a vampire hit squad intending to destroy the SCU. Thinking I was invincible..."

With an abrupt sweep of her hand, she brushed away tears. "Just as surely as if I'd stabbed them in the heart myself, I caused my parents' deaths. I brought about my sister's suffering all these years. My own arrogance destroyed my family."

He rubbed his neck, which was rife with tension. He wanted to hold her tight and take away her pain, but because of her agitated posture, he assumed she wouldn't appreciate anyone's touch, least of all a vampire's. "Why didn't you tell the SCU about your abilities? Surely they would have believed you then."

"I told a senior staff member about what happened, though I left out the part about being telepathic. Patrico died in the same manner as my parents before he could speak to the others. The vampire would have killed anyone else I tried to alert. I still hadn't learned his name. Not until the chief revealed it."

This still struck Daemon as odd. How would the chief have discovered the vampire's name so easily, when a huntress with telepathic abilities could not? "Do you know how the chief came to discern his name?"

Her brows knit in a deep frown. "You're thinking the police chief was manipulated. That Stevens was. Maybe so. Or maybe someone he turned or someone who had once been his friend squealed on him." She wrapped her arms around herself. "Krustalus said I'd find out his name soon. I'm certain he's the one, and how the chief or Stevens knew doesn't concern me."

"But it should, Tezra." Daemon finished dressing. "You have to prove he's committed murder. The SCU will have no recourse but to condemn you for murder should you kill him without proving he's committed a crime."

"He won't get away with their murders or any of the others he has committed. He's cunning, but I'm certain he's still killing. He has to be stopped. Soon, by God, he'll slip up, and I'll meet him in the flesh."

Daemon couched his disapproval, though another thought nagged him. What *was* Krustalus's game? "You said Krustalus taunted you. How?"

Tezra glowered at Daemon. The tension in his neck returned when he imagined what the vampire might have done to her. The notion she had to prove Krustalus had killed anyone quickly went out the window, and he was ready to terminate the vampire himself. "Tezra?"

"He touches me when he's in the form of mist."

Daemon's temper grew. "How do you know this? Couldn't it be just your imagination?"

"Forget it! You don't believe me anyway."

He couldn't forget it. He wanted to discover just how far the bastard had pushed himself on her, but his own anger was too near the surface to deal with it objectively. "Did he bite you, Tezra?"

She swallowed hard and shook her head again.

"Tezra?" He touched her arm but she didn't pull away this time. He embraced her, attempting to coax the truth out of her. "What happened?"

She wouldn't speak.

"If he's bitten you, he may believe he's laid claim to you. At least in his sick mind. I have to know if he's done anything to you to see where he intends to take this."

"He's never bitten me! Don't you think I'd remember something like that? I wouldn't ever have let him get that close."

"He touched you in mist form," Daemon reminded her. "And from there he could easily have become a man, touching you just as intimately, except in human form."

She wouldn't look at him, and he suspected the worst. "When did he bite you?"

She shook her head. "He didn't."

Tilting her chin up, he attempted to will her to be honest with him, but that impenetrable wall of hers blocked him. "All right, then." It wasn't. But he'd get the truth from her hopefully sooner than later. "What about your sister?"

Tezra turned away, her voice filled with regret. "I've had the world's best psychiatrists work with her with no discernable progress."

He knew a promising way to bring her sister out of the darkness—most likely at great sacrifice to himself and even greater to Tezra. Frankly, after his last three disastrous relationships, he wasn't interested in repeating his mistake. Yet a strange gnawing emptiness filled him with an unfathomable sense of disquiet. Just the bloodlust, just the hunger, he told himself, attempting to convince himself that was all it was about her that made him yearn for intimacy with the huntress.

She pushed her dark hair away from her face in such a sexy way, he groaned inwardly. His hard body couldn't take much more of her sweet fragrance or her alluring actions.

"I vow I will help you with finding a way to connect Krustalus with the crimes. In the meantime, you will remain here and—"

"Absolutely not." She crossed her arms, lifting her breasts. Her eyes narrowed with defiance.

"I told you last night, I expect your obedience in all matters."

"This is not the Dark Ages, and you won't keep me here against my will a second longer."

"Not even if I help you to solve the crimes?"

"I won't be locked away—"

She quit speaking when they sensed two vampires approach his house.

"Your brother and friend, Maison, are here again?"

Daemon motioned to the bedroom. "You will stay here and behave, or I'll return you to the cellar."

"I need a shower and a change of clothes."

"My brother will have your bag. I'll bring it up momentarily.

You may use my bathroom to shower." The thought of seeing her rubbing soapsuds over her soft, naked skin instantly aroused him again. Envisioning his hands soaping up her breasts, bringing her nipples to twin, rosy peaks—

Releasing a heavy sigh, he dissolved into mist and reappeared in the greatroom. *"You may enter my home freely, Atreides, Maison,"* he communicated before they asked.

"Trouble's brewing," Maison warned as he and Atreides appeared in front of Daemon.

And she's upstairs, Daemon thought privately. He took her suitcase from Atreides. "I shall return and hear all the news in a minute."

"She's attempting to pick the lock on your patio door." Atreides's voice and expression were hard.

With his acute hearing, Daemon had recognized what Tezra was up to at once. "Of this, I'm deeply aware. I shall see to the vixen."

Tezra considered the lock on the patio door, having already determined she couldn't pick the lock on the bedroom door. But then she sensed Daemon in the room—no anger though, just conceited amusement. Straightening and turning, she shot him her best glare.

"Looking for something?" He wore a bigheaded smirk. "Bathroom's in there." He set her suitcase down and motioned to the other door as if she were a moron. "If you need me to help in any way, you know how to call me. Extra towels are in the linen closet. Anything else?"

She grabbed her suitcase and brushed past him, not meaning to, but his body blocked her path, and she wasn't watching his smug expression one more minute.

"I've been told I'm awfully good at soaping hard-to-reach spots," he added, his voice taking on the earlier seductive tone.

She glanced back at him, not believing he'd say such a thing to her, knowing how much animosity she felt for him. Did he think because she had slept with him, she was now interested in his great body and wanted more? Not that she wouldn't want a great body like that making wild and passionate love to her, but...but...how could she lose her mind over a vampire's hot physique?

She couldn't fathom why he would be interested in her in particular, except maybe he was still hungry and would want anyone's blood. "You'll show me the latest tissue samples after I get cleaned up and changed."

His eyes darkened but glistened with amusement. She didn't figure her words would convince him to do anything he didn't want to. But she felt some satisfaction in making her wishes plain to him anyway.

"If you are thinking of escape, don't. Vicious animals protect the grounds from intruders."

A ruse? Though she'd heard some vampires used trained pit bulls or dobermans to guard their premises.

Well, Daemon was back to being egotistical and controlling, which suited her fine. She could deal with him better that way. Otherwise, he threw her off-kilter, and she wasn't sure how to take him. He bowed his head and waited.

She stalked into the bathroom, then slammed the door with such force it rattled the window. She swore she heard him laugh. She examined the window. *Barred.* She ground her teeth.

A whirlpool tub big enough for two dominated the room with its swirling chocolate marble like fudge ripple ice cream—her favorite flavor. Gold mirrors hung above two marble sinks set off by shining gold faucets. Encased in clear glass, a separate shower sat on the opposite wall. Jeez, the vampire had nicer stuff than she had—standard chrome faucet on a standard single sink. One porcelain tub/shower unit, one chrome mirror/shelf unit. Period.

She turned on the shower, then while the water whooshed down the drain, disguising the noise she made, she searched all the cabinet drawers for something she could use on the door lock. Not finding anything, she considered breaking the glass patio door, but then what? He'd be one pissed-off vampire.

Exasperated, she yanked off her clothes and heard movement in the bedroom. Daemon was listening to what she was up to? She climbed into the shower and glanced down at the peach shampoo sitting in a shower organizer. *Peach?*

She ran the shampoo through her wet hair and washed her face, brushing the silky soap over her breasts.

"Call me if you need me," Daemon suddenly said, then she

sensed he had vanished.

Just as quickly, she sensed Krustalus outside the house again. Her eyes shot open, and soap slipped into them. Cursing under her breath, she hurried to rinse the burning soap out of her eyes and then from her hair. She expected the bastard to speak to Daemon, to ask for entrance, to keep his communications secret from her, to show how superior he was. *And clever.* Daemon must have known he was here too, and that's why he had left so suddenly.

"Tezra, love, how are you?"

When Krustalus communicated with her instead of Daemon, her heart sped up, and she shot out of the shower. Until she realized she had no weapons. Then she spied her bag, and a flicker of hope came to her. Dripping water everywhere, she yanked open the zipper. Inside, she found her swords, their shining metal gleaming in the bathroom light. *Yes!*

A situation of neglectful assumptions? Atreides probably had assumed Bernard would have removed the weapons from her bag. Daemon would assume Atreides had totally disarmed her. Thank God vampires could be as disorganized as members of the Special Crimes Unit at times.

After hastily drying, she dressed in black denims and a cowl-neck pink cashmere sweater, then slipped on a pair of low boots.

Krustalus hadn't spoken to her again. She imagined Daemon was communicating to him in private somewhere else because she couldn't detect either of them. She shoved one of her swords underneath the mattress in case she got caught. Then she'd have a backup if she needed it—*if* Daemon didn't kill her for what she was about to do.

Heart hammering, she rushed to the patio door, grabbed a brass umbrella stand and bashed it against the glass. Nothing happened to the damnable glass.

She searched for something harder. The crystal lamps, though heavy, might shatter first. The mahogany stepping stool beside the high bed? She tried lifting it. Too massive to hoist against the patio door.

She rummaged through Daemon's closet. Shoes and clothes from sporty to dressy, like any well-dressed man owned. She peered into a darkened corner of the closet. A wooden box sat half hidden beneath his trousers. Opening it, she found a huge assortment of keys, different kinds from every period, it seemed. Long, short, fat, skinny, tiny, huge, brass, iron. One by one, she tried them.

Half an hour later, she kicked the box aside and grabbed the umbrella stand, readying it for another bash. A vampire suddenly hissed behind her.

Her heart lurched, right before his huge hand engulfed her wrist.

Chapter Five

When Daemon agreed to meet Krustalus at Popia's Wharfside Restaurant, he'd had one goal—to find out if the vampire had murdered Tezra's parents. If Krustalus had committed the crime, he would be far too clever to trip up unless his conceit got the best of him. But learning that the bastard had touched Tezra intimately without her permission took the game to a different level.

He assumed from the way she acted that Krustalus had bitten her. Daemon figured Krustalus wanted her—not dead as he had first presumed, but as his mate. If Krustalus thought he could intimidate the woman without consequences, let him tangle with an ancient more his match.

Seated next to the expansive windows overlooking the rugged Oregon coastline, Daemon tapped his fingers on the table. He considered the antique-looking coins—replicas of ones he'd used three hundred years earlier—buried in the clear plastic tabletop, nestled against dark, seasoned wood trimmed by a white braided rope. He glanced at his watch. Krustalus was fifteen minutes late.

The sound of conversations and the aroma of fresh fish frying in spicy sauces filled the air.

Daemon tuned out the background noise and watched the clouds building, darkening, casting shadows across the foaming waves. If Krustalus wanted to win his favor, making him wait *wasn't* the way to do it. But another notion bothered Daemon. Was the vampire surprised to learn of Daemon's association with the huntress? He hadn't seemed to be. In fact, it was almost as though he was engineering a confrontation with Daemon.

"Would you like to order something to drink?" a waitress asked, breaking into his thoughts.

Drink?

He studied the girl's throat revealed by a low-cut blouse, listened to the blood pumping through her veins, saw the pulse beckoning to him.

"Water," he said, and turned away.

He had to feed soon, he admitted, because he hadn't noticed the girl's face, breasts, legs, nothing, just the tempting pulse in the veins of her neck. The gnawing in his belly wouldn't go away until he fed.

He tapped his fingers on the table again and glanced out the window at the panoramic view of the Pacific Ocean. The waves in a never-ending fluid motion rolled in, tackling the boulders in their path, receding and coming in for yet another charge. The salty spray shot upward with the clash—an image worth capturing with his paints.

"Ahh, Daemon," a woman said, distracting him.

Before he acknowledged her, he recognized the sensuous lilt to her voice. Lichorus stood before his table, her black eyes challenging, her raven hair straight, dangling past her slim hips. At five-eleven, she could have been a runway model. Instead, the vampiress preferred being a vampire's pet.

"Lichorus." Daemon bowed his head slightly in greeting.

"I hear rumors. Ugly rumors."

Daemon figured what the gossip was about—Tezra, a member of the Special Crimes Unit, locked up in his home, a battle of wills between them. "Word spreads quickly."

"Already dissension is building among us." Lichorus pulled a seat out for herself. "Do you mind?"

He motioned for her to sit. "Make it quick. I'm meeting with Krustalus." And it better be soon, dammit.

Her dark eyes narrowed while she took her seat. Did she know Krustalus? With a movement designed to entice Daemon, she licked her red-frosted lips, but he wasn't interested.

His gaze dropped to the pulse in her neck. Normally anyone would satisfy the hunger, but all he could think of was Tezra's sweet blood. All blood had a distinctive taste. The smell of hers was like copper and wine, the taste as sweet as the richest burgundy...he couldn't get it out of his mind.

"Daemon, I believe my lover knows who killed the police officers."

Instantly, he sat taller. "Who?"

Exaggerated by three-inch red polished nails, Lichorus's long, thin fingers reached out to him across the table. She scraped them over his hands. Finding her action annoying, he pulled away.

She offered a simpering smile. "I've tried to find out from him, but he doesn't...trust me. He believes I still have a thing for you." Her lips turned up more. "Imagine that."

Daemon's stomach roiled. "What makes you think Mustaphus knows? If he's so secretive—"

"He's not very good at covert operations. From time to time he makes a slip. He communicated with another vampire but didn't funnel his thoughts directly to him. Mustaphus related how thrilled he was the killer had been so successful."

"This in itself means nothing. Several admire the killer's boldness. That doesn't mean they know who it is." Unable to determine if Lichorus was lying or not, Daemon leaned back in his chair and studied her reactions closely.

"Why keep his communications secret for the most part, then? The other kept his talk channeled. But, darling, there's more. Mustaphus knew where the police officer had been murdered *before* it was announced on the news this morning."

"Several of us knew of the murder before it was reported."

Lichorus gave a wicked smile, a gleam in her eye.

"Well?

She shrugged. "Let me amend my comment. He was there *before* the killing took place."

Daemon stiffened his back. "You are certain?"

"Reasonably."

"But it still doesn't prove he had anything to do with the killing or that he knew who had committed the crime, unless he was there while it occurred. Why didn't you report your suspicions to Maison?" Daemon asked, incensed that anyone would conceal the bastard's actions. '

"The deed had already been done." Lichorus circled an embedded coin in the table with her fingernail. "Word is the SCU is frantic Tezra Campbell is missing. They're concerned the vampire serial killer has murdered her or taken her hostage."

Lichorus's lips rose. "But we know where she's currently residing, don't we?" She shrugged. "I believe there is much more at stake here. Those involved don't realize how dangerous a war would be. They're arrogant enough to believe the vampires would succeed and rule."

"What would you want in return for the information?"

"Why, darling, as loyal as I have always been to your rule..."

He lifted a brow. "You know better than to play games with me. I recall a time when a few hotheads pulled their support, and you were at the forefront of that movement. Hell, if you hadn't turned the others in, proved you could still be useful and sworn your allegiance again, I would have had no choice but to eliminate you back then."

She hissed. "How can you get caught up in a dalliance with another huntress? You're playing with fire again."

"Temper, temper, Lichorus." Certain she would tell everyone she knew and the word would filter to the killer, he set the trap. "She's in my custody for her protection until I discover who killed the police officers. If he wants her, he'll have to come and get her."

"You are into bondage these days, my prince? I would be happy to oblige."

"I'll keep that in mind." Daemon bowed his head, formally announcing their discussion was at an end. If the vampiress wished to provide him information free of conditions, he would be willing to listen, but he would not be cowed into an agreement with her.

Before Lichorus responded, Tezra channeled a scream into Daemon's thoughts.

In Daemon's bedroom, the vampire tightened his grip on Tezra's wrist, numbing her hand. She dropped the umbrella stand. Before she could spin around and see the menace, he wrapped an arm around her throat. Squeezing, the bastard attempted to choke her into submission. Her mind blackening and in panic, she thrust her free elbow hard into his gut.

Grunting, he loosened his grip.

Grave mistake on his part.

She twisted around and saw the tallest vampire she'd ever encountered, topping Daemon by several inches. With heated blue eyes and extended white fangs that looked like they'd never touched an ounce of coffee, he was the first vampire she'd seen wearing a buzz haircut. Dressed in a black leather jacket, padded vest, boots and leather pants, he seemed as shielded as a knight in chain mail.

His unusual appearance startled her so, she stared at him, slack-jawed.

Grave mistake on her part.

Seizing her shoulders, he slammed her back against the glass patio door, sending a shard of pain slicing down her spine.

Unsheathing her sword, she screamed telepathically at Daemon, the bastard, for leaving her. The vampire giant was too close for her to swing her sword to any great advantage. With the glass pressed hard against her back, she couldn't move her arm up enough to thrust. Despite lack of maneuverability, she finally managed to slice at the ancient vampire's side. With her free hand, she shoved his massive chin up so he couldn't bite her.

A losing battle. So much bigger than her and an ancient male, the creature quickly wore her down. Her arm shook while she tried to hold his face away. She slashed the sword again at his waist only to make negligible cuts in his jacket.

Pressing closer with his extended canines, he threatened to rip out her throat. His breath smelled of iron, of blood—he'd recently fed.

Unable to free herself, she struck him again with her sword. Then to her horror, he released her shoulders and grabbed her face. He turned her chin to the side and licked her neck.

The torture before the bite.

Daemon suddenly appeared next to Tezra and yanked the sword out of her hand. "Dammit, Voltan. What the hell's going on? You're supposed to be protecting her."

This giant-sized oaf was supposed to protect her? She couldn't stop trembling, and if she had her sword back, she would make short work of Daemon for leaving her with this gargantuan vampire who was about to kill her.

"Well?" Daemon's face darkened with anger.

Voltan looked back at Tezra. "She would have broken your patio door, Prince Daemon. I merely prevented it." He bowed his head to Daemon, then he lifted thick, shaggy brows and eyed Tezra with disparagement. "She needs a tighter leash. Do you wish me to confine her to the dungeon?"

She fisted her hands at her waist. This vampire was even more conceited than Daemon, if that were possible.

"No, I don't want her in the wine cellar, for now." Daemon examined the sword's razor sharp blade. "Where did she get the hunter's weapon?"

Gladdened she'd had enough foresight to hide the other sword, she smiled inwardly.

"When I found her trying to break out, she already possessed the sword. Didn't your brother first take her into custody?"

"Yes, but Atreides should have disarmed her. Who brought her to him? Her hunter friend?"

Daemon faced Tezra, his dark eyes nearly black, studying her as if trying to learn the truth through reading her mind. All he'd find was an impenetrable wall.

"She didn't have a sword when I brought her here, so her bodyguard was not as solidly under Atreides's control as my brother thought." Daemon glanced around the room, then motioned to the bathroom. "Her suitcase. Check it. Make sure she has no more weapons."

As if she'd be dumb enough to leave one in there.

Voltan stalked into the bathroom. "My lord, the wench has made a mess of your bathroom. Water everywhere."

Daemon reached out to touch her cheek. "You smell of peaches, Tezra."

Furrowing her brow, she took a step out of his reach. Before she could make a catty remark about his choice in shampoo fragrances, he grabbed her wrist. "You haven't eaten."

Her teeth clenched as she tried to yank away from him. "Neither have you."

"You're right." His eyes darkened, he watched her like a vampire desirous of a quick fix would, intent on willing a human to offer blood in exchange for sexual pleasure. "I'm afraid you've spoiled my appetite."

She stopped struggling. "What the hell does that mean?" Yet she had an inkling. He wanted her blood, but he'd better not *even* think such a thing.

Drawers and cabinets opened and shut in the bathroom.

Daemon broke the intense eye contact between them and turned his focus on the bathroom. "Discover anything, Voltan?"

His guard walked back into the bedroom and shook his head. "Nothing, my lord."

"Find my brother. Tell him I need to see him and Maison in an hour."

Voltan bowed and still hovered a foot taller than her. "Yes, my lord." After casting Tezra a disdainful look, he vanished.

Daemon pulled her close, then took her into the whirling blackness that enveloped those who traveled in the way of the vampire. They materialized this time in an oversized kitchen that seemed to have two of everything: stoves, fridges, microwaves and miles of black slate counters.

When he released her, she grabbed an edge of the island to steady herself. "You and who else eat here? The whole vampire clan of Oregon?"

An almost imperceptible smile touched his lips while he reached into one of the fridges. "We have celebrations here from time to time. Don't you like to cook?"

Her brows rose. "Don't get domestic on me. Where did you go? Why did you leave me alone with that gigantic ape?"

Daemon lifted his hand to silence her.

"I'm not one of your courtiers. Why didn't you tell me you were the reigning Prince of the Americas?"

"In response to your question about the gigantic ape, Voltan is one of my most loyal friends. Saved my life countless times before we fell to the plague. Once our genetics were mutated by the virus, he rescued me in a number of skirmishes until we were no longer fledglings. Maison and Atreides had other business to attend to. They cannot always—"

"Babysit me?"

"You're way too much of a woman for me to take that comment seriously. Salmon?"

"Why haven't you fed? Really?"

"I told you." He put the fish in a pan when she didn't answer his question. "You've spoiled me for anyone else."

"You would have to taste my blood, to..." She touched her lip. "How did I bite my lip?" Her voice shook. "You didn't..."

"I didn't suck, if that's what's bothering you. I stopped the bleeding."

"You shouldn't have." She was certain her blood couldn't have made him lose his appetite for anyone else's, but the idea he had tasted hers at all made her uneasy. "Why haven't you fed for some time, anyway?"

"The killings. How can a vampire look humans in the eye without them worrying he or she might be the serial killer? All it takes is one to damage our reputation. I vowed to limit my feeding as much as possible until this matter is cleared up."

"But you can't. Not forever."

"Do you have so little faith in me? I will discover who the killer is shortly." He began to fry the salmon. "Spinach?"

She twisted her mouth in thought, then tucked her hair behind her ears. "Where did you go?"

"To see Krustalus. But he did not show." Daemon's jaw ticked.

"I told you he was a bastard."

His expression dark, he didn't say a word. After a few minutes, he set the food on the table.

"I want to see the tissue samples you stole." She sat at the dining room table, big enough to seat twelve.

"There's a way to deal with this situation." Daemon sat opposite her.

"Taking down Krustalus?"

"No. This has to do with your sister."

She narrowed her eyes. Bargaining with a vampire— especially one who was holding her hostage and seemed to want her for more than a quick taste of her blood—couldn't be a good thing. "Go on."

"To reach your sister, someone would need to conceal her bad memories. If I turned her, I could help her, but in the state she's in, I couldn't get her consent."

Tezra's blood sizzled. "Turning her would violate both your laws and ours. Which is why your brother will be in big trouble if the SCU learns he tried to turn Bernard without his approval."

"As far as Bernard is concerned, he's been released.

Besides, he already had vampiric roots."

"What?" Tezra's mind raced, her thoughts flooded with memories. She didn't recall any instance that would indicate Bernard had vampire family ties. "You're wrong."

"You know how the SCU feels if they learn any of their members have vampire genealogy. Where would his loyalties lie if it came to a question of family over duty?"

"I-I don't believe you."

"Bernard hid his secret well, but Maison knew his maternal grandfather—a vampire. He'd had a love affair with a woman, Bernard's grandmother, but the vampire died at the hands of another before he could turn his lover."

"Bernard's telepathic," she said under her breath. "I thought he had the ability because your brother had turned him."

"No. Bernard hid this fact from you and everyone else he knew. He couldn't risk having anyone dig into his family ties to learn why he had telepathic abilities—because he was of mixed heritage. In your case, I've discovered your deceased aunt was a telepath, and that's why you have the ability."

"You've been investigating me?" She hated how shrill her voice sounded.

He gave her a mysterious smile. "What if you'd had vampiric roots as well? One never knows, now, does one?" He ate another bite of his salmon.

Her fork clattered to the plate, and she clenched her fists. "You can't turn my sister."

"I'm not saying anyone should turn her, only that it would be a way for someone to shield her mind from the trauma. If her thoughts could be controlled, the painful memories hidden, maybe you could reach her telepathically and she could return to our world."

"I can't do away with the emotional injuries she's sustained. And I can't contact her telepathically. I can only speak with someone who has telepathic abilities. Though I've tried to reach her mind, to learn what she's thinking, I can't. Not with the way she's been traumatized. Her thoughts are nonsensical, useless or totally blanked out."

"Since you are her sister, she would more than likely open her mind to you. But you need to shield her from the horrors that paralyze her and allow her to see who committed the crimes."

Tezra frowned. "But I told you I can't do that."

He didn't respond, the look in his eyes unfathomable, the expression on his face formidable.

Her mind swirled as she considered what he was thinking. Then it dawned on her. "Oh, no, no, no." She waved her hand at him. "You would have to turn me into a vampiress!" She glared at him. She hated him for suggesting such a thing, yet she realized his plan could mean the difference in a living death or real life for her sister. Her throat clogged with tears.

"As a vampiress you would be able to control her thoughts to a degree. To free her from the trauma. It's the only way I know to bring her out of the darkness."

She'd always sworn she'd do anything for her sister, anything to give her life back. Now she had the opportunity? A life for a life?

She swallowed hard. It was only fair, since it was her folly that had caused her sister's suffering and their parents' death.

"There's something else."

"What?" Tezra asked, her voice hollow. She didn't want to become a vampire, not in her worst nightmares, but for her sister...

"If your sister is able to speak again, she'd be able to testify in front of the SCU High Court and tell them the name of the vampire who killed your parents. Justice would prevail."

"What about the chief? He said Krustalus was the killer."

"And you trust him?"

"I have to speak with him, learn how he knows." Then a distasteful thought flickered across her mind. Wouldn't Krustalus be surprised if she came after him with a set of fangs? She rubbed her temple. If she didn't rein in her darker side, she'd be no better than the murdering vampire.

Glowering at Daemon, she wasn't sure who she was madder at—him for suggesting she be turned, or herself for getting into the predicament she was in by taunting Krustalus so long ago. "I suppose you'd be the one to turn me."

Daemon leaned back in his chair. "I no more want to change you than you want to be turned."

After the way he'd acted toward her, like he wanted to taste every inch of her, she didn't believe him for a second, yet his words fed into her insecurities. No one wanted to risk being with her, not even a blasted vampire, once he learned she'd been instrumental in her parents' deaths.

"Who then? Your brother? That beast you called Voltan? Maison?"

"No one. It was just a thought." Daemon finished his salmon.

The vampire was so infuriating, Tezra bit back the urge to slug him. "Why the hell did you bring it up then?"

"It was an option. But..." He shook his head. "It wouldn't work."

"Why did you say it would work then, if it wouldn't?"

"I doubt it's ever been tried before. Beyond that, the matter of turning you isn't a good idea." He reached for her plate. "Done with your food?"

"Turning me isn't a good idea, why?" Not that she wanted to be turned, but what did he think? That she'd make a lousy vampiress? That being with her was too risky?

He grabbed her wrist just as she sensed a vampire lurking near the house. "You'll return to the bedroom, then I must take care of other business."

Chapter Six

Tezra attempted to jerk free from Daemon's grip, but he moved her in his vampiric way before he released her in his bedroom again.

"You know you're infuriatingly controlling, Daemon. Don't you *ever* drag me off like that again. And what the hell do you mean by saying turning me wouldn't be a good idea?"

The fire in her emerald eyes, and her words, amused him. He gave her a sinister smirk. "So now you *want* to be turned?"

"Of course not."

"That's why it wouldn't work." Daemon sensed the vampire who had arrived had vanished again and assumed Krustalus had his own people checking out his safeguards, looking for weak links, a place that would afford him the opportunity to get to Tezra. Daemon opened the patio door and motioned for her to join him on the balcony for some fresh air. Her skin had become so pale, he was certain his suggestion to turn her was making her ill, which hadn't been his intention.

No matter how much he'd thought about it, he couldn't come up with a better solution. Except he'd vowed never to turn another woman for as long as he lived. Despite this, he couldn't allow anyone else to change her, to control her or to force her to be his mate. On the other hand, he assumed the guilt she felt concerning her sister would never be appeased until she set her sister free and the SCU found her parents' murderer accountable.

Which meant Daemon was damned if he helped her and damned if he didn't.

"If you turned me, what would the consequences be for you?" she asked softly, looking out at the vista.

Her question stunned him. He understood her agonizing over her sister, the killer, the effects being turned would have on her emotionally and physically. Not in a millennium would he think she'd be concerned about the impact it would have on him.

"I'm not sure what you mean."

She looked at him with a questioning gaze. "Except in Bernard's case, I've heard vampires would rather die than turn a member of the SCU who targets vampire renegades."

"True." Daemon wasn't going to deny it.

"Then your people wouldn't be happy with you."

Personally, there was more at stake for him than that. "Changing you isn't feasible." He rested his arms against the railing and looked in the direction of the evergreen forest that framed his backyard, the peace and tranquility only an illusion. Beyond the forest he knew renegade vampires were planning some kind of mischief. "I'll find the evidence you need and take care of Krustalus."

"What about my sister?"

"When I take Krustalus into custody, she'll be able to verify it's him and seeing him as a menace no longer, maybe she'll get well."

"Renegade vampires can't be taken into custody. They'd just, *poof*, vanish. And if you terminated Krustalus first, he'd be a pile of ashes, and there would be nothing left for Katie to identify." She shook her head. "In any event, she's been traumatized enough. It wouldn't work. And you know it."

He knew it, and that was the point he was trying to make. He couldn't think of any other way to deal with Katie's problem except to change Tezra. Yet it wasn't a sure solution either. What if a vampiric Tezra still couldn't reach Katie?

Tezra paced, silent, chewing her bottom lip.

The thought of licking her lip came rushing back to mind. But when he sensed another vampire's approach, he pulled her into the house and shut the door.

She folded her arms. "If I agree to be turned, I won't be forced into being your mate or anybody else's."

Not about to give an inch on this, Daemon stood taller. "Living the life of a vampire can be tenuous at best. Some vampires prey on the fledglings, which is what you'd be for a good century. I wouldn't turn you then leave you to fend for yourself. You'd have to be...hell, what am I saying? I'm not turning you. End of discussion."

She raised her brows. "Fine. Go about your business, why don't you? And while you're at it, I'll look at the tissue samples you stole."

He couldn't fathom what she was up to, but her words reminded him of his brother when he was bound and determined to do something Daemon didn't agree with. Speaking with an ancient authority, he offered no room for argument, simply stating, "You won't be turned."

He transported himself to the greatroom, then slipped her sword into the hidden panel next to the fireplace. He would protect her, help her, but he would not allow her to be another vampire's mate.

He made a telepathic call to the vampires to spread the word. *"Death to any who try to turn the SCU investigator, Tezra Campbell. All will obey me in this."*

Once again, he felt he was tumbling down the dark chasm after a mate, but this time he was determined not to make the same mistake again.

Tezra paced across the darkly woven Turkish rug as soon as Daemon vanished. *"Okay, so where are the damned tissue samples, Daemon?"*

He didn't respond, and she ground her teeth.

Then she glanced at the patio door. Had he locked it? Her heart hammering, she opened the door as quietly as she could, worried the door hinges might squeak. Yet, subconsciously she suspected a trick on Daemon's part.

Not bothering to close it for fear a click might give her away, she rushed across the balcony and peered into the woods that surrounded the property—guarded, he'd said, so she needed a weapon to venture there.

She ran back into the bedroom, pulled on her leather coat and yanked the spare sword out from under the mattress. After attaching the sheath to her belt, she returned to the balcony. Evergreen vines wound through a wrought iron trellis attached to the house, perfect for use as an escape ladder. As long as the rungs didn't suffer from corrosion, she figured they would hold her weight.

She swung over the top of the railing and let herself down. The toes of her boots felt for the first rung. Gingerly, she tested her weight on the metal. When it didn't give, she eased down. Her boot slipped on glossy leaves. She lost her footing and stifled a wild cry of alarm. With a thud, she landed on the grass. Panicked that she'd be discovered, she hurried to her feet and crouched in place.

Darkened windows all across the back of the house made her skin tingle. She felt like a fish in an aquarium. Daemon could be watching her from anywhere.

Surely if he saw her, he would stop her flight. Yet she halfway suspected he planned the whole damned thing.

For now, she had one goal in mind as she dashed for the woods—focusing on her mission. Time to track down Krustalus and end his miserable life.

The autumn midday sun couldn't part the thick gray cloud cover, and the mist still clung to the ground, rising three feet from the wet grass. The forest itself appeared dark, deep and ominous, but her only concern now was freedom and slowing the thunder of her heartbeat for fear Daemon would hear it no matter how far she ran from him. She wished the legend that vampires could be exposed to sunlight and burst into flames was true. She'd have another way to terminate Krustalus.

Nearly to the fringe of the forest, she hoped to find a way off the property under the cover of the trees.

But as soon as she reached the comforting shade of the pines, a low, threatening growl warned her she wasn't alone.

Maison and Daemon watched Tezra through the greatroom windows. He shook his head when she made a dead stop at the edge of the forest.

"She's been allowed to run, why?" Maison asked.

"She needs to discover for herself that not only is she protected here, but she's unable to leave."

Maison folded his arms and rocked on his heels like he always did when he was worried. "Lichorus is pretty incensed.

She's stirring up dissenters."

"Tezra needs my help." Daemon would not ask for anyone's approval.

"To discover the identity of the vampire who killed the police officers, I know."

"To bring down Krustalus."

Maison stared at Daemon, his blue eyes wide. "What has *he* done?"

"Maybe killed her parents and before this, other humans."

"You don't know for certain?" Maison sounded concerned and angry at the same time.

"Her sister does. She's been traumatized and can't communicate with anyone. If Tezra was one of us, maybe she could reach her and learn the truth about the murderer."

Maison cursed under his breath. "Damn, Daemon. You cannot consider turning her for that reason."

"How in the hell did she get another sword?" Daemon mused, ignoring his friend's comment when she whipped the steel out of its sheath and leveled it at the first of the wolves.

"You vowed you'd never turn another human after the last three times. You cannot change the huntress."

"I can think of no other way."

Tezra twisted around, keeping the snarling wolves, now eight of them, at bay. She didn't attack them, only remained in a defensive posture.

Despite her angry words concerning Krustalus, Daemon didn't feel she would kill him in cold blood without first proving he truly was responsible for murdering her parents and others.

"What if *I* turned her?" Maison asked. "I wouldn't claim her, just change her so she could help her sister. The clans of Oregon wouldn't care if I did so, as long as she consents."

The thought of his longtime friend tasting her blood made Daemon's turn slightly green. "No."

Maison's brow furrowed. "What difference would it make?"

Daemon couldn't answer. The woman had burrowed under his skin, and no matter how much he felt she'd be his undoing, he didn't want anyone else to have her.

"You've already decided this?" Maison asked.

"If you turned her but didn't take her for your mate, others would undoubtedly try. She would be a prized vampiric possession, don't you agree?"

Maison gave a stiff nod.

Tezra swung around when a wolf behind her got too close. She called out to him with soothing, coaxing words of praise.

"Ancient vampires wouldn't give her a choice. She couldn't stand up to them."

"She has agreed to this permanent bond?" Maison asked.

Daemon gave a dark laugh. "Of course not." He motioned to Tezra, her sword poised. "That's why she's playing with our friends and not waiting for my love bites upstairs. But the truth is I've told her I wouldn't change her."

Taking a deep breath, Maison nodded. "Then all is not lost."

"Meaning?"

"There's hope she won't succumb to your desires, and you will not have to break your oath to yourself." Maison rubbed the back of his neck like he always did when he was getting ready to reveal something he wasn't sure Daemon would take well. "Do you know she was in a special home for troubled teens for two years following her parents' deaths?"

"Why?"

Maison lifted a shoulder. "She was troubled."

"What did the records say?" The fact she hadn't had a family to care of her during her formative years bothered Daemon. Even though he was the bastard son of a king, his father had provided for him and Atreides in a castle befitting the ruler of the land. Their duchess mother and her family supplied the warmth and loving the two growing boys needed until she died. Then his uncle had taken care of them. He couldn't envision Tezra living in an ice-cold environment, especially after her parents and sister had been taken from her.

Maison cleared his throat. "She escaped from the home several times but was easily recaptured."

Now Daemon saw why Tezra fought confinement.

Maison turned to watch her. "She always went straight to the hospital where her sister was sent. The staff from the home alerted the hospital, and when she arrived they took her back into custody."

"Was she allowed to visit her?"

"No. They restricted Tezra to the home. One of the staff said allowing her to visit her sister would be tantamount to rewarding her dysfunctional behavior."

Daemon fisted his hands. "Dysfunctional for wanting to see her sister?"

"Yes. The first time they had to wrench her away from her sister's embrace. They said it caused problems with the younger sister, that it was too traumatic for her to see Tezra."

"Too traumatic to separate them, they meant." Daemon had every intention of overstepping his bounds and straightening out the home, or shutting it down. He took a deep breath to settle his anger. "What else did the records say?"

"She is a very talented weapons expert. They couldn't pit her against females, only the more capable males. They said it was due to the anger she harbored. They trained her in criminal investigations because she tested off the scale in that subject, but several of her instructors recommended she continue with the huntress training she'd started before her parents were murdered."

"Was she ever destructive?"

"They felt she might be somewhat unstable."

Daemon raised his brows.

"She insisted a vampire had killed her parents when they knew it couldn't be since the murderer hadn't killed them like a vampire would and hadn't taken their blood either. They called her delusional."

Daemon snorted. "No more delusional than you or me."

"I must see to other matters. With your permission, I will take my leave." Maison bowed, and Daemon reciprocated.

When Maison left, Daemon opened his patio door and ditched his clothes. The mist enveloped him, shielding him from prying eyes before he shape-shifted effortlessly into a wolf. Bounding across the yard in his thick brown pelt, he headed straight for Tezra. He'd made it clear to his guards that should she take a jaunt through the woods there would be hell to pay if anyone injured her. Yet, he still worried one of his vampires might take their guarding mission a little too far, especially now that she was armed.

All eight wolves turned their attention to his loping gait, and he warned them, *"The lady is not to be harmed, only stopped. Just stay out of her sword's path."*

When she twisted her head around to see what caught their eye, her mouth dropped and she took a step back.

Yes, here comes the big bad wolf, darling. Meet your adversary, he thought. *Round two.*

Chapter Seven

Great, just great. If it wasn't bad enough that vampires in the form of eight gray wolves surrounded Tezra in the forest shadows, now an even larger one advanced on her. Except that he was more of a sable brown mixed with deep reds, the tips of his coat black, and his face a cream-colored mask, making him stand out among the rest. *Daemon.* The sunlight glinted off his dark brown eyes, and his mouth seemed to smile, which did nothing to still her racing heart.

Before he reached her with his long gait, his sable coat glistening in the filtered sun, Atreides appeared in front of her and bowed his head slightly in greeting. She quickly stepped back.

"Where the hell did you get a huntress's sword?" Atreides asked.

With a brow raised, he shared eye contact with the large wolf. The other wolves dispersed, headed across the property. Dismissed, most likely.

"Daemon's guards warned me you were out here, and I came to escort you back." Atreides's jaw tightened. "The SCU sent hunters in search of you. You have to tell them you're safe."

Oh hell, that's all she needed—the SCU dictating to Daemon. That would really go over well. "Let me go, and that will be the end of their concern."

"I'll be glad to release you when the killer of the police officers is dead," Daemon communicated to her. The brown wolf melted into mist, then transformed into his human form—his very naked human form. She couldn't help but look at the whole of Daemon, every gorgeous muscle taut. He looked ready

to pounce...on her.

A heated flush spread through her. What was there about him that made her dissolve under his heated scrutiny? She'd only had a couple of hunter lovers to compare him to—and they were conceited to the max. Interested only in one thing—she learned after the fact—having sex with a willing huntress. *Bastards.* Quick, like a swordfight with a vampire, in and out and finished.

Daemon relieved her of her sword and handed it to Atreides. "Next time, make sure she is *totally* disarmed." He seized her wrist.

"Let go of—" Darkness swallowed her next word, and in the next instant, she stood in Daemon's cavernous bedroom with him.

"Daemon, what should I do about the SCU? Lichorus has threatened to tell them you're holding Tezra hostage. If they take you into custody, our people will revolt," Atreides said from downstairs.

Lichorus? Who the hell was that? Refocused on the immediate concern, Tezra didn't want to escalate tensions between the SCU and Daemon and his people when he was only trying to keep her safe.

"I'll talk to them, convince them I'm all right." Her gaze drifted to his body—hard and controlled—yet she figured if she touched him anywhere, he'd lose the restraint he seemed to have. So why was the thought so appealing?

His touch tender, Daemon ran his hand down her arm. "All I want is to keep you from being the vampire's next victim."

His words and actions thawed the ice wall surrounding her heart, yet she still craved freedom. Being imprisoned by him was too much like when she was in the teen home under guard.

"I have to research the crimes." She had to remain focused on her mission, not give in to the sexual craving he'd aroused.

She didn't like being under Daemon's thumb, but the alternative? The SCU would lock her away so she couldn't go against their rules any longer. She took another look at Daemon's physique, which brought a lift to his lips. She made the decision, right or wrong. She'd stay with him. At least she thought Daemon would let her continue her work, albeit under his control. The SCU? They'd stop her.

"You will let me conduct my research, right?" Her words

were spoken as a promise rather than a question.

His dark eyes hinted at amusement.

She took his subtle response as a yes. "I'll tell them I'm secure in your protective custody. They won't like it and will insist you hand me over for safekeeping."

"I'll keep you safe." His eyes entranced her, and he drew close. A shiver of need rippled through her. He gripped her shoulders, and the touch of his strong hands triggered the desire to experience the shared intimacy of lovers, to feel the burning passion grow between them.

She blinked away tears and studied the flecks of gold in his dark chocolate eyes. His thumbs rubbed her shoulders, warming her to the marrow. But then he turned away from her and pulled a phone from a drawer. Wordlessly, he handed her the receiver and lifted a brow.

Hoping this wasn't a mistake, she dialed the administrative head of the SCU. "Julie, it's me, Tezra."

"Where have you been? Half the hunters in the state are searching for you. Senior Council Member Ingrid is furious you were trying to solve the police murders."

Tezra could envision Julie twisting her shoulder length hair around her fingers like she did when her nerves were on edge.

"I'm safe. Have them call off the search."

"A vampiress reported that you'd been taken against your will by a vampire named Daemon. Senior Member Ingrid says he's one of the most powerful in this country. How can we know you're there voluntarily?" Julie nearly whispered the question as if she was concerned the vampire would be listening in on the conversation.

Which he was.

"I have to go, but no, he's not holding me hostage."

"The senior staff will want you here to tell them yourself," Julie said.

Tezra knew then Julie believed she was being held hostage.

"Listen, he and his people are keeping me safe. And he's helping me catch the murderer of the police investigators. I've got to go, really. Tell them I'm fine. I'll get in touch with you when we have some answers."

"The SCU won't like it." Julie's voice sounded low and irritated.

"The killer's after me. It can't be helped. I'll be safe—"

Julie cleared her throat. "The senior staff will send hunters to check your story."

"We'll be in and out investigating. So we won't always be at Daemon's place."

Julie snorted. "All my best, sweetie, and be careful. Even with the vampires watching your back, one of them is the killer."

"I'll keep in touch." Tezra hung up the phone and handed it to Daemon.

He set it on the dresser, then ran his hand over her arm, his eyes smoky with desire. "What now?"

She tilted her chin up. "I want to look at the tissue samples." No way was she going to tell him she wanted red-hot sex with him.

His brows rose. Well, hell, he asked! Or had he realized from her expression what she'd been thinking? Her skin heated with mortifaction.

Daemon wrapped his arms around Tezra's waist. Her traitorous body responded to his touch as if she were the lock and he the key, and with one twist they fit together in perfect synchronization.

She hadn't been with a hunter in so long and it was always strip-and-do-it. No foreplay. No building up to the big crescendo. Just strictly get the business out of the way. Sure, the guys seemed perfectly satisfied, but she'd felt...*used*, afterwards, though she'd thought she would have felt something more. Loved, wanted. Wasn't to be.

"Are you sure all you want to do is look at tissue samples? Nothing else?" He pulled her hair away from her neck and held her firmly. His tongue swept down her throat.

She closed her eyes and shivered.

Of course she was interested. Damned interested. But how could she justify sexual relations with a vampire? Not any vampire, though. The prince of all the American clans. *Daemon*. The only man she'd ever felt so drawn to.

A part of her desired to be wanted, to be cherished, protected and respected for who she was, despite what she'd done to her family.

Daemon reached up and ran his hands over her breasts,

massaging, lifting, weighing them, stealing her thoughts.

More than ever, she wanted the intimacy Daemon offered her.

He pressed her mouth with a kiss, hard and unwavering, demanding and possessive. She shouldn't have loved it. She should have resented his rapaciousness—how he plundered her like no man had ever done, would never risk doing without her consent. Instead, Daemon lured her in. He wove a silken web of charm securely around her like a warm cloak on a bitter cold day.

She battled the burning urgency that consumed her and refused to give in to her baser longings. Yet her fingers itched to comb his unbound hair, and she yearned to press against his firm, naked body.

His velvet tongue, tasting of the richest wine, probed hers and intoxicated her. He slid his hands down her arms and caressed. The cashmere sweater slipped against her sensitive skin as she—a telepath who could not be hypnotized by a vampire—fell under his charm. A split second of panic made her feel vulnerable to his vampiric magnetism. Then she realized he couldn't control her in that way, nor she him.

Leaning into his kiss, she gave in to the lust. She wouldn't allow herself to call it anything other than a raging desire to satisfy primitive needs. She wouldn't fight the growing attraction any longer. Her fingers gripped his back and held on as she teetered precariously at the edge of a jagged cliff.

His mouth shifted down her jaw, and she closed her eyes, knowing the bloodlust called to him, compelling him to feed. Her pulse pounded in her ears, and the sound must be an aphrodisiac to him.

Worse, she tilted her chin up and offered herself to him, encouraging him to take her while she raked her fingers through his sable hair, fanning the satiny strands over his broad shoulders.

Daemon's tongue traced her throat, sending exquisite shivers down her skin. His hands shifted to her breasts, his fingertips caressing her swollen nipples. She moaned as his touch destroyed any last resolve to keep him away.

Without warning, he suddenly separated from her, muttering under his breath in some ancient language, and she guessed by his angry tone it was a curse.

His jaw ticked, his smoky gaze refocused on her, the heat in his eyes still simmering. He communicated his thoughts to his brother, "*Tell Lichorus all is well with the SCU. I'm sure this will make her feel much better.*"

Lichorus again.

Before she could question who the troublemaking vampire was, Daemon took her face in his hands and leaned over to kiss her.

His heavy erection pressed against her belly. Her own panties were damp in anticipation. Jeez, what was she thinking? She wanted to help her sister, destroy Krustalus, ensure the SCU didn't turn Portland inside out looking for her, and so what does she do? Offers her throat and everything else to a vampire.

His powerful fingers chased away the tension in her shoulders. What she wouldn't give for a man's touch like that every evening after a day of investigations.

He kissed her mouth, stealing her breath. Controlled, he pressured her to respond. Shaking loose her reservations, she kissed him back. Her tongue tangled with his. Her body molded with his hard form. Wanting all of him, she craved the intimacy only lovers captured.

He slipped her sweater over her head, then plied her mouth with his heated kisses. Her fingers explored the fluid way his biceps moved, strong and resilient. He growled and reached behind her for the fastener on her bra.

"In front," she said against his mouth.

With a snap, he unfastened the bra and tossed it away. Afterwards, he moved so fast, before she knew it she was naked in his arms, then on the bed.

His arousal pressed into her waist, his dark eyes nearly black. His jaw tightened, and she assumed his canines itched to extend, but he fought revealing them.

She looked away from his entrancing gaze, knowing his hypnotic qualities could compel most humans to his will. "W-will you make love to me?" She ran her fingers over his chest, touched his nipples with feather-light sweeps of her fingertips, forcing him to growl. "Will you?"

"Why?"

His erection pressed against her, and she wanted to feel him deep inside her. Why? She knew he wanted her. She knew he'd had lots of lovers before, had to have, as ancient as he was. So why not have an experienced lover like him? No commitment. No one would ever know.

But more than that, she desired to learn why her grandmother had fallen for a vampire. If the one she'd loved was anything like Daemon...Tezra was beginning to understand the compelling attraction. She wanted to know why blood bonds offered their blood so readily—drawn to the vampire's power. She craved feeling real pleasure like hunter lovers had denied her.

Or was she the one who was incapable of having great sex? Something psychological that impeded her happiness? She had to know.

She got up the nerve and said, "I've never..." She meant to say, "...had a lover who was all that great," but Daemon smiled, the look as self-satisfied as ever, as if he knew.

She shoved at him to get him off her. "Forget it. Let me up."

"You'll permit me to feed?"

"You won't turn me." Even though she wanted him to. Whatever it took to rescue her sister. Once he made love to her, would he change his mind? She was willing to risk anything.

"I told you I wouldn't. I'll make love to you, feed and...nothing more." The glint in his eye suggested amusement, intrigue and something else. Conceit, most likely. Arrogance, that after he made love to her, she wouldn't want anyone else.

He kissed her more slowly now, not in such a rush. As if he believed he'd won her over already, or maybe he realized he had one shot to prove to her she'd want no other.

She folded her arms beneath her head.

He stopped and looked at her, a smile tugging at his lips. Ooh, he could be so exasperatingly superior.

"What?" she said, her tongue laced with poison.

"You would enjoy the experience more if you participated."

"What you mean is *you* would enjoy it more. I don't want to get you so stirred up that you forget you're only making love to me this one time."

"I won't forget. Participate, or not. I'll enjoy watching you take pleasure anyway."

He gave her a devilish smirk as if he didn't think one time would be enough, then touched his lips to hers while his hands moved from her shoulders to her breasts.

She took in a deep breath of him, memorizing his scrumptious spicy scent, the feel of his hands caressing her breasts, the way he moved against her, hotter than a summer drought.

His eyes clouded over when she combed her fingers through the silky strands of hair, and his fingers stilled on the tips of her breasts. Breathless, he waited, and she realized then how much her touch affected him. *Power.* Having control over the ancient one incited her to touch him more. She ran her hands over his back, the muscles tightening, tensing.

His body had stilled, but now he rubbed his erection against her waist. His mouth moved lower, trailing kisses along her throat, down her breastbone, then fastened to her breast and suckled, long and hard. Bliss stroked her nerves, pleasuring her like never before.

"Do it," she whispered, her voice lost with the feelings he elicited from her, her nipple puckering into a hardened nub, the other waiting in hopeful expectancy.

He smiled at her, then switched to the other breast, giving it its due. "Patience."

Patience wasn't one of her virtues either. She pressed against his arousal, attempting to push for a quicker resolution. His lips turned up darkly, and his fingers drew lower as hers moved down his waist, tracing the hardness to his buttocks. God, if she could only have a butt as sinfully firm as his.

He shifted off her, and she worried he was going to stop. She held onto him, her lips parted to object, until he slid his fingers over her mound, down, dipping deep inside her, stroking, retreating.

Barely breathing, she tensed, squeezing his buttocks. His fondling intensified the feeling of near euphoria, higher, higher. She reached for the peak.

Shifting, twisting under his fingers' skillful touch, pushing against him, wanting more, she craved having him deep inside her at the same time.

"Make love to me," she whispered.

"I am," he said, his voice husky and deep.

He held himself back with the utmost restraint, his neck so tense it looked like it could snap. Why?

The bloodlust. He was keeping his canines from extending.

He wanted to make love to her like she'd asked, wanted to pleasure her first to allow her time to change her mind.

But she wouldn't change her mind.

"Make love to me, Daemon, and feed. I offer my blood to you freely." And my life for one of a vampiress, if she could convince him to do the deed.

"Hmm, Tezra." He renewed his strokes, the kisses. He teased her nipples with his velvet tongue, then sucked on them with a vengeance.

And she felt in heaven, craving more and more, like an addict needing a fix.

She rocked against his fingers, trying to push the climax. She climbed to the top of the peak, felt the exhilaration, the warmth wash through her like a warm Caribbean wave in summer. She moaned his name with exquisite pleasure, never having experienced anything so satisfying. Delightful aftershocks rippled through her body.

Daemon's eyes smiled, and his lips curved just a hint. She loved how he seemed to take pleasure in pleasuring her, just as he said he would.

Not wasting another second, Daemon pushed the siren's legs apart with his knee, then worked his way between them. "We will *only* make love and I'll feed, but I won't change you," he reassured her, having lost the battle to keep his distance the minute she said she wanted him.

He desired to take it slow, but her willingness and soft moans had pushed him faster than he'd intended. His damnable canines threatened to extend, and fighting them had given him a painful crick in the jaw.

He couldn't refuse to make love to her and feed, not the way she'd aroused him, yet he couldn't calm her like he could any human. If she grew scared when he bit her, he could hurt her, bruise her, tear her skin unnecessarily.

"Tezra." He stroked her hair and kissed her lips. "I won't be able to stop once I start. I haven't fed for too long."

She caressed his face, her green eyes dark with desire. "I want you to, Daemon. Please."

He nuzzled her cheek, gently moving her face to the side to expose her throat, testing her resolve. "Sweet, Tezra, relax." He spoke calmly, with patience, though he couldn't control his canines much longer.

She took several deep breaths.

Touching her throat with light sweeping strokes of his tongue, he centered himself between her legs and entered slowly. She sucked in her breath. He backed out and tried again, slipping into her velvet glove, the territory a tight fit. Stroking his back, she kissed the top of his head, spreading her legs to open herself up to him further, encouraging him to continue. Her pelvic muscles tightened, narrowing the passage to nearly impassable.

"Relax," he whispered against her breast, his tongue teasing the raised nipple, so delicious to taste. When he tugged on it with his lips, her pleasurable moan stirred his libido more.

He lifted his face and studied the way she breathed so quickly and her pulse fluttered rapidly under the skin. His teeth extended, his mind no longer in control, he tilted his head back, closed his eyes and thrust his erection deep inside her.

She gasped but held him tight. He pulled out slowly, then buried into her tight sheath, drawing out the pleasure.

Her vitality called to him, begged him to take his fill. He licked the sweet skin of her throat, preparing himself to take some of her life force, to share another experience with her, to love her completely the vampire way.

He pricked her skin with his canines, and her eyes opened, startled, but she couldn't object, not as far as he had gone. His erection pulsed as he dove into her heat, farther and deeper, then he sank his canines into her neck. She sighed with gratification, the way a blood bond did when a vampire pleasured her.

"Oh, Daemon." She thrust her hips against him, making him finish what he'd begun. She touched his waist with tender strokes, titillating him.

Her blood tasted like the richest burgundy wine, satisfying the craving he had for her...for the moment. Yet, for an instant, he had the insane urge to take her for his own.

He licked the drops of blood, sealing the wounds while he continued to thrust into her. Then with a headiness he'd never experienced, waves of heat flowed through every pore, his skin saturated with sweat.

With one last push, his seed spread through her. He sank against her soft, warm body, covered lightly in perspiration and the fragrance of peaches and Tezra's sweet sex.

She came again, her muscles clamping over his erection, holding tightly, claiming him for her own. He'd never felt so satisfied, so complete, yet with a sinking feeling, he knew nothing could ever come of his relationship with her. He rolled onto his back and pulled her on top of him.

He hadn't planned for Lichorus's telepathic communication, and he was glad the vamp sent the message straight to him so that Tezra didn't hear it. *"I have discovered information about the police killings. If you meet me now, I will give it to you, my darling prince."*

"You will give it to me now, Lichorus, unless you do not stand by me as you have promised."

He could almost sense her smiling, but would the vamp give him the news or not? Or was it just a ploy on her behalf to stir up more trouble?

"Give her up, my prince, and I will tell you anything."

Daemon sensed Lichorus's trap, closed his eyes and wrapped a wall around his mind to terminate her communication with him. He would not be misled by her now or ever.

Tezra gave a sad smile and closed her eyes, but not before he saw the moisture gathering in the corners. Her warm tears dropped on his bare chest, nearly unmanning him.

Her silky skin rested against Daemon's. Her shallow breath tickled his chest, and her springtime fragrance scented the air. He ran his hand down her back with a gentle caress, his thoughts in turmoil. "Did I hurt you?"

"No." She sniffled.

"Did I push too fast?"

"I-I shouldn't have wanted this. Not when everything's so wrong. I don't deserve..." Shimmering with tears, her eyes locked on his for an instant, then she looked away.

Before Daemon could respond, she left the bed and quickly dressed.

"Tezra—"

She waved her hand to silence him. *Him!* The leader of the vampire clans in America!

"Where are the stolen tissue samples? I need to look at them." She kept her eyes averted as if she was ashamed of herself.

"What don't you deserve, Tezra?"

But she wouldn't say. He realized then as much as she needed to heal, she needed someone who would be her mate forever. Not someone like him who had no intention of taking a mate again. So why did he feel like he'd slipped into the bloody pits of hell?

Downstairs the doorbell rang, and Atreides warned, *"Five armed hunters at the door, Daemon. I don't think it's a social visit."*

Chapter Eight

His thoughts focused on the hunter menace standing at his front door, Daemon dressed in a flash. But Tezra grabbed his arm before he could leave the bedroom, her eyes reflecting deep-seated worry.

"Let me speak with them first," she implored.

He brushed the hair away from her cheek. "They can't take you away from me. *From here,* I mean," he amended, hating that he'd made the mistake. "I can provide better security for you than they can."

"I agree. I want to stay with you. Until the murderer is eliminated."

"All right. We go together, but I won't back down concerning you staying here with me." He wrapped his arm around her waist and pulled her close. As soon as he did, he regretted his action. She melted in his embrace, and he was reminded she needed someone to care for her more than he could commit to.

Transporting her to the front door where Atreides and Voltan stood silently blocking the hunters' entry, Daemon felt white-hot tension in the air. He quickly released Tezra, severing their connection. He wanted to shove her behind him so he could protect her from the hunters, but fought the urge. They were not here to harm her, he assured himself.

One of the older hunters, gray-haired but tanned and trim, gave Daemon a cursory look, then turned his attention to Tezra as if the ancient vampire was of no consequence. But Daemon knew damn well the hunter wasn't that naïve.

"Tezra Campbell, we're here to escort you safely to SCU headquarters."

"Thank you, Gavin, but while the killer vampire is on the loose, I prefer remaining here under Daemon's protection."

"I would speak to you alone," Gavin said.

Before Tezra could reply, Daemon said, "No."

The look she gave him could have sliced a watermelon in two. "I've already told you I intend to stay here," she said to Gavin.

"You're not...yourself." Gavin glanced at the vampires, emphasizing his point.

"I'm not under their control, if that's what you're inferring."

One of the hunters unsheathed his sword with a whoosh. Voltan drew the one he had at his back, and Daemon's canines instantly extended.

"The senior staff wants to speak with you," Gavin said, his tone more conciliatory. "If they agree, you can return here."

Daemon intended to tell the hunters, tactfully, where they could go, but Tezra took the lead. "Have them call me, and we'll talk."

"You face expulsion," Gavin said, his voice hard.

"Hmm, well, if Krustalus—my parents' murderer—gets hold of me, expulsion from the SCU will be the least of my troubles. Tell Senior Staff Member Ingrid that I'm staying here until Daemon takes down the killer." She patted Daemon's arm, surprising the hell out of him. "He'll watch out for me until then."

Gavin's gray eyes narrowed while he considered Daemon. "What if he's in league with the killer?"

"Like they're all cut from the same evil cloth, right, Gavin?"

He gave a haughty snort. "Coming from you, that's laughable."

Tezra's cheeks colored. "I'm staying here." Before anyone could say anything more, she slammed the door in the hunter's face.

"That went well," Atreides said, then looked out the peephole. "They're arguing about what they're going to do now."

"Watch them. Let me know if they pull anything." Daemon said to Tezra, "I have the tissue samples in my office, if you'd like to look at them."

"You know I would."

His thoughts shifting over different worst-case scenarios,

Daemon walked Tezra down the hall. Like most SCU staff, Tezra didn't care for vampires, and after what had happened to her parents and Krustalus taunting her over the years, Daemon understood her animosity. But sticking up for him in front of Gavin and the other hunters took real courage. She had to know her words would get back to the SCU, which wouldn't sit well with many. It more than pleased him to think he'd had a positive effect on the way she felt toward some of his kind.

He guided her into his office and immediately thought of how hers had looked—light and airy with paintings of windswept beaches and seagulls heaven bound. Of light oak wood file cabinets and a desk cluttered with typed papers, record files and handwritten notes. Bright yellow sticky notes had covered the edge of her computer monitor. The screen had been filled with the scene of a tropical island paradise. Cozy and small, a guest bedroom turned office. Homey and scented with Tezra's sweet fragrance.

His office? Large, dark heavy wood, antique, neat, not a paper or pen out of its designated place. Outfitted with the latest in computer equipment. Luxuriously furnished, the brown leather desk chair, a high-backed recliner built for comfort. The massive furniture polished to a brilliant shine with lemon-scented cleaner. Paintings of dark-forested scenes hung on the walls, and the music of the ancient Celts was piped in to give an old-world feel. Even if he had to change with the times, he preferred to surround himself with some of the ages he'd lived through.

"They'll be back and cause more problems, you know," she said, her voice filled with soft regret.

"Yeah. Hunters are as tenacious as a mongoose with a snake. Once they discover their prey, they won't let go."

She looked up at him, her eyes sparkling with humor. "You're saying I'm like a snake, and they want me dead?"

He gave her a small smile and motioned to his chair, a veritable throne in this day and age. "They don't want to give you up. What if you worked for my side?"

"But you're the good guys. I mean, you're not rogue vampires."

Not exactly the good guys, he noted with wry amusement. "What if we formed our own task force to take down renegade vampires and cut the SCU out of the business?"

"So why haven't you done it before?"

"Like humans, not all vampires are suited to policing the world. Each of us has our special interests."

"And yours are?" She sat at his desk.

"At the moment, protecting you and finding the killer."

"And ruling your people." She opened the first of the reports concerning the tissue samples from the dead police officers and began to read over them.

He couldn't help thinking how much she changed the feel of his office—the smell of peaches lingering in the air, the sight of her fuzzy pink sweater against the dark brown leather chair and her jeans-clad buttocks pressed against his seat, the sound of her light breath and her enchanting pulse, always beckoning to him. His office would never seem the same.

More than that, he couldn't get his mind off the way she fell under his spell when they'd made love. So eager and responsive...every kiss, every touch made him crave even more. Here he'd hoped taking the plunge would have revealed a woman who couldn't meet his expectations. When in truth, she had exceeded his wildest dreams.

The way she pulled her hair behind her ears, chewed on her bottom lip, ran her long fingernails over the notes, made her look sexier than hell.

She tilted her head to the side, looking puzzled. Then she narrowed her eyes. "Some of these are *my* slides! When the hell did you steal them from my apartment?"

"You needed them *here*. And here are the samples from the dead police officer outside your apartment." He motioned to a table where a microscope and slides caught her attention.

For a moment, she stared at them, then looked at Daemon. He again waved at the samples. "See if you can learn anything from them. You're the expert, after all."

She made a face and he figured she thought he was mocking her. After living so many centuries, he'd learned a wide variety of occupations, some of which came in handy now and again. So yes, he was somewhat of an investigative expert, but two heads were definitely better than one. Her gaze shifted to the official police files sitting next to the microscope.

Looking back at him, she parted her lips, her eyes questioning.

He shrugged. "Files on the murders. We'll need to see all

the evidence if we're to solve this case."

"The chief gave them to you?"

"Borrowed. I don't trust him, Tezra. It's just too convenient he found out who murdered your parents. I don't like expedient solutions."

"As much as I hate to admit it, you may be right."

He studied her glum expression and wondered what kind of a relationship she'd fostered with the chief. "Why do you say that now?"

Sighing, she examined the slides. "I'm a friend of Mandy Salazar who speaks very highly of him. She's a police dispatcher and has been for years."

"For more than ten years?" He couldn't help but wonder if the earlier police killings were related to the recent ones.

She lifted one of the slides and placed it under the microscope. "A carefully calculating vampire committed the first murders and tried to make it look like a hunter's vendetta. The new ones are done by a raging vampire, no finesse at all. I'm almost certain two different rogue vampires killed the police officers."

Folding his arms, Daemon tilted his chin higher. "We have already discussed that the killer could have changed his MO. Was Mandy Salazar working for the chief when the other officers were murdered?"

Tezra didn't look at him, but nodded.

"And?"

"I didn't know her early on. I was only sixteen at the time and she was twenty-two. While I was trying to learn what I could about the first police murders, I chanced to meet her. She said the chief had been under a lot of strain before the killings, and she was afraid this would break him."

"A lot of strain."

"Yes, she figured it was concerning family issues. You know, most often that's the case. Anyway, he kept pretty quiet about it, though she could tell something was wrong because he'd become moody and ill-tempered when he normally was a pretty cheerful guy. I've never known him as anything but somber and serious. I can't even imagine him being jovial. But I questioned some others, and they said the same thing, that it was like a storm cloud had settled over him and changed him permanently."

"Before the killings?"

"Yes."

"And then?"

"For a while things were worse. She said it was really bizarre. She went to get a cup of coffee in the break room and three policemen there immediately silenced their conversation. At first, she just figured they were talking about some woman they'd had sex with or something crude that they didn't want her to hear, but then one of the men was murdered. Two weeks later, another one was. And you saw what happened to Officer Stevens."

"So Mandy thought maybe a connection existed between the murders of the three men and the secret talks they'd had."

"Yes." Tezra sat back on the leather chair. "I assume the police officers had murdered a vampire friend of his, and he took revenge. When I began investigating Krustalus, he murdered my parents as a warning. The point is why would he wait ten years, change his MO, and begin killing again? It's got to be someone else."

Daemon looked at the files, then back to Tezra. "You alluded to the possibility that the earlier case had something to do with the chief."

"Oh, yes. Well, after the men were murdered, the whole police force was antsy. The chief pretty much barricaded himself in his office for weeks, then when no more killings occurred, he started to lighten up. Except he never did return to his cheerful self."

"Not enough evidence to make anything of that."

"Like I said, I figured the drastic change in his mood probably had something to do with his family life. So I began to investigate that." She flipped through the files and read through each page like a speed-reader would.

"And?"

"I'm afraid there was nothing much there. He had a wife and two young sons. No mistresses that I could discover. I checked out his financial status. No gambling debts or substantial money crisis that would account for his behavior. His parents were both alive and well. No problems with the in-laws, another source of contention in bad marriages. He genuinely seemed to love his wife and children."

"Any siblings?"

She looked up from the files. "A sister and her husband who were both police officers."

"You know, Tezra, getting you to reveal what you suspect is like getting blood out of a tomato."

"Nothing there either." She closed the file and opened the next one. "The brother-in-law was well-liked and is still with the police force. The chief's sister committed suicide some years ago."

"Suicide."

She paused in her reading. "Yes, clinical depression. She'd been on medication and took an overdose."

"When?"

"A year after the killings."

Daemon rubbed his chin while he considered the information. "Why was she depressed?"

"An organic thing, apparently. Nothing going on in her life. Oh, she couldn't have children, so I suppose that could have been it."

"And her husband? How did he feel about the matter?"

"Broken up about it. Same thing with the chief. Mandy told me she figured his sister's suicide would send him over the edge. But apparently, he got over it and got on with his life."

"Lots of siblings don't get along."

"I wouldn't know. My sister and I always did." She looked up at him. "What about you and your brother?"

Daemon gave a sardonic smile. "When he's not getting himself into trouble."

"Oh?"

"Usually over blood bonds. The women he chose to be blood bonds; sometimes their boyfriends didn't like it."

"Did he use his charms to get the women to agree?"

Daemon shook his head. "He's always had a way with women, even before the plague made him vampiric. But in truth, the vampirism does accentuate the ability, and we really haven't a lot of control over it."

She *hmpfed*. "That's like saying you have no control over what you eat or—"

Daemon chuckled darkly. "That is not what I'm saying at all."

"Sounds like it to me."

Touching her cheek with his fingers, he grew serious. "You will have the same effect on men, though from what I've seen, you already wrap them around your finger and render them senseless."

"In your imagination."

He leaned down, pulled her hair aside and kissed her neck. A shudder went through her as her hands stilled on the file she'd been reading. "I have heard the humans' crude comments concerning you, Tezra. It is not just my imagination." He sighed, deeply exasperated, knowing if any man approached her in an attempt to fulfill his sexual fantasies with the huntress, Daemon wouldn't be responsible for his actions. "You still haven't told me why you think the chief might have had something to do with the vampire killings of his police officers."

She closed her eyes and took a deep breath, then opened them and studied Daemon. "I think like you do—he has a connection or he wouldn't have gotten Krustalus's name so easily. I think the chief knew his name all along, but worried there wasn't anyone who could or would be willing to take the vampire down until now."

Daemon opened his mouth to speak, then his lips turned up a notch. "I like it when we're on the same path. But you still don't think the crimes are connected? What if the recent murders triggered Chief O'Malley to contact you?"

"It's possible the chief was concerned Krustalus was at it again. I'm wondering if they'd had somewhat of a truce. The police officers murdered Krustalus's friend, Krustalus took revenge, the chief turned the other cheek, end of investigation. According to these files, the inquiry into the murders was hastily conducted, then the cases were filed away as unsolved, as if no one even wanted to get to the bottom of them. I have no idea about the Council of Hunters' investigation concerning my parents' murder, except that they questioned several hunters who were borderline rogues. Again, the results of the inquiry were inconclusive. Anyway, that's what I'm speculating for now about Krustalus and the relationship he has with Chief O'Malley." She took a deep breath. "Thank you for 'borrowing' the files and letting me look at them."

Daemon bowed his head in acknowledgement, but she was too busy reading the paperwork to notice. He intended to transport himself to the greatroom to allow her to look at the records alone, unsupervised. He had high hopes she felt more agreeable toward him, though he chided himself for having any feelings of the sort.

Before he left, Atreides spoke to him privately. *"Daemon, the hunter named Gavin is calling on his cell phone in the front courtyard, but I can't tell what he's saying. They're not leaving though. At the same time, Voltan's overseeing matters out back."*

"Prince Daemon, hunters have made their way through the forest, but our guards have advanced," Voltan warned.

Daemon ground his teeth. *"I'm coming."*

Tezra studied the glass slides containing the tissue samples under the microscope. Safe and secure for the moment.

"I'll be right back." Daemon vanished before she could answer.

As soon as he appeared in the greatroom, she yelled, "Wait, Daemon! Where are you going?"

Wolf form, or vengeful vampire? Daemon grabbed his favorite bastard sword from the rack next to the patio doors. With a blade sharply honed and a more impressive size than most of his ancient weapons, either swung two-handed or single-handedly while carrying a shield or another weapon, he gripped the leather hilt. To Atreides, he said, "Keep an eye on the hunters out front and inform me if they make a move. And don't let Tezra leave the house."

Her footfalls raced down the hall, but before she could reach the greatroom, Daemon motioned to Atreides, vanished and reappeared in the mist near the edge of the forest. He wasn't about to get into an argument with Tezra over whether she could come with him. Protected in the house was the only place he wanted her to be.

Five hunters stood their ground near the edge of his property. In the form of wolves, Daemon's vampire guards kept the hunters from advancing in the direction of the house.

His sword readied, Daemon stalked toward them with Voltan at his side. "Trespassing is a crime, gentlemen."

The hunters held their swords outstretched, trying to keep the wolves from tearing them apart. The hunters barely looked in Daemon's direction.

"I'm within my rights to have my people shred you into bite-sized pieces. For all I know, you are hunter renegades, have to be if you're trespassing without a warrant."

"The word is you have Tezra Campbell, an SCU investigator, locked up in your home. We're within our rights to remove her from it," the tallest of the five men said.

"We should kill them, my prince," Voltan said. "Let me have the tall one. He is more my size."

No one Daemon knew was close to Voltan's nearly seven-foot height.

"*Daemon!*" Tezra screamed at him telepathically.

Daemon turned his attention to the house, sensed Tezra's anger, but she wasn't scared, which probably meant only one thing. His brother was confining her to the house. "If any of the hunters slice at my guards, kill them," Daemon told Voltan.

He returned to the greatroom and found Atreides pinning Tezra facedown on the couch, her cheek pressed against the cushions, her hand behind her back, elevated so she couldn't squirm loose.

"Let go of me!" she screamed.

Atreides, red-faced and with clenched teeth, growled. "She tried to chase after you. I told her you wished her to stay safely in the house, but she wouldn't cooperate."

When he released her, she jumped off the couch and swung her fist at Atreides's face.

Interceding on his brother's behalf, Daemon grabbed her wrist and pulled her away. "I thought you wished to see the evidence from the officers' killings."

"I want to know what's going on with the hunters outside. You can't kill them, Daemon, or they'll call you and every one of your people rogues and issue a termination decree for all of you."

"I'm touched you're concerned for my welfare."

She jerked her wrist free. "I don't want you killing them."

Daemon motioned to his back door. "The hunters have no business trespassing on my land. They've been told repeatedly you are here of your own freewill by your own admission. Despite being a vampire, I have rights."

"Yeah, well, maybe I need you to live a little longer so you can keep me safe."

He couldn't help but smile. "I have no intention of dying by a hunter's sword. But Voltan sometimes needs a chain to keep him in line. I wish to return to the problem out back, but if I cannot be assured you'll stay put..."

She folded her arms and looked more cross than ever.

He turned to Atreides. *"Keep her here."*

Atreides gave him a smug smile and bowed his head.

Then Daemon vanished and returned to Voltan's side. The tallest hunter spoke on his phone, attempting to keep it private, but Daemon's attuned hearing caught most of the conversation. Someone was ordering the siege to cease. *Smart move.*

The hunter shut off his phone. "We'll be back." He and his men turned the way they'd come, and Daemon's wolves loped back to their posts.

Voltan resheathed his sword. "What was the woman's problem?"

"She intended to save me, but Atreides wouldn't let her."

Voltan gave a short bark of laughter.

When Daemon and Voltan reached the greatroom, Atreides was pacing. "Apparently when you put out the ruling no one would turn Tezra, Lichorus assumed you were claiming Tezra for your own. Anyway, she just informed me she'd tell the SCU, and she's not one to issue idle threats."

"Who is Lichorus?" Tezra asked, her voice highly agitated.

"A vampiress who's stirred up enough trouble to warrant my action." To Atreides, Daemon said privately, *"Relay to Maison he's to take Lichorus into custody."*

Atreides bowed his head to Daemon, then stalked toward the den.

"I have to visit my sister at Redding Hospital," Tezra said. "I see her every day without fail—except since I've been in your *protective* custody. Someone have a car I can use?"

Instantly suspicious, Daemon suspected she had other motives. Afraid the SCU would be too much for him to handle? Not a problem. Concerned he wouldn't give her enough freedom? If so, she had that right.

"Car? We generally prefer vampire transportation. No traffic jams, no red lights, no tailgaters and no high gas prices," Daemon said.

She folded her arms. "I like driving from place to place; gives me time to think about the cases I'm working on. Why don't you leave me off at my apartment, I'll pick up my car, see my sister and return here afterwards."

"Voltan, you come with us."

"I want my weapons back," Tezra said, her voice deepening. "And my cell phone."

Atreides rejoined them. "Maison's bringing Lichorus in as soon as he locates her."

"My cell phone?" Tezra asked Atreides.

He slipped it off his belt. "Okay with you, Daemon?"

Tezra grabbed for the phone, but Atreides moved it beyond her reach.

Her face reddened.

"Let her have it."

"And my weapons?"

"Later." Daemon pulled her against him, and his body reacted to her with rabid attraction. She only made him feel this way because he hadn't had a partner in so long—it was nothing more than lust, pure and simple. He refused to be drawn into another deadly relationship. Besides, she needed so much more from a male companion. Determined not to get sucked into traitorous thoughts of another mating, he whisked her away to Redding Hospital.

The hospital looked like it was washed in a coating of fresh milk—everything was white, the walls, floors, even the garments the staff wore. Someone had the notion that colors would upset the patients, which Tezra thought was the most inane idea anyone ever had. Even flowers left by family and friends had to be regulation white.

A little wobbly from the teleporting, she stood with Daemon and Voltan outside her sister's door while she gathered her composure. Her sister seemed to enjoy her visits, though bringing two vampires along put Tezra on edge. She reached for the door and Daemon said to Voltan, "Stay here and let no one in."

Releasing the door handle, she frowned at Daemon. "You shouldn't go in either."

"You can't go anywhere without me or one of my men."

"You *can't* enter."

Daemon quirked a brow. "The killer could be in the room

this very moment, waiting for you. You're not going anywhere without one of us. That's my final word."

Whirling about, she grabbed the door handle, her stomach tightening into knots. Since the killings, Katie had been locked away in the hospital and never saw another vampire. In fact, no one but Tezra visited Katie. As far as everyone else was concerned, Katie didn't exist, didn't share their world, didn't need their words of comfort.

Tezra entered the sitting room and smiled at Katie, curled up on an overstuffed chair, wearing a pair of white sweats, her red hair braided. Her eyes lighted, then rapidly shifted to Daemon. She seemed curious, not afraid, and Tezra assumed she thought because Daemon was with her, so he wasn't anyone to worry about, thank God.

He bowed his head slightly, and Tezra wanted to slug him for greeting Katie in the vampire way.

Katie's eyes widened, and she gasped. Tezra crossed the floor, knelt beside her and held her hands. Now twenty-two, Katie was a beautiful woman. If Tezra could only draw her out of her shell. Stifling tears that always pricked her eyes when she visited Katie, she knew if she lived to be a hundred, she'd always feel the same sorrow for what she'd done, wishing she could do anything to save Katie from a life of nothingness. But now she had a hope of bringing her out of the abyss.

Tezra knew she had to do it.

But first, as soon as they finished their visit with her, Tezra would see Chief O'Malley. If he could prove Krustalus was the murderer...

She feared revealing the killer to Katie wouldn't bring her out of her silent world. Tezra felt she had no choice but to try the option Daemon had suggested.

"This is Daemon, a...friend of mine," Tezra said.

Katie looked at him again.

Tezra settled down with her and shared entertaining pieces she'd found on the Internet, leaving out any mention of the gruesome world she surrounded herself with. She didn't party, date, eat out or have fun. Her sole relentless focus was investigating vampire crimes and helping Katie to the best of her ability—though it was never good enough. Nothing but making Katie whole would ever be good enough.

Her phone vibrated against her waist, and she pulled it out.

Out-of-area call. Just like six other missed messages she'd had. Telemarketer, no doubt. She poked the on button, prepared to tell the rude caller she wasn't interested in whatever he was selling when Chief O'Malley's deep voice penetrated her defenses. "Come see me. Cafferty's Tavern now, and come alone."

Before she could respond, the phone clicked dead. Chill bumps erupted on her arms. The chief's message eerily mirrored Officer Stevens's call to her.

"You can't go," Daemon said. "Alone, I mean."

Katie's eyes widened, and she opened her mouth to speak, but when Tezra saw her reaction, Katie averted her eyes and clamped her mouth shut.

"Katie, did you want to say something?"

For a glimmer of a second, Tezra thought there might be a breakthrough. Though she'd seen Katie react mildly to situations before, she'd never seen her respond in such a pronounced way. Yet as before, Katie stared at her lap and withdrew into her private world, her emotions shut down.

"Katie, I've got to take care of some business, and I'll return later."

Katie's gaze shifted back to her.

Keeping her eye on her sister's reaction, Tezra said to Daemon, "I have to see him alone. I'm sure it has to do with the case."

"No. You put your life at risk the last time, and I won't—"

Tezra glanced sharply at him, but again turned to see how Katie was taking it. She'd switched her attention to Daemon, waiting for him to finish what he was saying.

"We go together or not at all, Tezra."

"All right. You watch my back, for now. But if he doesn't show because you're with me..." Tezra gave him a warning look, then leaned down and hugged Katie. "I'll return as soon as I can."

Katie wouldn't let go of her hand, and Tezra's heart sank. She was sure Katie possessed some sense of time, and they hadn't visited long enough.

"Honey," Tezra said, her voice choking, "I'll be back."

Daemon touched Tezra's arm, and Katie looked alarmed.

"She seems upset. I thought she never showed any

emotions."

"She doesn't, normally. Though on occasion she's shown a hint of them. The psychiatrists say it's natural, like mimicking behavior and doesn't really mean anything."

Tezra gave her another hug. "We'll be back. Soon."

When she couldn't break free of Katie, Daemon took Tezra's arm. Immediately, Katie let go. Daemon led Tezra out of the room and shut the door.

Her heart in her throat, Tezra stared at the door. "I can't stand seeing her like this one more day. I have to speak to the chief. If we learn he has no proof..."

In her worst nightmares—and she'd had enough to fill several lifetimes—she didn't want to be a vampire, but she was resigned to it anyway. "I just think he's involved somehow," Tezra said.

"Did you find anything else besides what you told me before?"

"Krustalus wears Green Irish Tweed, the same cologne my father wore—it's one of his macabre games. The night Officer Stevens was murdered, Krustalus wore the same scent. Stevens wasn't wearing any—he was allergic to most fragrances according to his wife. Yet, I distinctly smelled sandalwood near Stevens's body. The killer's scent, not Krustalus's. So there must be two of them."

The thought of Tezra in the warehouse district with two murdering vampires chilled Daemon's blood. If he'd been responsible for her, he would never have allowed her to meet Stevens there. *He* would have taken care of the matter.

Daemon let out his breath in exasperation and wrapped his arm around her to take her to Cafferty's Tavern. How fragile she seemed where her sister was concerned.

Hell, she *was* his responsibility. Once Krustalus came to his house and made his connection with Tezra known, it became Daemon's business. He released her. "You stay and visit with your sister. *I'll* speak with him, *alone.*"

He intended to get the answers he wanted *without* an SCU investigator breathing down his neck. If she got pissed off at him—well, more so than she already was half of the time—she could turn him in for human rights violations in the event he had to resort to forcing the truth from the chief. But Tezra's safety was more of a concern, and he smelled Krustalus's hand in this.

She gave Daemon a look that could change a man into a toad.

But then she slipped her arm around his waist with a lot more strength than he gave her credit for. "If you think I'm staying behind, think again. I'm going with you. And that's *my* final word."

Chapter Nine

Daemon wouldn't be dictated to, not by any vampire or even one sexy special crimes investigator. Before he could say so, Tezra said, "Chief O'Malley wanted me on the case. He'll speak with me. You're a vampire. Why should he talk to you?"

Because Daemon could force him to? "Why does he want you on the case so badly?"

"Krustalus killed my parents! The chief wants me to stop the murdering bastard, and I'm the only one who believes he's involved. That's why."

Reaching down, Daemon touched her silky hair. "I want to help you and Katie." He pressed his head against her chest and listened to her rapid heartbeat. Then he lifted her chin and looked into her eyes, which were filled with condemnation. "Against my better judgment, I'll take you with me. But know this, Tezra, I will use whatever means necessary to force the chief to tell me the truth."

"Fine, no problem. Let's go."

He gave her a hard look. "As an investigator for the SCU, you're supposed to frown on actions like that."

She hmpfed. "I'll frown deeply while you question him if it makes you feel any better."

She tightened her grip around his waist. The treacherous notion of hauling her off to his bed sprang to mind.

Mist coated the entire warehouse district in a leaden, wet blanket and everything was deathly silent. When Tezra,

Daemon and Voltan approached Cafferty's Tavern, a couple of blocks from the police killings, the icy air sent a shiver through her. Daemon reached for her hand and she was certain he regretted taking her.

"I'm cold, not afraid," she said.

An obscure smile curved his lips while he and Voltan scanned the area.

"When we return, I want my weapons back," she snapped, hating that he thought she was afraid, though she did feel more vulnerable without her sword, despite having vampire bodyguards. But she wasn't scared!

Daemon opened the metal door to the bar, the rusted hinges sending a creak echoing across the narrow street where several pickups parked curbside. Despite the sleaziness of the place, business appeared brisk.

When they walked inside the dimly lit building, all conversation faded and everyone looked them over. A scantily dressed woman, the only other female in the room, set a tray of beers on a marred table with a clunk.

Tezra brushed past Daemon and the murmurs began. He seized her wrist and she frowned up at him. He didn't lighten his grip. Possessiveness or protectiveness? She should have been annoyed, but instead she felt as though he genuinely cared for her. Nobody had acted that way toward her in a very long time, and she hated how much she craved it.

Voltan's heavy step followed close behind.

"He plays cards back there." Tezra motioned past a bar stretching across the room to a door in the back. She recognized some of the men as off-duty cops, others probably closer to the criminal element they arrested during duty hours, though maybe some were undercover.

"You've been here before?" Daemon asked, his voice surprised.

She shrugged. "Not to drink, but yeah, when I investigated the first of the most recent police murders."

A burly cop stood and moved into their path. His neck was about as thick as his waistline, and the image of a gruff bulldog came to mind. He gave Daemon a sinister look and smiled at Tezra. "Investigator Campbell, the chief's busy."

"We have an appointment."

"Chief's busy," the officer repeated.

"Step aside," Daemon said, as if the guy was just one of his minions.

Voltan moved closer. Though the policeman attempted to stand his ground, everyone watched the situation with wariness, but no one else came to the man's aid. Voltan towered over the guy until he finally lifted a massive shoulder and sat.

Daemon opened the door to the backroom, and four men looked up from a game of cards. Chief O'Malley sat at the far side of the table, facing him. More gray seemed to stripe his fiery red hair than the last time Tezra had seen him a few days ago. He glowered at Daemon and Voltan, then he shifted his attention to Tezra.

He motioned to the other men. "Can you give us some privacy for a while?"

"Sure, Chief."

"Yeah, we'll get a drink."

Though several half finished and empty bottles of beer sat on the table already, the men moved past the vampires, giving them a wide berth, and the last man winked at Tezra. "Campbell."

Daemon turned his head so quickly, he looked like he intended to bite the guy.

She squeezed Daemon's hand, which brought his attention back to her, then the cop shut the door with a jolt.

"Tezra, gentlemen," Chief O'Malley said. "What can I do for you?"

He acted like he'd never called the meeting, and now Tezra wondered if he had.

"Stand outside the room, Voltan," Daemon said.

Voltan bowed and did as he was told.

"Could you please tell us how you knew Krustalus murdered my parents?" Tezra said, her voice sugar sweet in an attempt to get him to reveal the truth.

The chief's bushy brows rose. "How would I have known that?"

Wrong answer.

Daemon moved so swiftly Tezra only heard O'Malley's chair crash on its back. In the next instant, Daemon pinned the chief against the wall, his hand around the chief's throat. "Tell...me...the truth."

"H-he told me to say he was the one."

"Why?" Daemon growled.

"H-he said it was a long-running game he had with Ms. Campbell. I had to tell her."

A game—the bastard. Tezra's heart sank. "So you have no evidence. Nothing to prove he was the one. Did he appear before you?"

"Yes, he came to me," the chief choked out, his eyes bulging.

"And Stevens, how come *he* knew?" she asked.

"Krustalus told him to tell you. I didn't know he was going to kill Stevens."

Daemon released the pressure on the chief's throat, though he didn't let go.

"So then Krustalus returned and ordered you to tell me the same thing?" Tezra asked.

"No. I mean, he told Stevens in front of me. After you called and said Stevens was dead, I wanted you to catch and...terminate the bastard."

Wary that this was another of Krustalus's games, she didn't trust the chief in the least bit now. "I'm not a huntress."

"Mandy says you were trained as one before the SCU switched your job. I figured you'd have reason enough to want him dead."

She sure as hell did, but no one would use her to bring Krustalus down for their own dark purposes.

"What was the connection between your police officers and the killer?" Daemon asked, his voice as smooth as black velvet but as deadly as the honed edge of a steel blade.

"No...no connection."

"There had to be a connection," Tezra insisted. She wanted to mention how Mandy had overheard the police officers talking, then all of them ended up dead, but she thought better of it in case the chief was involved.

"Nothing I could discover," the chief sputtered.

Not getting the answers she wanted, she focused to read his mind when Voltan relayed, *"Everyone's clearing out. Looks like we're in for some trouble."*

"Krustalus," Daemon said, and Tezra sensed him nearby too.

She barely breathed when the number of vampires with him increased by several. "Did you want to meet me here because Krustalus made you call me?"

"No," the chief said.

Daemon squeezed the chief's throat tighter.

O'Malley grappled with Daemon's fingers. "Yes," he croaked. "He said it was part of the game."

Daemon released him, then joined Tezra. "We return now."

"But if Krustalus is here, we could kill him. Well, I could help if you'd given my swords back."

"I wouldn't risk it. There are too many with him." Daemon telepathically communicated, *"Voltan, we return home."*

But Voltan was already in a fight to the death and Daemon cursed under his breath. *"Atreides, Maison, send men to Cafferty's Tavern. Now!"*

Slipping Tezra's wrist daggers out from underneath his coat, he handed them to her.

Relieved and surprised, she raised her brows, then hurriedly strapped the wrist blades in place.

Daemon yanked the door open and kept Tezra by his side. Krustalus wasn't in the bar, but several others were and some of them were attacking Voltan. The others waited patiently to get a piece of the action around the perimeter of the melee.

Like a choreographed dancer, the. giant swept around, clanking his sword against his attackers' weapons.

"Stay close," Daemon said to Tezra, then swung his sword at a vampire. With one swift strike, he severed the vampire's head from his neck.

Tezra dodged a vampire who tried to grab her wrist. Then she twisted around and hit him in the chest with her dagger. As soon as the blade reached his heart, he dissolved into ashes.

Only five of the vampires remained when Krustalus appeared. At once, she smelled her father's cologne on the bastard and knew it was him. But he was taller than she had imagined, his hair darker, his eyes smaller, and his chin longer with a cleft the size of the Grand Canyon dividing it.

"Sorry," he said, whipping out his sword, his black eyes sparkling with humor as he shifted his attention from Tezra to Daemon, then back to her again. "I had some other pressing business. Why don't you come with me, dear Tezra, and

Daemon and his friend can live?"

"Seems you and your thugs are outnumbered," Tezra said as Voltan killed another.

Krustalus flexed his muscles and moved toward her with vampiric speed.

Daemon, who'd been fighting with two vampires, killed the one and left the other for Voltan, then moved in between Tezra and Krustalus to shield her.

"Why don't you pick on someone more your own size, Krustalus?" Daemon sliced at the rogue, but Krustalus dodged the strike.

Krustalus's thin lips turned up slightly, but his eyes remained ice cold while he slid out of the blade's path again. "You want the huntress for your own, yet she is a dark huntress—a borderline renegade." He lunged with his sword, but Daemon struck it with his own, knocking it out of his path.

"You have already taken several women for your own and it hasn't worked out, from what I understand, my prince."

What was that all about?

Tezra tried to get around the two of them to help, but Daemon effectively kept her behind him. Suddenly, four more vampires appeared and when one came for her and another tried to strike Daemon from behind, she wondered where the hell Daemon's reinforcements were.

The vampire seized her arm, and she quickly cut it. "Behind you, Daemon," she screamed.

But because he had to concentrate on the ancient in front of him, the vampire behind him stabbed him in the back.

"No!" Tezra finished off the one who tried to grab her and attacked the backstabber.

"The huntress will end up like the other women you have mated, Prince Daemon," Krustalus taunted.

Daemon struck Krustalus's sword hard with a clank. "So why would you want the lady?"

Tezra stabbed the vampire who'd struck Daemon but missed his heart. She swore under her breath and attacked him again.

"She will obey me. I'm not as soft as you," Krustalus promised.

Suddenly, Atreides, Maison and a flurry of other vampires

appeared in the bar. Krustalus gave a wicked smile. "Later, Tezra love. You and the others cannot always watch your back." Then he vanished along with what was left of his vampire minions.

"I'm sorry." Atreides grabbed Daemon's arm when he looked ready to collapse. "Your telepathic communication was scrambled by Krustalus's vampires. We weren't sure where you were."

Tezra sheathed her daggers and wrapped her arm around Daemon's waist. "Are you going to be all right?"

"We go home," he said in an annoyed tone of voice.

She wasn't sure why he was mad, whether it was because he'd been injured, his brother and his people hadn't shown up soon enough, he'd missed taking Krustalus down, or her concern about his welfare. But she was angry too.

She'd have given about anything to see the murderer of her parents turned into a pile of ashes.

"Daemon—" She didn't get a chance to say anything more as he pulled her hard against his body and took her into the dark abyss.

∽

After teleporting through a vortex of blackness, Tezra found herself in the middle of Daemon's bedroom again, dizzier this time. Voltan was speaking with Atreides and Maison downstairs, explaining what had happened in the bar.

"You shouldn't have gone with me, Tezra." Daemon collapsed on a chair, his look stern but pale.

Before she could respond, a tall, thin man dressed in a tux and carrying a black bag appeared next to him. Daemon greeted him with a bow of his head. "Doc."

"I understand you've been injured, Prince Daemon." The doctor quickly dispensed with the small talk and helped Daemon out of the chair, then removed his coat and shirt.

"A mere inconvenience." Daemon cast an arrogant smile at the doctor.

The man considered the wound and gave his head a slight shake, but hurried to clean it.

"Will he be all right?" Tezra asked. She assumed Daemon

would be well enough once his vampiric healing abilities took over, though his face was ice white, and he looked ready to crumple.

The physician cast her an inquisitive look, then dismissed her question and said to Daemon, "She's not one of us. She's...the huntress?"

"Special Crimes Unit investigator by occupation," she corrected him.

His mouth curved up a little while he bandaged the wound, stemming the flow of blood. Afterwards, he gave Daemon a bag of blood and bowed his head. "The wound should heal within the next twenty-four hours, but I suggest you stick to much more passive pursuits until then."

The doctor glanced at Tezra, then vanished.

"Are you all right, Daemon? Do you want to lie down?"

Still pale as death, he shook his head and sat back on the chair.

"All right, then." If he wanted to pretend to be Mr. Macho, fine. She might as well get on with business. "About this matter with Krustalus—the chief has no proof that he murdered anyone. It's just the chief's word that Krustalus told him he was the killer. The vampire could easily deny it."

"I assumed as much, but the next time I tell you what to do, you'll do it." His eyes narrowed and focused on hers.

Tezra ground her teeth and bit back what she wanted to say. Her sister's dilemma was too important to quibble over whether Daemon thought he could control Tezra's actions or not.

"One of Krustalus's men could have spirited you away. I knew it was a setup, and next time I tell you to do something—"

She folded her arms across her chest and disregarded his scolding. "Listen, I don't believe a perfect solution will ever avail itself. There's only one way to deal with this. You have to turn me."

Daemon shook his head.

Once she made up her mind—damn the consequences—there was nothing stopping her. She was not taking no for an answer from him or anyone else. She was bound to bring her sister out of the darkness—and if it meant being changed, fine. She'd do it. "If changing me doesn't work, Daemon, there will be hell to pay."

Daemon's lips rose in a slow, lazy smile. Arrogance became him. "You presume too much." Rising from the chair, he took her hands and kissed her lips, no pressure, gentle, unassuming.

She pulled away from him and crossed the floor to the patio doors. "You said I had no other option. Why did you bring it up, then?" Taking a settling breath, she looked out at the forest. "I *have* to free Katie from this nightmare." When Daemon didn't say anything, she said, "You must have changed dozens of humans before. Why not me?"

His eyes darkened.

She folded her arms. "Okay, you know my past. Tell me what went wrong when you changed a woman."

With one fluid move, he closed the gap between them. His mouth claimed hers, and his hands caressed her shoulders. She wanted to melt under his touch, but the issue of his turning her needed to be resolved. *Dammit.*

Grabbing his strong hands, she stepped back from his kisses. She was certain it was the bloodlust calling to him. "Tell me what happened."

His jaw tightened. Keeping his teeth sheathed, or annoyed she'd question him?

"You have to tell me why you won't turn me, or let someone else do it."

He growled something foreign, then straightened his broad shoulders. "When a vampire turns a human, it has to be mutually agreed upon. The vampire seeks a mate; the human wishes the vampire to be his or her mate in return. The rogue vampire is the exception, turning a human either against her will or letting her flounder on her own afterwards. That behavior is condemned."

He sat back on the chair, but she noticed his color already returning.

"I don't want to be anyone's mate. I just want to be turned. Well, not really, but I don't feel I have any choice if I'm to help my sister."

"Therein lies the problem. As a fledgling, you'd be at the mercy of rogues if you weren't under a vampire's protection as his or her mate. But the other difficulty is your reluctance to be turned. No decent vampire would change a human who didn't wish it."

She didn't have a choice. Didn't she already say so? And she didn't want a mate! Attempting to get her annoyance under wraps, she drew close to him, crouched and circled one of his shirt buttons with her fingertip. "Not all vampires turn an individual and then make him or her their mate."

"In those cases, the human pays the ancient vampire for his or her services for some mutually agreed upon consideration to make the mortal semi-immortal without the tie. They're a...different class of vampires. Not totally accepted by most."

"I don't understand."

Daemon shrugged. "Vampires as a class are not accepted by many so we tend to be...clannish. When a human is turned who is not mated for life with a vampire, they are considered outsiders. Occasionally, a vampire loses a mate and will accept an outsider for his or her own. But this rarely happens. The practice of turning humans for monetary gain or some other form of consideration and not taking them for mates isn't well received. We...have rules we abide by. When humans are changed who don't become part of our society, they avoid being governed by our rules and often become rogues."

"So if they're outsiders and vampires don't want them, why couldn't I be one of those? From what you're saying, an ancient wouldn't be interested in me." Sounded like the best scenario to her. She wouldn't be ruled by anyone then, and everyone would leave her alone. She'd have some new abilities that would give her some advantages, if she avoided thinking about the consequences. She could save her sister and—

Daemon let out his breath. "Hunters or huntresses rarely choose to become vampires, but in every known case, they've been selected as mates. You would not be considered an outsider because you're a huntress, and a rogue ancient could very well desire you, Tezra."

She was certain he wasn't telling her the whole truth, but she didn't know enough about this aspect of their society to know for sure what he *wasn't* saying. "All right, so what happened when you turned a woman?"

His eyes burned with a flicker of flame, but then his gaze shifted to her fingers trailing down his shirt. "They *wished* to be turned, not the same as you. They each *desired* to be my mate."

"They?"

He looked up at her. "Three. Three times I chanced taking a

human mate. Three times it led to disaster."

She let out her breath and touched his cheek with a tender stroke. "Maybe changing someone like me who doesn't fit your perfect profile will work better. I won't become a bad mate, because I won't be yours anyway."

He growled and caught her hand. "You're not listening to me, Tezra. I wouldn't change you, then allow you to roam freely without my protection."

"Add *controlling* to your growing list of undesirable traits, up at the top with arrogant and impatient."

He gave her a sinister smile.

"So, what happened to the others?" she asked, not wanting to hear she might have to fight a former mate of Daemon's if she learned he changed Tezra and didn't like it.

"Those of us who were turned by the plague centuries ago learned to live with the changes, or died trying. But vampire-turned humans sometimes become power hungry. Sometimes they turn into rogues."

Her mouth dropped. She couldn't imagine anyone Daemon had loved turning renegade. "The three women you changed?"

He nodded. "It doesn't always work out."

"You think I would be like that?" Her words were threaded with disbelief. Well, not that she was perfect but...

"You have a history of...disobedience."

She narrowed her eyes, instantly undoing her attempt at placating him.

"You would have to obey me, and I know you wouldn't."

She clenched her teeth against saying anything that would make him change his mind, but the memories of living in the home under strict rules rushed back to her all at once. Obeying Daemon, being ruled by him, didn't appeal, and she wasn't about to allow it.

He lifted his gaze from her sweater to her eyes. "I wouldn't take you for my mate."

"Not your mate?" she asked, her voice elevating too much. She didn't want to be his forever, but the notion he'd changed three women he wanted to live with for an eternity but wouldn't change her hurt—putting it mildly. Which was crazy because she shouldn't have cared one iota.

He shook his head. "I vowed never to take another."

"What happened to the other three?"

"Dead. Rogues are terminated. Either by hunters or vampires. Though in the case of newly turned vampires, the one expected to do the job is the one who turned them."

"You did it?" she asked, half whispering the question.

"I should have realized they couldn't handle the change. I should never have turned them."

Reaching up, she untied the leather strap holding his hair back. The satiny strands fell free and caressed his shoulders like she wanted to. "I won't become a rogue."

His eyes darkened. "You want to kill Krustalus with or without proof he's the murderer."

She combed her fingers through Daemon's dark hair, and his eyes clouded with desire. "I'm not like the other women," she mouthed against his lips. "I don't want power, or immortality or anything but to help my sister."

"You're already a borderline rogue, Tezra." He rose to his feet, placed his hands on her shoulder and kissed her throat, stealing her breath. "Everything about you warns me to take a step back and keep my distance." He pulled away, his eyes clouded with lust. "We're going to have to find another way."

"Add pig-headed to your list of foibles," she growled, glowering at him.

He studied her, his face expressionless.

"Fine, just fine. Take me back to see my sister. I'll visit with her for another hour like I normally do, and then...well, then we're going to discuss this some more. Just because you have some mating phobia, when I've already said I don't want to be your mate, well, that's your problem. And dammit all, I'm not a rogue, and I wouldn't become a rogue. Well, sometimes I get pretty pissed off, but doesn't everybody? Hell, of course everyone does occasionally. It doesn't mean—"

Daemon took her hand and pulled her close, his touch tender. Her eyes moistened. His mouth covered hers, and she leaned into his kiss, cherished the feel of his silky skin against hers, the heat of his body, the arousal she'd stirred.

"I'm sorry, Tezra," he said.

Before she could react to his making her feel small and unwanted, he transported her to Redding Hospital.

The blackness dissipated, and she was momentarily

disoriented, her stomach still reeling with the vampiric travel, then she realized she stood before her sister's door. Voltan stood behind them, ever on guard. Letting out her breath and still peeved with Daemon, Tezra grabbed the knob and opened the door.

She expected to see her sister staring into space as she usually did when Tezra visited her in the evenings before one of the staff put Katie to bed, New Age music softly playing on her CD player. When Tezra found the sitting room empty and deathly quiet, panic seized her. She dashed into the adjoining bedroom, but found no sign of Katie. Nothing was out of place. The snow white bedcover was undisturbed. The white petal roses tinged with a hint of pink she'd brought Katie the day before fluttered under the heating vent, perfuming the air with their tea-scented fragrance. The plastic chair still sat next to the bed where Tezra often read to Katie at bedtime. Nothing was out of the ordinary.

Only Katie's absence.

A new trickle of dread wormed its way down Tezra's spine. Attempting to squash the chill spreading through her, she hoped that maybe one of the staff had taken Katie to the common room to be with other residents. But Katie cringed in crowds, and Tezra was certain her sister's behavior hadn't miraculously changed within a couple of hours.

Tezra ran out of the room and into the hall, trying to sense if she could feel her sister's presence anywhere. Daemon shadowed her, and Voltan's heavy footfall wasn't far behind.

"What's wrong, Tezra?" Daemon reached for her hand.

She wiped away tears, hating herself for getting emotional, likely over nothing. She couldn't sense Katie anywhere. "I'm afraid Katie's left the building. I'll die if Krustalus has taken her."

She grabbed Daemon's hand and hauled him with her, maneuvering down the labyrinth of halls past a tennis court-sized cafeteria filled with white plastic chairs and laminated tables.

She pulled him into a large room, where several residents sat playing cards or watched television from a half ring of white vinyl couches. Katie wasn't among them.

Tezra's head pounded. "Nobody else would have taken her." Whipping around, she headed for the administrative office to speak to the woman in charge, Mrs. Wither, an unsmiling middle-aged woman who Tezra felt should have retired years ago.

Ready to tear anyone apart who had allowed someone to remove her sister from the facility, Tezra harbored a shred of hope Katie was still in the building. "What if Krustalus knew or suspected what we were up to? What if he figured out that I might be able to reach her mind and find proof he was the killer?"

"I should have taken her to my house into protective custody," Daemon said with dark regret.

"Damn, I can't believe I put my sister in further peril." She vowed with all her heart to set things right with Katie, if she could only reach her in time.

Voltan interjected, "What do you wish me to do, my prince?" His voice was shaded in anger, and she figured if someone had taken her sister, whoever did so wouldn't stand a chance against the giant. And she'd be there to back him up.

"Stay with us for now."

Tezra stormed into the administrative office. Mrs. Wither, tall and thin with bulging black eyes, choppy brown hair and an exaggerated under-bite, nearly dropped her cup of coffee. She reminded Tezra of a startled Pekingese.

"What are you doing in here?" the woman snapped.

Tezra's emotions were tied to her with barely a thread. One last tug and she'd lose control. "Where's Katie Campbell?" she asked in a fairly reserved manner, though her blood boiled.

Mrs. Wither backed into her desk, her face as white as the crisp suit she wore.

"Where is she, and don't make me ask again," Tezra growled.

"Patrico Sargento signed the release papers and—"

"Patrico?" Tezra squeaked. Her knees buckled, but Daemon grabbed her by the waist and steered her to a chair.

"Patrico?" Daemon asked Tezra. "The SCU senior staff member that you said was murdered?"

"Yes, ten years ago." Tezra's voice was hollow, and she felt sick to her stomach. Her thoughts swirled. "Patrico can't just take her out of here. He has no authority. Besides, he's supposed to be dead. "

Mrs. Wither's eyes looked like they were going to pop out of her head. "Mr. Sargento had credentials." She grabbed papers off her desk and shuffled through them. "Here. Power of attorney." She looked perfectly pleased with herself. All nice and official, as if she had done nothing wrong.

"I'm Katie's only living relative. He can't have gotten a power of attorney to take care of her. Hell, he's dead!" And if he really wasn't, Tezra would strangle him once she got hold of him! Rubbing her temple, she massaged the colossal headache pooling there while she scanned the papers.

Daemon took Katie's picture attached to the paperwork and handed it to Voltan. "Warn Maison what has happened."

"Tell him what, my lord? That a dead hunter removed the huntress from the facility? Or that Krustalus has her?"

Daemon frowned at him. "That someone has taken her, but we can't be sure where or who has done such a deed. Reproduce this and send word I want her located and returned to me at once. Arrest whoever has her."

"Even if it is a hunter who holds her hostage?"

"Hunter, human, vampire, anyone."

"Yes, my lord." Voltan left the office and discreetly vanished.

Daemon ran his hand over Tezra's shoulder and asked the administrator, "Where did Patrico take her?"

"He said the SCU wished to see her."

"Didn't you think this odd? She doesn't communicate at all. Do they often send their people here to see her?" Daemon asked.

"He has visited her before on occasion."

Tezra glowered at the woman. "Why did no one tell me?"

"I...well, I..."

"What did he look like?" Daemon asked, his voice calm but low, like the rumble of thunder from far away, foreshadowing the appearance of a dangerous storm.

"Tall, short strawberry blond hair, scar on his right cheek."

Tezra couldn't stop the shiver trilling down her spine. "It can't be Patrico. He was murdered right after I told him how the vampire killed my parents." Yet the description fit, and again she felt like she was going to throw up. "I have a photo of the senior staff at my apartment. Council members serve on the board for five years, but the headquarters issues a new group photo every year for the new members on the staff. I need you to take me to my apartment, Daemon. We'll bring the photo back here and see if Mrs. Wither recognizes him." She took a deep breath, hating what she knew was an inevitable part of the job. *"Then we go after his family. Hunters are extremely family oriented. He has to have had some contact with them."*

Though if he had, his family members could be protective to the point of being dangerous.

"What about the Council? Don't you want to check with them first to see if Patrico was bringing Katie to them on the off chance he was telling the truth?"

"If they had anything to do with covering up Patrico's death, what does that tell you about the Council? Do you think they would declare the hunter dead, then have this same hunter pick up my sister to meet with them when she can't even communicate?"

"I respect your understanding of the Council and its members and abide by your decision, Tezra." Facing Mrs. Wither, he said, "We'll be back with the photo to see if you can identify him."

The woman folded her arms. "My shift ends in half an hour. I'll be gone if you haven't returned by then."

"Wrong answer," Tezra bit out. "You'll wait for us until we return. Do you understand?"

The administrator quickly nodded.

Daemon escorted Tezra into the hall. "We go to your place." He hesitated and touched Tezra's cheek. "Are you ready?"

"Yes, let's hurry." But she couldn't get over the shock of Katie being gone, and her stomach hadn't settled from traveling the last time. Every minute Katie was missing meant she could be traumatized all the more. Tezra couldn't get rid of the feeling that she might already be too late.

Daemon pulled Tezra close, then whisked her away to her two-story brick apartment complex. The lights were on in nearly every place but hers, making it appear as dead and deserted as she felt.

When they entered the apartment, more pronounced side effects from moving in the vampire's way from one place to another—the disorientation, nausea, headache—assaulted her. For a moment, she tried to get her stomach under control and clung to the wall.

Daemon turned on the light for her benefit. She gasped. Eyes wide and barely breathing, she took in the destruction— her furniture in ruins, glass tables smashed, couches torn, the stuffing shredded, books ripped apart. Tezra leaned against the wall and closed her eyes, trying to get her physical discomfort under control while her emotions ran wild.

Daemon didn't say a word but moved so swiftly into her kitchen his appearance blurred. *"No one here,"* he announced, sounding relieved.

Her stomach settled some and concerned whoever had trashed her apartment might have found her hidden investigative files, she practically flew into her bedroom, feeling Daemon's presence behind her.

Feathers were strewn about from her down pillows and comforter, her curtains were in shreds, mirrors were smashed, and drawers were scattered in splintered remnants all over the carpet.

Who would have destroyed her place? The SCU? Krustalus? She didn't think either would have done such a thing.

Enraged, she reminded herself all that mattered was finding Katie unharmed. She stalked into her closet and poked at a cedar panel, which opened and a secret compartment containing her work appeared. She reached inside and pulled out her files. "Pays to be careful," she grumbled under her breath.

She cleared a space on the floor and started teleporting through the contents. When she found the photo she was looking for, she handed it to Daemon. "I need to keep these papers somewhere safe. It's the only evidence I have for the investigations I've worked the last four years."

"We'll return to my house first and put them in a secure place."

Before she could brace herself, Daemon returned her to his greatroom where Maison and Atreides were having a heated discussion.

"He's headed down the same path of destruction as before," Atreides said, then grew silent when he saw Daemon.

Again, Tezra felt horribly unsettled. She fought a new bout of nausea but hid it from Daemon, not about to be left at home while he questioned Patrico's mother. Yet her head swam, and speckled lights danced in front of her eyes. She didn't think she could take much more of Daemon's way of travel. But Atreides's words bothered her too. Was she the reason for Atreides's comments about his brother? She was certain that's who he was talking about, especially when she saw the heated look on Daemon's face.

"Safeguard these." Daemon handed the files to Atreides.

"I'm going with you." Atreides passed the documents to Maison, looking a bit contrite. "Voltan gave us the word."

Tezra clenched her teeth and braced herself for vampiric travel again.

Daemon didn't know what to think of the situation, with someone from the SCU being involved in Katie's abduction and the deceit concerning Patrico's death...but for now, he worried even more about Tezra's state of mind.

"You can come with us later, Atreides." Daemon wrapped his arm around Tezra's waist and returned her to the hospital's administrative office.

Mrs. Wither was no longer in her office.

Daemon rubbed Tezra's back, but his action didn't alleviate the tension straining her muscles, and she looked awfully pale. "We'll find Katie, if it takes—"

The woman walked back into the office and cried out, dropping her cup of coffee. The mug shattered on the linoleum floor, and the black liquid splattered all over her white pumps and nylons. "I...I didn't expect you'd return so quickly."

Daemon shoved the photo at the woman. "Is this the man?"

"I think so. He appeared older, but then—" she pointed to the year of the photo and said, "—this was taken ten years ago."

Tezra looked at Daemon, her green eyes narrowed and dark, but she clung to him as if she needed his support. *"We have to see his mother. She's a retired SCU huntress, so we have to take precautions."*

"Thank you," Daemon said to Mrs. Wither. He escorted Tezra from the room, appreciating the logical way in which she tackled the investigation despite how upset she appeared. "I can guess what you're thinking, but we don't know that he has anything to do with your parents' murder."

"Why fake his own death? Why take my sister when we're so close to revealing who the killer was?"

"All valid points, Tezra, but we don't know all the facts, and jumping to conclusions—"

"Isn't an investigator's way. Yet I don't feel like much of one right now."

"I'd say you're doing a remarkable job under the circumstances. We go home first, let my brother and Maison know of the situation, then we'll take it from there." He hoped he could convince her to stay there while he and his brother spoke with Patrico's mother. He definitely wanted his brother's backing and Voltan's support for additional muscle in the event the SCU *had* solicited Patrico to abduct Katie.

As soon as they returned to the house, Tezra freed herself from Daemon's grasp, though she stumbled and appeared not at all well. Again, he felt she should remain behind.

"Where are my swords?" she asked, her voice harsh as she looked from Daemon to Maison, Voltan and Atreides.

"It wouldn't be wise to arm her," Atreides said. "Remember, she threatened our guards the last time she had a sword." He motioned to Voltan. "And she made mincemeat of his leather jacket. If she gets hold of this Patrico, no telling what she'd do to him in her present state of mind, particularly if he's unarmed."

Tezra took a swing at Atreides, and he moved so quickly, Daemon didn't have time to react. Trapping her shoulders against the wall, Atreides held her firm. "You know," Atreides said in a low, husky voice, "your actions are tantamount to a vampire's sexual foreplay. If you were a vampiress, I'd have pinned you to the couch and shown you how powerful an ancient male vampire can be." His eyes sparkled with devilish delight. "If Daemon hadn't already laid claim to you, I'd assume you were trying to entice me. However, be forewarned, huntress, do not try this with other ancients. Many would not be as controlled as I am."

"Daemon hasn't laid claim to me," Tezra growled.

"Release her," Daemon said, not willing to disagree with his brother over the enchantress. He had not claimed her for his own, but he didn't figure anything he had to say would convince his brother otherwise. However, he fully intended to have a word in private with him once they'd cleared up this other matter.

Maison stroked his chin, considering the situation with

reserved thoughtfulness. Voltan stood with his arms crossed, waiting for the end result.

Atreides released Tezra, but she swung at him again. Daemon caught her wrist this time and pulled her away from his brother. "Save your energy, Tezra."

Atreides's small smile faded, and this time he addressed Daemon. "Three hunters came here looking for Tezra while you were gone. They said Lichorus has made a formal complaint to the SCU and accused us of trying to turn her against her will. The SCU Council members don't believe she's here of her own free choice."

"Did you tell them where I was?" Tezra asked, rubbing her temple, and Daemon assumed a headache was brewing in that pretty head of hers from all the anxiety she felt.

He could tell she wanted to strike out at anyone who was involved in taking her sister from the hospital, or anyone who would try to stop her in locating Katie. Something else seemed to be troubling her, yet as usual she kept her thoughts shielded from him.

Atreides tilted his head to the side in a condescending manner. "No. The SCU has no jurisdiction here without a warrant."

"I want my other weapons." Tezra took a menacing step toward him.

Daemon shook his head. Then she poked her finger into his chest. "*You* have my favorite swords. Where have you hidden them?"

Her dark curls tangled over her shoulders; her cheeks flushed in anger. Every inch of the inferno-tempered woman tantalized him. Atreides was right—Tezra truly didn't realize how she taunted him.

Atreides channeled his communication solely to Daemon, "*Lock her in the cellar before she causes the situation to become even graver. Maybe we can discover some clues without putting her life and yours in danger. She's too hot-tempered over her sister's abduction.*"

Daemon considered the wild look in her eyes. His word should be law. Not so with Tezra. Was that what appealed so much? She was like the river—shifting, dangerous, out-of-control. He agreed with Atreides about Tezra's temper and wanted to leave her behind with protection. Still, she might be able to reach Patrico where Daemon and his kind couldn't.

"Give her swords back to her, Atreides. She needs her weapons for the trouble I'm sure we're bound to get into. We'll go to Patrico's mother's home and hope the SCU hasn't already gotten wind of our plans."

Chapter Ten

When they arrived at Patrico's mother's blue and white colonial, Voltan and Atreides watched for Patrico in the event he tried to leave or enter around the side or back of the house while Tezra pushed the doorbell. Maison sat in the form of a raven on a nearby rooftop, watching for vehicles approaching the house—mainly concerned SCU hunters might arrive any minute.

Tezra's face was so pale Daemon worried traveling with her in their way was making her sick, but he knew he couldn't have talked her into staying at his home. In any event, he figured she would get farther with Patrico's mother than he and his vampire companions could.

When she reached up to push the ringer for the fifth time, Daemon took her hand and kissed it.

A fiery blaze burned in her expression like she wanted to devour him in one bite.

A white-haired woman with a benevolent, Mrs. Santa Claus kind of face, opened the door with a squeak.

He assumed the woman, wearing a floral housecoat and fluffy pink slippers, was Patrico's mother. A strong fragrance of perfume surrounded her like an invisible cloud of flowers. Mrs. Sargento gave Tezra a tentative smile, then glanced at Daemon.

The look of recognition in her eyes told him a lot about her. What was a vampire doing visiting a retired huntress? And why was Tezra here? He felt the woman knew a hell of a lot about Katie's disappearance. Using his vampiric abilities, he attempted to read the woman's mind. For an instant, he gathered a thought—Tezra was one of them. A huntress turned vampire. And then a brick wall like the one surrounding Mrs.

Sargento's backyard rose to shield Daemon from reading any further thoughts. Fine. He'd get the information out of her one way or another.

The way Tezra was studying her so intensely, Daemon assumed she was trying to read her mind also. "Mrs. Sargento," Tezra said, "I learned your son is alive and well."

The woman's face turned into a mask of white marble.

"Patrico has my sister." Tezra's voice was even, not accusatory. "Why did Patrico take her, and why was his death faked?"

"You're mistaken. He's dead. How could he have taken your sister from the hospital?" Mrs. Sargento vehemently shook her head, loosening a curl from her bun. "That's absurd."

"When was the last time you saw him?"

"At his funeral." Mrs. Sargento avoided Tezra's hard look.

"Closed casket. Did he fake his death or was the SCU in on the charade?" Tezra asked, and Daemon was proud of her for being so controlled in her questioning. Not even a hint of emotion coated her words.

"I don't know anything about this." Yet Mrs. Sargento's voice quaked.

Again, he tried to read her thoughts, but she blanked them. Daemon rubbed Tezra's arm but willed Mrs. Sargento to reveal the truth. *"Tell us where Katie is, and we'll be on our way."*

But the woman was a huntress, and he couldn't force her to reveal anything she didn't want to.

Tezra's back grew rigid and she said through clenched teeth, "Tell me where Katie is, Mrs. Sargento. The vampire who's after me could very well be targeting her now."

Tears dribbled down the older woman's cheeks. "I...oh, Patrico. If he got involved... I-I told him not to do this. I warned him the vampire... Oh, what has he done?"

"He apparently wanted to protect my sister," Tezra said, but from the way she was scowling and the tone of her words, Daemon didn't believe she truly felt Patrico stole Katie away from the facility for her own safety.

Tezra folded her arms and looked even more cross. "But I fear Patrico has only made it worse for Katie. Please, tell me where he is."

Mrs. Sargento reached out and touched her hand. "You're

not one of them?"

"No. I just need to make sure my sister remains safe from the likes of the vampire who murdered our parents."

The woman chewed on the inside of her cheek, then let out her breath. "He'll be here in about an hour. He didn't mean any harm."

"I only want my sister back." Tezra's voice attempted to appease but had a sharp edginess.

Daemon relayed the word to his vampire companions, proud Tezra could move the woman to tell the truth without violence when he couldn't entice her with his vampiric abilities. Now to confront Patrico.

Having a hard time believing Patrico was truly alive after all these years, Tezra stared at Mrs. Sargento.

"Is he coming here with Katie?" Hope instantly renewed. A chilly breeze played with her hair, but as angry as she was, she didn't imagine even sitting in the middle of a frozen iceberg would cool her down. On top of that, she felt like her stomach was still back at Daemon's house, or maybe at the hospital before that. The constant transporting was making her discombobulated.

"I don't know." The woman looked at the porch.

"Does anyone else realize your son is alive?"

The elderly woman shook her head. "They think he's dead."

Tezra took a breath of relief, glad the SCU wasn't in on some cover-up.

"Are we finished here, Tezra?" Daemon asked. He seemed anxious to leave.

She nodded. *"We need to return before the hour is up though."*

"Most assuredly."

"If you think to warn your son that we've been here, remember this, Mrs. Sargento. The vampire is after me, and most likely my sister now too. We're the best chance Patrico has against the menace. I doubt the killer will let Patrico escape unharmed again."

"Yes." Mrs. Sargento wiped the tears from her eyes with the back of her sleeve. "I-I imagine what you say is true, dear. I'm–I'm so sorry about your sister and you. Believe me. I only wanted my son to remain alive." She turned and headed into her home. "I'm so sorry."

Mrs. Sargento shut the door behind her, and the lock clicked.

"Will she warn Patrico?" Daemon asked, his voice worried.

"I don't think so. He can't just get rid of Katie now—at least I don't think he would be capable of doing anything so cowardly as that. And I truly believe Mrs. Sargento feels we'll protect her son from Krustalus."

"Still, I wish I could have wiped her mind of our visit. It would have made things simpler, more secure." Daemon wrapped his arms around Tezra and held her close, his warmth like a blanket on an icy day. "My home," he ordered Atreides, Maison and Voltan.

This time she tensed for the next wave of discomfort.

When they arrived in his greatroom, Tezra collapsed on the nearest sofa. Unable to stand, she tried to hide her physical distress while Daemon sat beside her. Dizzier than before, she took a moment to focus on her surroundings.

"We'll return within the hour. It was too risky for us to wait around, but in the meantime, I need to know more about your dealings with Krustalus, Tezra. You said he'd been murdering humans and you overheard his telepathic communications?" Daemon asked.

Everyone observed her as if she were on trial, making her skin prickle with annoyance. "I heard him speaking to someone about the killings. Until I told him I was listening." And she hated herself every day for the stupid thing she'd done.

"What was the pattern of the killings?" Daemon took her hands and gently massaged them.

The friction helped to chase away the chill in her fingers but did nothing for her queasy stomach. She took a deep breath, hating to relive the murders she'd kept alive in her memories so she could catch the murderer. "The victims were killed two weeks apart." Exasperated, she pulled her hands free from Daemon. "What has this got to do with Patrico absconding with my sister?"

"What tie would the police officers have with the vampire?" Daemon asked.

Tezra wrapped her arms around herself. "I keep thinking maybe they killed his vampire friend."

Atreides swore under his breath. "Like the police officers

killed our uncle."

Tezra glanced at him and saw the anger in his eyes. Hell, the way he looked, he could have been a rogue himself.

Daemon growled at him. "They made a fatal mistake, but we don't kill policemen in retaliation."

Then a new thought occurred to her and a chill centered in her spine and radiated outwards. "When did your uncle die?"

"Six weeks ago."

Not liking the coincidence, she swallowed hard, but nothing would ease the dryness of her throat. "The timing is right for the recent police killings. What if the killer murdered them because he was a friend of your uncle's and sought vengeance? Do you know which policemen killed your uncle?"

"No. Afraid of retaliation, the police department withheld the names, and since Uncle Solomon is my relation and I'm the head of the family, it was left up to me to learn of them. I felt there was no need. We do not kill humans to avenge our kind when the case was purely an accident. But now..." Daemon's voice was terse, his eyes black as a river at night. "Maison, find out which officers killed Uncle Solomon."

"I'll check into it," Maison said and vanished.

Tezra's cell phone jingled, and her heart leapt into her throat. She looked at the Caller ID, but the name and number were unlisted. "Hello?"

"It's me, Bernard." His voice was again gruff. Same old Bernard, and she was relieved to hear him sounding like his old self.

"What's up, Bernard?" If he was calling, it couldn't be good.

"You have to turn yourself in," he said, serious as could be.

"Turn myself in?" She faked a laugh. "I'm investigating a murderer, and I have to turn myself in?" Telepathically, she slipped a message to him. *"Why didn't you tell me you had a vampire grandfather?"* She didn't mean to sound accusing, but did he believe she would think ill of him because he didn't have pure blood?

Then again, she'd been pretty untrusting of vampires after Krustalus killed her parents.

"H-how can you telepathically communicate to me?" he asked.

"Are hunters listening to our telephone conversation?"

"They've tapped my phone."

"I've already told Julie I'm safe," Tezra assured Bernard over the phone. "Don't worry about me. If I try to leave the safe house, the murderer will track me down. You were right. I'm offering myself as the bait. We'll get him soon."

"Dammit, Tezra. Dammit to hell!"

Now that was the Bernard she knew.

"You can't go offering yourself up like some damned sacrificial goat."

"Goat, as in stubborn? Lamb sounds sweeter."

He growled.

"I've learned Patrico's alive, and he's taken my sister hostage."

For a minute, Bernard didn't say anything, and Tezra thought they'd been cut off. Then he cleared his throat and said, "The SCU has issued a warrant for your arrest, stating that you've been turned and are in league with the criminal element." Again, a significant pause ensued, then he added telepathically, *"And dammit, Tezra, Patrico's dead. Everyone knows that."*

"I *haven't* been turned, and I'm *after* the criminals!" Though if she could change Daemon's mind, Tezra had every intention of being turned. *"And for your information, Patrico apparently doesn't know he's dead! The hospital administrator verified he took Katie."*

Daemon ran his hand over her hair and kissed the nape of her neck. "Are you certain Bernard can be trusted?"

Tezra covered the mouthpiece. "My gut instinct tells me yes."

"Yet you willingly went with him when I sent him for you," Atreides warned. A superior smirk crossed his face.

She scowled at him, but Bernard distracted her. *"If you haven't been turned, how can you communicate with me like this?"*

"I can't explain right now. I hope to catch up with Patrico soon, but if something happens and I miss him, can you find out anything about him?" To give the hunters listening in on their phone conversation something to overhear, she added, "Tell Julie I'll be in to the office soon."

"I'll let her know you said so. Take care, Tezra." Bernard

again channeled his thoughts to her. *"I'll find out what I can about Patrico. He'll wish he was still dead if he's harmed Katie in any way. You can count on it."*

"Thanks, Bernard." Tezra spoke to him privately. *"Be careful. I'm not sure who can be trusted."*

The phone clicked off, and she worried whether she should have put her trust in Bernard, given that the SCU wanted her in custody now. She knew all Bernard ever cared about was her safety, and if he didn't believe she was safe, he might relay to the SCU Council everything she had revealed to him.

How could the SCU want her in custody? Well, not like they hadn't pulled stuff like that before in the name of state security. Give someone a little bit of authority and—

"I'll wait near Mrs. Sargento's house and let you know when Patrico arrives," Maison said to Daemon.

"We'll be there shortly," Daemon responded and patted Tezra's hand.

Maison vanished and Atreides said, "Can we trust Tezra's bodyguard?"

Tezra couched her annoyance. Only *she* was allowed to suspect Bernard's actions, not some vampire who didn't know anything about him.

The sound of vehicles pulling up into Daemon's circular drive caught their attention. Daemon moved with vampiric speed and peered out the front picture window. "Three black SUVs."

"The SCU," Tezra said, barely breathing, but before she could see anyone's reaction, Daemon pulled her from the couch and took her into the swirling black void.

Bewildered, she found herself standing beside prickly holly shrubs enclosing Mrs. Sargento's front yard. Wood smoke from a nearby chimney drifted on the frigid breeze, scenting the air, and the sound of footsteps hurrying toward the front door of the house caught her attention.

"Tezra, I'm right here." Daemon touched her shoulder.

The front lamp was out, and except for the neighbors' lights casting a pale glow at the edges of the property, she could barely see anything. Everything happened so quickly after that, events blurred.

Someone let out a strangled cry, and before she could respond, she was whisked away again into darkness.

Tezra didn't catch Daemon's controlled command, but the next thing she knew, he led her to a black leather couch where she collapsed, her mind frazzled.

"We're at Atreides's home." Daemon crouched in front of her, caressing her hands.

Voltan held onto Patrico's arm where they stood a few feet away. Patrico's blue eyes couldn't get any wider, and he ran his free hand through his long, curly, strawberry blond hair.

Daemon grasped Tezra's hands, his face drawn with concern. "Your fingers are ice cold and you look pale as death. Are you all right?"

Her mind and stomach swirling, she sat dazed. "Transporting so quickly and so many times makes me feel like I've been on a horrible roller coaster ride that won't end." Yet she refused to give in to her human weakness and turned her attention to Patrico. "Where's my sister?" She tried to stand, but her head felt like it could float away.

Daemon gripped her hands tighter and made her stay put. "I'll do this my way." He faced Patrico and instantly unsheathed his canines. "Where is Katie?"

Patrico lifted his chin higher and stared Daemon in the eye, daring him to proceed with his threatening posture. When he didn't answer, Tezra tried to get him to talk. "I only go after the bad guys. You know it. The SCU knows it. But you've taken my own flesh and blood. Not to mention you've faked being dead all these years. As far as I'm concerned, you're as evil as the one who killed my parents."

She didn't really sense that about him, but she had to use whatever leverage she could to break through his defenses and make him see the truth concerning Katie. She attempted to read his thoughts, but it was useless. Hunters from an early age learned to control their thoughts around vampires.

"By all accounts you're already dead. No one saw you tonight at your mother's house because it was too dark. Someone will inform the hospital administrator that a person made up to look like you stole your identity and took my sister. You're a nonentity like her. No one will miss you, and your mother will be compelled to accept as true that you died ten years ago like everyone else thinks. Is that what you want?" She hated to bully him, the only person who had believed her when her parents' tragic murders occurred. "I want to help my sister.

I love her. Can't you understand that?"

Daemon interceded. "Tell us where she is."

Patrico ground his teeth but didn't respond.

Tezra let out her breath. *"Why the hell can't you see that I'm only concerned about my sister's wellbeing?"* She delivered the message telepathically in frustration, not expecting him to hear her. But when his eyes widened in response, she stared at him in disbelief. *"Are...are you telepathic?"*

His jaw dropped.

Tezra couldn't believe it. "You're telepathic too."

"I thought they'd changed you, turned you. I thought you were in league with Krustalus."

"No, no. Daemon and his people took me in to protect me from the bastard. Years ago, I thought I could make Krustalus slip and give me his name. I taunted him with my telepathy." Tears filled her eyes. "I was so stupid, and he proved to me how powerful and cruel he is. You know what happened with my parents and with Katie. What you probably don't know is that he's stalked me for the last ten years—persistently tormented me in return for my arrogance."

Patrico took a heavy breath. "I should have done something to protect you, Tezra. It was my fault you had to face the demon vampire on your own. Four-oh-five Seabreeze, Seaside. That's my home. That's where Katie's sleeping."

"All alone?" Her heartbeat accelerated.

"Let's go," Daemon said.

She knew what was coming next, and she was certain she couldn't take much more of it. But no matter the momentary consequences, she had to be with her sister.

Daemon pulled Tezra from the couch and held her securely. "Sorry, Tezra. No more transporting after this."

"Buy a car..." Her words faded as she slipped away.

The next thing she recognized was the salty air and smell of fish. The moisture-laden cold clung to her while they stood on Patrico's faded gray cedar porch overlooking the Pacific Ocean, as Daemon kept his arms tight around her.

"Invite us in, Patrico," Daemon said, his tone dark and persuasive.

Tezra barely held on to her wits and almost forgot what they were doing here while she watched the foaming waves crash against the rocky beach.

"Invite us in," Daemon said again.

His demanding tone finally filtered into her foggy brain. "Hurry, Patrico. Let us in." She clung to Daemon's firm body like a vine needing support. His warm touch kept her vaguely in this world. Her mind blurring between reality and a dreamlike world, she had wicked thoughts of getting naked with the man who could bring her body to a fevered pitch.

Voltan still held onto Patrico's arm, though the hunter seemed as lost as Tezra felt.

"Patrico." She clenched her teeth against new waves of nausea swamping her. "Let us in."

"Come in," he muttered, fumbling with his key. As soon as he unlocked it, the party walked into the house, and Patrico relocked the door behind them.

Her mind a jumble, her legs gave out and Tezra collapsed. Blue and white couches, white wood floors, seascapes decorating the walls and a white brick fireplace filled her vision for an instant. Then a black satin sheet wrapped around her—shutting out the light, Daemon's concerned communication and the rest of the world, until even his warm touch vanished into the lightless void of space.

"Dammit to hell!" Exasperated with himself for compelling Tezra to transport their way, Daemon carried her to the couch, her face ashen, her body limp.

"I'll search for her sister in the rest of the house," Atreides offered. "I sense a woman sleeping nearby."

Voltan forced Patrico to sit on the striped couch opposite where Tezra lay on a matching loveseat.

"What will you do to me?" Patrico's tone was dull.

"If you hadn't taken Katie in the first place—" Daemon growled.

"Katie's here." Intrigue laced Atreides's words. *"Sleeping soundly like a redheaded goddess."*

"She is strictly off-limits, Atreides." Daemon didn't disguise the annoyance in his communication. He turned to Patrico, the man's eyes filled with worry. "It's time you answered some questions."

Daemon moved Tezra so he could sit with her, then placed her head on his lap, wanting the closeness, to touch her, to listen to her breathing and feel her pulse to ensure she would be all right.

"What do you want to know?" Patrico matched Daemon's glare, yet he sat hunched over—and looked soundly defeated.

Daemon imagined Patrico was around his mid-forties. A T-shirt stretched over his broad, hard chest, though he had a soft, rounded face like his mother's. "According to Tezra, a vampire was supposed to have murdered you after she told you about her parents' deaths. So what exactly happened?"

Patrico drummed his fingers on his lap and stared at the wood floor. Then he lifted his gaze, his eyes heated. "Though it is no concern of yours..." He turned his attention to Tezra. "I don't want her to suffer for my lack of courage any longer."

Daemon sifted his fingers through Tezra's hair. He concentrated on her subtle peach scent, her unhurried breath, the twitching of her eyelids, making her long lashes flutter. "Continue."

Patrico tried to stand, but Voltan laid a hand on his shoulder, and the hunter remained seated, though he scowled at his guard. "Ten years ago, my buddy, Fish, and I'd been drinking at a bar in the warehouse district. We came across a vampire in an alley. The vampire's mouth was bloodied, and he was leaning over a woman lying dead on the asphalt. 'What the hell do you think you're doing?' Fish asked him. Fish pulled out his blade and stumbled toward him. The vampire bared his bloody teeth and disappeared. I thought that was it. One more woman dead. The sixth in a string of murders committed close to bars. The vampire had done the killing, but we were too late to do anything about it.

"But then another vampire appeared half hidden in shadows, his lips smeared with fresh blood. And I realized in my booze-soaked brain that there were two vampiric predators, not just the one as we all had assumed. Before I could react, he swooped down on Fish, broke his sword arm in two, then bit into his throat and tore out the jugular. Releasing my friend, who fell limp to the ground like a discarded rag doll, the fiend faced me. Immobilized, I was too drunk to wield a sword, even if I could have pulled the damned thing from its sheath."

"Who was he?"

"Mustaphus. The vampire conveyed to me, 'You live, hunter, because I, Mustaphus, choose to let you live.' But he spoke silently, telepathically. He had no way of knowing I could 'hear' his words. Conceited bastard."

An image of Lichorus at the restaurant, speaking about her lover, came to Daemon's mind: *Mustaphus knew where the next police officer would be murdered before it was announced on the news this morning.*

"You never reported Mustaphus's crime?"

"No. How could I? Fish and I shouldn't have been drinking on duty when we were investigating the barfly murders. Instead, I let on that Fish had left me and I found him dead near the woman's body, no vampires in sight. If I had told the SCU what I had seen with my own two eyes, I'd never have been appointed to the senior staff. And as Tezra well knows, I could never tell anyone of my telepathic abilities. Had I said I knew the man was Mustaphus, the SCU would have wondered how I had known and why the vampire let me live. I was in line for the only available seat on the High Council in two days' time. So I fabricated my involvement."

Patrico took a deep breath. "When Tezra came to me with her story, I had to vindicate myself and help her prove she spoke the truth. It didn't matter that I was a member of the Council. She was too vulnerable, spunkier than hell, but investigating her parents' murder could have easily gotten her into hot water, and I wanted to help her."

"Why did you believe her when no one else did?"

Patrico looked past Daemon as if he were reliving it again. "After she told me what had happened, but before I met her in the warehouse district, I heard the vampire telepathically threatening her. I didn't realize she had the ability. I thought he was making silent threats like Mustaphus had done when he had spoken to me. She didn't respond, or if she did, she directed her message to him."

Daemon blew out his breath. "You saw him?"

"No. I only heard his communication."

"And you did nothing to protect her and faked your death?"

"The killer thought the drifter he'd murdered was me. The victim was the same build, a redhead, standing near where I was to meet Tezra. She hadn't reached the location yet, but when she did, she found the man so mutilated no one could tell the difference. I persuaded my mother to agree the man was me, to ensure the vampire didn't come after me again. I was certain the vampire wanted to convince Tezra that anyone who tried to help her would meet the same fate. I assumed she would give up her search. I should have known better.

"But, I…well, I was afraid. Anyone who shows fear in the face of danger is expelled from the elite organization. So you see, I was already dead." Patrico shrugged. "The longer I lived the lie, the easier it was. I've made a nice life for myself as a psychic. Only my mother knew I was still alive, and she wanted to keep me that way."

"You left Tezra to fend for herself, dammit. How could a hunter and senior staff member leave a teen who'd lost her parents to deal with an ancient vampire alone?"

Patrico avoided eye contact. "It's something I've got to live with."

As far as Daemon was concerned, it wasn't enough.

Voltan shoved Patrico's shoulder, his canines extended. "You don't deserve to live." Wearing leather "armor", his angular jaw set and steely blue eyes hardened, Voltan looked like he belonged in the dungeon, torturing enemy prisoners.

"Why visit Katie?" Daemon asked.

"I wanted to help her and Tezra, but I didn't know how. No one but Tezra came to see Katie so I visited her from time to time. I'd hoped…well, that maybe I could help her come out of her shell since I'd failed her sister."

"Then why remove her from the hospital?"

Patrico fisted his hands and stared at the floor. "The word on the street was Tezra had joined a group of vampires and had been turned. I thought the vampire who'd murdered their parents had finally taken Tezra for his own. By removing Katie from the hospital, I thought I could finally do my part and at least save her where I had failed with Tezra."

"Save Katie from the killer?"

Pinning Daemon with a glare, Patrico said, "Yes. I thought he was coming for her."

Thankful the hunter wasn't against them, Daemon rose from the couch. "Voltan, have Patrico retire to bed and watch him."

"I'm on your side. Let me help you to take down Mustaphus and the other."

Daemon studied him for a minute but wouldn't give him

the satisfaction of his decision, then lifted Tezra off the sofa. *"Atreides, call for backup to conduct perimeter watch."*

"What are you going to do with the hunter?" Atreides asked.

Daemon carried Tezra down the hall, the feel of her soft body, her light breath, stirring his need to protect and care for her. *"Help him regain his courage."*

Chapter Eleven

When Daemon laid Tezra in the king-sized bed in Patrico's master bedroom, her eyelids fluttered open, and he hated that he had awakened her.

"Katie's all right?" she asked, her voice sultry and sexy.

He nodded and slid her boots off, depositing them on the floor with a clunk.

As if she were shocked awake, Tezra jumped off the bed and in a flash, headed for the door. "Is she asleep?"

"Yes. How are you feeling?"

"Wiped out. I guess I'd make a lousy vampiress after all." She sounded annoyed with herself as she yanked the door open.

How could she always see herself in such a negative way? She'd make one hell of a vampiress if she didn't turn rogue.

"As a vampire, you wouldn't have any side effects." He followed her down the hall to the first guest bedroom. "I shouldn't have moved you so much without allowing you the time to adjust. It was entirely my fault."

She didn't say anything, but pointed to the correct room with a questioning glance.

"She's in there, perfectly safe."

Tezra's concerned expression didn't lighten. She twisted the doorknob with care, then opened the door slowly and peered in. Once she observed her sister sleeping in the queen-sized bed, her posture relaxed. She closed the door without making a sound.

"You need to rest after all the transporting you've been through. Not to mention it's late." He led Tezra back to the master bedroom, hoping she'd get some much-needed sleep.

When he closed the door, she headed for the bed and collapsed. She lifted the edge of her sweater. Intrigued, he focused on her garment, though he knew he should let her sleep while he served as her bodyguard.

"Do you need some help?"

She gave him a wicked smile.

Instantly wary, Daemon said, "I'm not turning you."

Frowning at him, she shrugged. "Whatever."

He slipped the sweater over her head and cast it on a chair. "Patrico said Mustaphus killed his hunter friend and committed the barfly murders ten years ago."

She growled. "Then he lied back then. Said Fish had gotten away from him and later Patrico found him dead."

"Yeah, he was afraid he'd lose his position on the Council because of his cowardly actions—not to mention he was drunk and couldn't have fought the vampires if he'd wanted to. Though it's no excuse—he left you alone to fend for yourself."

She touched her belt buckle. "As much as I hate what he did, I imagine he hates himself even more." She fingered her belt. "Wanna help?"

His gaze shifted to hers, her green eyes sparkling with impish delight.

She shrugged. "Or not."

He unfastened her belt and pulled her pants past her hips.

She patted the bed. "Wanna join me?"

Join her? "What's on your mind, Tezra?" He hoped she wanted the same thing he did, but where women were concerned, he could never be certain no matter how many centuries he lived.

Her lips curved up. "Come to bed, Daemon. There's room for two."

"To sleep," he stated, though he waited for her to verify that's what she had in mind.

"It's late. Katie's asleep. For the moment, everything's quiet. So, yes, why not sleep?"

Disappointed she didn't want anything more, Daemon removed his clothes, turned out the light and joined her in bed. *One time*, she'd said. Only one time for sex, though he knew she was right. The more he was with her, the more he wanted of her.

"Where are you?" she whispered.

He still didn't entirely believe her motives, nor did he trust himself not to give in to the sexual cravings and bloodlust she stirred in him. When he didn't move toward her, the mattress jostled. She laid her head against his chest, her fingertip tracing his abdomen, rousing him.

Only intending to hold her, he wrapped his arms around her. It would never be enough. Yet he wouldn't succumb to the illicit reactions she prompted in him, and he closed his eyes, fully determined to sleep.

One time wasn't enough, Tezra thought wryly. She shouldn't have chased after the prince of the American clans, shouldn't have solicited his touch, but she wanted him, just one more time. She was certain the sensations wouldn't be as strong, nor the sex as good—just old hat, liking eating the second chocolate bonbon, more filling but not as tantalizing and satisfying as the first. But she wanted proof. And she still wanted to convince him to turn her.

At first Daemon barely responded to her touching him, until she licked his nipple. He sucked in his breath and his stomach tightened. He pressed heated kisses on her throat, her shoulders, her breasts, sent sparks of desire tingling through her veins. Even now with blissful expectation, the short curly hairs between her legs dampened. He kissed her cheeks, each kiss lingering and erotic as if his velvet touch memorized the impression of her skin against his, cherished it and wanted more.

His leg shifted and propped possessively over hers.

She ran her hand over his perfectly toned back and his erection prodded her waist. "Hmm, Daemon." She'd never been with anyone who responded so quickly to her sexually, who wanted to please her as much as he seemed to enjoy being with her. She loved how that made her feel so wanted. But would he ever agree to change her?

He lifted strands of her hair and took a deep breath. "Sweet, silky delight." He touched her breast and ran his finger over the extended nipple, sending a shiver of need through her.

She responded by caressing his thigh, so titillating pressed against hers.

He groaned and nudged his leg between hers. Trailing his

fingers over her jaw, he kissed her mouth at one corner, then the other. Every touch was amative, sensual, calculated to make her feel sexy and desired. When she was with him like this, being his mate didn't seem so bad even if he said he didn't want her to be his. He licked her skin, feathering kisses down her neck to the breastbone, sending liquid heat spiraling through her.

He gently rubbed his thigh against her sensitive nub. Moaning, she leaned against him and encouraged his stimulating action. She barely breathed when he slid his fingers down her stomach, lower, until he ran them through her short curly hairs.

"Tezra."

He licked her nipple. Closing her eyes, she savored his mouth scandously clamping down on the tip. She reached lower and stroked his stone-hard arousal, forcing him to groan. He *thought* his rule was absolute, but her simple touch unraveled him. She smiled at the contradiction.

He removed her hand from his erection, and he tugged tenderly at her nipple with his teeth.

Both nipples instantly firmed and begged for more of his touch. With a deep breath, she pulled at his leg, encouraging him to join with her.

His hand moved to her waist, but he didn't take her despite her encouragement. Leaning forward, he touched his forehead to hers. "You said only once."

"A woman can change her mind." And if he didn't go through with it after already getting her this worked up, she wouldn't be responsible for her actions!

His deep chuckle tickled her. He pressed her legs apart and settled in between, his movements rushed as if he feared she'd change her mind.

He slid his erection inside her. Driving her hips for maximum penetration, she savored his thickened shaft reaching deep.

Meeting her impetus with faster thrusts, he matched her drive and willingness with his own, rubbing his pelvis against her mound. Then he slowed. Her heart sank when she thought she was losing him.

She held onto his back, digging her fingernails in to force him to continue, but he pulled out despite her efforts.

Confusion and upset reigned.

Before she could ask what was wrong, his mouth tackled hers with fervor. His fingers caressed her most sensitive spot, wringing her body until she clambered for the peak. Only a little higher. She moaned his name, her body hotter than a fire's white flames, their hair and skin damp with perspiration, the sun nearly within reach. The jolt of inspiration, of exhilaration and of being loved while he put her needs before his, washed over her with a mixture of euphoria and complete satisfaction. "Bite me."

"You wish to offer your blood?"

And more, if she could convince him. She nodded, certain he wasn't ready to turn her yet, but the ache to feel the sensation intensified, triggering a surge of new need. She understood now why blood bonds offered themselves to the vampires—for the sexual pleasure they received.

Entering her again, Daemon resumed his thrusts, deep, penetrating, almost desperate.

His hands stroked her hair, then pushed it aside, and he licked her neck. Trying not to think about his feeding off her, she ran her hands over the muscles of his butt, concentrating on the way he moved, hard and determined. A prick on her neck was all it amounted to, like the infinitesimal sting of two mosquitoes situated slightly apart. Then warmth spread through her body, and a calm like she'd never experienced before flooded every cell.

She tightened her legs around him, pressuring him to find release in her.

Peacefulness and serenity filled her while he sucked from her throat, drawing her blood, his thickened erection still thrusting deep inside her. When he pumped his seed into her, her heated body reached heavenward again. She moaned, satiated with pleasure.

His mouth still claimed her throat, his touch as sensuous as when he sucked on her breast, tingling and titillating. Her mind drifted, circling the stars and the moon, floating past the constellations, sparks of light falling to the earth, and nothing but joy could touch her.

With a sigh, Daemon licked her wounds, sealing them. Pulling her against his body, he vowed never to take her again. Being with her was too tempting. He couldn't risk it, and he worried she was trying to use her sexual wiles to ensnare him to turn her.

She nestled against him, her breathing growing softer, her heart rate slowing.

Never again, he vowed. Never again, and he tightened his hold on her.

Gale-force winds pummeled the beach home, rattling the overhang over the back porch. A couple of hours later, Daemon sensed Maison speaking with Atreides in Patrico's living room. Daemon kissed Tezra's cheek, unwrapped his body from hers, then dressed and joined Maison and his brother.

Maison's hair dripped water and the bottoms of his jeans were wet. Raindrops puddled up on his black trench coat hanging on the arm of the sofa.

"What have you learned in your investigation concerning Uncle Solomon, Maison?"

"Tezra's hunch was right." Sitting on a sofa opposite him, Maison took a sip of wine, leaned back and stretched his long legs. "The murdered police officers killed Solomon."

The wind howled through a crack in the front door, making it sound as though angry spirits were warning them to get out. Rain driven at a slant pounded the picture windows, and Daemon left the sofa and took a look out one of them. The waves billowed into white frothing mountains in the blackness, but they were safe enough here for the moment.

Returning to the sofa, he considered Maison's words. Even though Daemon condemned the murdering vampire, the darkest part of him felt the officers deserved their just rewards for killing an innocent. Their uncle, for centuries their surrogate father, harsh at times, loving when they needed it, was the last of their natural-born kin. Life without his wry sense of humor or many words of wisdom would never be the same.

Daemon's gut clenched with the tightness he'd felt when he first learned of his uncle's death. Settling back against the couch, he attempted to release the tension in his spine and let go of the feeling of loss that swamped him all over again. "Tezra said Krustalus taunted her at the scene when Officer Stevens was murdered, but she was certain another vampire killed him."

"It's rare when serial killers work in pairs, but not unknown," Maison said. "Also, Atreides told me Patrico identified Mustaphus as his hunter friend's killer."

"Lichorus said Mustaphus knew about the officer who was killed at Tezra's apartment before anyone else did. If Mustaphus murdered him, it would stand to reason he killed the others."

"But Uncle Solomon never spoke of Mustaphus," Atreides argued. "If Mustaphus killed the policemen because they had murdered Uncle Solomon, he must have been a pretty close friend, don't you agree, Daemon?"

"I agree. We need to discover if Uncle Solomon kept a journal among his effects. Have some of our men go through the boxes in my cellar—see if they can find anything."

Soggy-eyed, Patrico dragged into the living room, combing his fingers through his tangled, shoulder-length hair. "I want a piece of him."

Voltan lumbered behind him.

Ignoring the hunter's comment, Daemon asked Maison, "Who did you speak to concerning the names of the police officers?"

"Chief O'Malley. He said when the officers killed your uncle it was a case of mistaken identity. They thought he was Mustaphus. Anonymous evidence was sent to the police department concerning the earlier killings and Mustaphus's home address was given. Solomon was visiting while Mustaphus had gone on an errand. Maybe he knew the police were coming for him?"

"The bastard."

"It's possible he was fully aware of the situation." Maison cleared his throat. "When the police arrived, Solomon opened the door to them. The chief said Mustaphus and Solomon were around the same age, both dark-haired, had dark brown eyes, same height and husky build. Solomon denied being Mustaphus, but the police officers believed he was the serial killer, trying to lie his way out of being terminated and knowing how dangerous an ancient could be, they took him down."

Daemon shook his head, his temper building. "That's not what the chief told us right after they killed Uncle Solomon. He said they'd gone to the wrong house, and he named some other vampire they were after—not Mustaphus. Someone we'd never heard of before. Since we could never locate the vampire, we assumed he had an alias." He glanced at Patrico seated in a chair between the couches. "You wouldn't happen to know who sent the police the anonymous information about Mustaphus, would you?"

Patrico's brows furrowed. "I couldn't let the bastard get away with any more murders. He never stopped, you know. He went after women who frequented bars, either alone or in pairs."

"So you were the one who got our uncle killed," Atreides growled.

"Hell," Patrico said, waving his hand, "he shouldn't have been friends with a serial killer."

Atreides's fangs extended, but Daemon held up his hand in warning. "Uncle Solomon wouldn't have known about Mustaphus's murders. You know how most serial killers operate. Their friends are often the last to know of their complicity in crimes such as these." Daemon poured himself a glass of wine at the bar.

"When I asked about the policemen's names, Chief O'Malley acted nervous," Maison said. "When you spoke to him after your uncle was terminated, the chief's explanation sounded reasonable. He was horrified by the mistake, probably because he feared retaliation. He would have done anything to bring your uncle back. But this time..." Maison lifted a shoulder. "I didn't trust him. He shielded his thoughts from me. Filled his mind with police business unrelated to your uncle's case, grocery lists, anything to keep me from learning the truth. So I used our form of persuasion and got the new answer."

"I asked him at Cafferty's Tavern if there was a connection between the vampire and his police officers, and he said no. Hell, I should have taken him with us and willed it out of him then, but in the ensuing fight he conveniently disappeared. So why was he protecting Mustaphus?" Daemon asked.

"Someone sent him death threats. Said they'd kill O'Malley's family. The chief didn't feel he had a choice," Maison said.

"Put out the word that Mustaphus is to be eliminated on sight for the hunter named Fish's murder. No need to involve the SCU in this one. If they learn he killed one of their hunters, no telling what the repercussions will be."

Atreides turned his head and looked in the direction of the hallway leading to the bedrooms. Daemon followed his gaze. Tezra leaned against the doorframe, her hair tousled. The man's black shirt she wore, probably from Patrico's wardrobe, covered her to midthigh and looked pretty damned hot.

"The storm woke me." She motioned to the crack in the front door where the wind continued to moan. "Then I heard a bunch of heated talking. Want to let me in on the secrets?"

Daemon poured another glass of wine and said to Maison, "I want the word to go out tonight."

"You've got it." Maison rose from the sofa, pulled on his trench coat and vanished.

"Voltan, return Patrico to bed." Daemon crossed the floor to Tezra and wrapped his arm around her shoulder. "I'll protect you from the storm."

She slipped the wine glass out of his hand. "This will help. But I want to know what was said."

He lifted her in his arms. "I'll tell you everything we know, but believe me, they're not the kind of bedtime tales that will help you sleep."

"If you have evidence concerning Krustalus and have put him on a termination list, it'll help me sleep."

She snuggled against Daemon's chest, and he was overwhelmed with how good she felt.

Too good. And dangerous. But he never wanted to turn the one he loved to spend an eternity with her only to have to eliminate her shortly after their vampiric mating. Never again.

Chapter Twelve

In the middle of the night, Tezra touched Daemon's chest, and he looked down at her. She seemed to be concerned about something. He certainly was.

"I want to know about Krustalus—when he approached you," he said again, hoping this time she'd tell him the truth.

She sighed deeply.

"Tezra—"

"It was like...he only came to me when I..."

"Was defiant, broke the rules, became a rogue?"

She didn't say anything, just continued to caress his chest with a light touch which was driving him mad. "Did he bite you, Tezra?"

"What difference does it make?"

"Bloody hell. Why wouldn't you say so before?" Daemon wrapped his arms around her, but she stiffened in his embrace. "When did it happen?" He suspected the worst, but tried to keep his emotions from getting away from him.

She rubbed his arm, then looked away.

"A long time ago? Recently? When? Where?"

"What difference does it make?" she asked again, except her tone of voice sounded defeated this time, soft and vulnerable.

He tightened his hold on her but she seemed in a different world. "When did he bite you, Tezra? Tell me."

She wouldn't say, and he kissed the top of her head. "Tell me what happened." He assumed she was reliving the memories, but when he attempted to read her mind, she kept him locked out.

"He came to you after your parents' murders, didn't he? He came to you when you were most vulnerable. Who took you in when Katie was admitted to the hospital?"

Tezra looked up at him, confused.

"Where did you live after your parents were murdered?"

She took a deep breath and looked away.

"You couldn't have stayed with relatives?" he asked. He knew she lived in the home for troubled teens, but he wanted her to tell him the whole story in her own words.

"I didn't have any left. My aunt was killed on a hunt and though her lover wanted to take me in, the higher-ups at the SCU wouldn't permit it."

"Why not?" He touched her cheek, but she turned away from him.

"She wasn't a blood relative."

"Was she a huntress?"

"Yes."

"So where did you go? Foster parents?" Which wouldn't have made any sense since they wouldn't have been blood relatives either, but he needed for her to tell him the truth.

She didn't say.

"To an SCU home?" He'd heard rumors that they tried to create the perfect hunter corps—stripping the children of their emotions so they could take down renegade vampires without remorse.

She swallowed hard.

He wanted to lash out at anyone who was involved with confining her to the facility and the ill treatment she received afterwards, but he shifted to another tactic, hoping to gain her confidence. "When Atreides and I were thirteen, my mother died of a fever, and we went to live with our Uncle Solomon. He was a hard but fair man, and we cared deeply for him. But during a battle with the Turks, Uncle Solomon was taken prisoner and—" He took a deep, calming breath. It didn't matter how many years he lived, he would never forget how terrified or isolated he'd felt.

"We'd always had a loving family's support up until then. But when our uncle's castle was besieged without him to lead his men, the castle finally fell and the Turks took Atreides and me prisoner along with a score of other men, including Maison and Voltan. We were confined in separate cells in a dungeon below a fortress. Imagine being immersed in the dark for days on end with the only sounds the squealing of rats scurrying across the cell floor and the groaning of fellow prisoners dying slow and hideous deaths.

"The rats carried the plague that changed us, you know. For a long time, I had no idea why I could hear the prison guards speaking on the other side of an iron door, or why I could suddenly see in the windowless cell below ground."

He paused. Tezra seemed to be immersed in his story.

"I grew weaker from the wormy gruel they fed us, but one day in desperation, I caught and killed a rat. After that, I asked Atreides—in my mind—if he was all right. *'I can't make it much longer,'* he relayed to me. He sounded on the verge of death and something inside me snapped. I had to do anything I could to save him, to save myself. Somehow, I managed to coax the guard who brought the next meal into the cell. I felt no remorse. In an instant, he was dead. I didn't even remember how he died, but just that he was standing one minute, the next he was lying lifeless on the floor.

"With the keys to the cells, I freed my brother, Voltan and Maison. Before long, we had freed all our men. We didn't leave any of our captors alive. I knew either they died, or we did. The choice was as simple as that."

"They...they couldn't stop me either," Tezra said, her voice whisper-soft, her head settling back on his chest.

Her touch was making him hot, but he squelched the rising lust for her and encouraged her to tell him what he wanted most to know—how intimate had Krustalus been with her? Was she his lover?

When she didn't say anything further, Daemon prompted, "They?"

"The...SCU home where I lived. I...I had to see my sister. But—but they said I...upset her. And they—they locked me in a padded room without windows down beneath the home. I could smell the damp earth around me, but I could hear nothing but my own screaming, demanding to be let out of the tomb."

She grew quiet, and he was about to ask her if she'd tried to run away when she said, "One of the caretakers invited him in."

"Krustalus? *Hell.*"

"I didn't know that was his name. I couldn't see him for the dark. He tried to control me, to control my mind." She looked up at Daemon. "Like you did. But he couldn't either. Whereas you were frustrated, my fighting him and succeeding amused him."

"He bit you while you were confined in the home's basement?"

"I don't remember." When he didn't conceal his disbelief, she scowled at him. "I don't...remember. I would have, wouldn't I?"

Daemon considered the situation for a moment, then said, "Normally if he didn't want you to recall, he could wipe your mind of the incident. But since you can fight mind control, no. But what if the SCU staff drugged you? You might not have been able to keep your shield up. Or what about when you slept?"

She stared at him. "Did you get past my barriers when I was sleeping?"

He remained silent.

"What did you find out about me?"

"You were having a nightmare—a recollection of Krustalus's threatening you and your response to him."

"I don't remember."

Daemon nodded. "Which is why I think he bit you while you were sleeping or drugged, and you only vaguely recall the experience. Or maybe you're repressing the memory. Did he only come to you the one time?"

"Several."

Daemon swore under his breath. "Then in his mind, he has claimed you. And he really won't like it that I took you under my protection."

"Too bad." She snuggled closer and wrapped her arm around Daemon's chest. "Too *damned* bad."

Daemon knew then he had to destroy the vampire at all costs before he had another taste of the huntress. Krustalus had claimed Tezra from the beginning, and he'd never give up wanting her.

❦

Early the next morning, Daemon mysteriously slipped out of Patrico's beach home without a word before Tezra woke, and no one would say where he'd gone. She couldn't help thinking he was trying to solve the crimes without her, as weak as she'd been when he'd tried to transport her his way. Instead of being a help, she was nothing more than a hindrance, which curdled her blood. She fingered a cup of coffee while she sat at the glass-covered dining table and studied Katie seated across from her. Patrico made omelets while Atreides served up toast. She choked down another mouthful of coffee.

Voltan was nowhere in sight either, and she assumed he was serving as Daemon's bodyguard, which didn't help to alleviate her concerns.

The storm had abated but the steady ocean breeze blew against the house and lowered the temperature. Before she could ask Patrico where the thermostat was so she could turn on the heater, it flipped on.

She considered Cynthia Stevens's words concerning her husband's death—*he'll kill them all*. Wanting to know if Cynthia knew anything more, Tezra left the table and lifted a handset from its stand. First, she called Mandy for Cynthia's number since she didn't have it on her, and then she called Cynthia.

"Hello, Cynthia? This is Tezra Campbell investigating—"

"Yes, yes, go ahead."

Tezra glanced at Katie who stared at her blue and white striped placemat, sipping her coffee. Atreides was watching Tezra, and even Patrico glanced in her direction.

"You said he'd kill them all. Could you elaborate?" Tezra assumed they knew now it was Mustaphus who had killed the men for revenge because the police had murdered Daemon's uncle. But she wanted final confirmation in any event.

"My—my husband was just doing what the chief told him to do. I warned him that he shouldn't have gone. That the police department should have turned the job over to the SCU—let them handle a rogue vampire. Let them make the mistake and kill the wrong vampire. But nooo, he had to go along with what the rest of them were ordered to do. The chief wasn't there. He didn't have to pay the consequences for his actions."

"Why didn't the chief turn it over to the SCU?"

"The chief wanted to make a name for himself with the department. He wanted to prove that they could do more than just regular policing. He was sick and tired of the SCU acting as though they were superior—that only they had the ability to deal with a vampire threat. The chief's feelings were infectious. Every man on the force felt the same way. But I think it went deeper with the chief, and my husband knew something about it. He would never say though when I'd question him about it. It was almost like the chief had a personal vendetta against this Mustaphus and didn't want to give up the kill to the SCU."

"Because he had killed his police officers?"

"Something that affected him years before this."

"But you don't know what?"

"No, I'm sorry, Tezra. I wish I could be more help, but watch out where the chief is concerned. I don't believe he's to be trusted. And it's more than just that he got my husband killed."

"All right. Thanks so much for your help. I'll call you later."

She hung up the phone and said out loud, though not to anyone in particular, "I need to talk to Chief O'Malley."

Atreides peered out the kitchen window. "You can ask Daemon when he returns."

She didn't need Daemon's permission, dammit!

Unable to decide what to do about Katie either, Tezra felt at a loss. Shouldn't Katie be in the hospital? Tezra couldn't watch her twenty-four, seven like the staff there could. And if Daemon wasn't going to turn her so she could help Katie, then she needed to return her to the facility. Yet she wavered about that too. Usually, she knew just what she wanted to do. See Katie, help Katie, find and prove a vampire was a rogue, notify the SCU that he or she needed to be terminated, locate and kill Krustalus.

Making love with a vampire—twice—was not part of her ordered way of life, and she still felt guilty for allowing herself any pleasure while Katie... She shook her head. She hated how indecisive she was concerning her sister.

She tapped her fingers on the table. "Do you have a car, Patrico?"

Atreides and Patrico looked at her, their expressions surprised.

"I...I should return Katie to Redding." The lump in her throat grew. She didn't want to return her to the hospital. Just having breakfast with her sister had brought a little sunshine into her life on the typical gray autumn day. But the SCU wanted to arrest Tezra, Krustalus taunted her at the most inopportune times, and well, there was no way she could physically care for Katie as much as she wanted to. She couldn't take her on investigations, and she wouldn't be safe home alone.

Patrico didn't say anything and flipped the omelets frying in a pan.

Atreides sat at the table and plucked a couple of pieces of toast from the platter, but Tezra walked into the living room, intending to locate Patrico's garage. Katie's disposition wasn't anyone's call but Tezra's, and she had every intention of using Patrico's car to take Katie back to the hospital. Then she'd go to the police station where she could question the chief with the new information she had.

When she reached the front door and grabbed the brass knob, Atreides's hand encircled her wrist, effectively stopping her. "Daemon wants you to stay here while he's gone."

Daemon didn't have any right telling her what to do. "I'm taking Katie back to the hospital. She'll be safer there than with me."

Without a word, Atreides escorted Tezra back into the dining room.

"Let me keep her here," Patrico offered, serving up the omelets.

She jerked her wrist free from Atreides, and he gave her a superior smile. "No, Patrico," Tezra said. "You work like I do. She shouldn't be alone."

"What if Krustalus comes for her?" Patrico asked. "Look how easy it was for me to take her from the hospital."

"The hospital staff won't be so remiss the next time," Tezra growled, but she had to admit Patrico was right.

"No? All Krustalus would have to do is will someone to invite him in. He's grown more aggressive, don't you agree? To get to you he might take Katie hostage."

Tezra slumped in her chair. The bastard haunted her sleep whenever she let down her barrier. He'd visited her on numerous occasions in the form of mist on gray days much more often than before.

"Yes," she reluctantly admitted.

"I worry now that Krustalus has told the chief to tell you his name, he intends to tie up all the loose ends." Dripping honey over his plate, Patrico waved a butter knife. "Mark my words."

Her expression blank, Katie looked at her plate and forked her cheesy omelets.

"Tezra, it's me, Bernard. Can you hear me?" Bernard telepathically communicated.

She glanced at Patrico, but he was busy eating. Atreides watched her though, suspicion written all over his face.

"Are you channeling directly to me?" She buttered her toast, pretending to concentrate on her breakfast.

"To the best of my ability. I'm only a quarter vampire."

"What have you learned?"

"Patrico's dead."

She stifled a dark laugh. *"Right, and his spirit is sitting across from me, eating breakfast. So what else is new?"*

"Hunters are still looking for you and your vampire accomplice. They now say you were in league with him from the beginning and stole Katie from the hospital but tried to make it look like you had no knowledge of it."

Great. *"We found Patrico, and Katie is here safe and sound."* But now Tezra knew she couldn't return Katie to the hospital.

"Great news about Katie!" Bernard paused and she sensed the tension in his thoughts, then he finally said, *"A vampire telepathically contacted me—said he was a friend of yours and wanted to meet with you to tell you his side of the story."*

Her heart hitched. *"Krustalus?"*

"He didn't give a name. Just said he wants to meet with you."

Just like Patrico said, he was tying up loose ends? *"Where?"*

"He'd tell you privately. He wanted you to come alone. But you can't, Tezra. It's a setup."

"I'm the bait, remember?"

"Dammit, you can't do it, Tezra."

Patrico pushed his plate aside. "I really think Katie should stay here. Atreides said your place was broken into and everything is a shambles. You and Katie can stay with me."

"Got to go, Bernard. Keep safe and stay in touch." Tezra turned to Patrico. "I agree Katie should remain here."

Patrico's mouth dropped open. Atreides's brows rose. Katie

sipped some more of her coffee and gazed at the remaining toast stacked on a platter.

"What?" Tezra said, her ire stoked. "When you're right, you're right. Krustalus could get to her. He's tying up loose ends like you said. She's safe as long as she has you and strong vampires like Atreides to watch over her."

"And you." Patrico looked like he didn't believe her sudden change in attitude any more than Atreides did.

She lifted her plate off the table, but Daemon suddenly appeared next to her and took the plate from her before she dropped it. After setting it on the table, he moved her into the living room. "You're like a drug I can't get enough of, you know."

Ditto, she wanted to tell him, a dangerous, uncontrollable, life-altering drug, but she didn't want it to go to his already big head. "Where the hell were you?"

His lips curved slightly. "No, hi, honey, how was your morning?"

She crossed her arms. "You're not my honey, and why the hell didn't you tell me where you were—"

He cradled her face in his hands, then silenced her objection with a sizzling kiss.

Closing her eyes, she leaned into the kiss, but then remembered Katie. Opening her eyes, she saw Katie watching, her mouth gaping wide. Atreides was watching them too, but she couldn't tell from his controlled expression what he was thinking. Patrico shook his head and returned to the kitchen, probably figuring she was a lost cause.

Flustered, Tezra pulled away from Daemon. A vampire killed their parents in front of Katie, and what the hell did Tezra do? Disgusted with herself, she snapped at Daemon, "Where have you been? The truth?"

"Checking Lichorus's old haunts and a few leads on Mustaphus. No success. When are you going to tell me about Bernard's communication with you? The truth?"

Atreides continued to watch them from the dining room and gave her a conceited smile.

Atreides had been able to listen in on Bernard's communication. Tezra lifted her chin. "Atreides—"

Daemon's expression turned hard. "Bernard told me. He said he didn't trust you to solicit anyone's help. He worried you'd get yourself killed."

"Traitor."

Daemon's lips curved in a self-satisfied smile. "He's a good bodyguard."

"Like hell he is. He's supposed to be loyal to me, not you."

"Let's walk along the beach." Taking her hand, Daemon pulled her close. *"Out of Katie's hearing."*

Tezra turned to her sister and gave her a reassuring smile, though she felt anything but. "We'll be right back."

"She likes to play Dominoes." Patrico pulled a carved wooden box from a drawer. "Don't you, Katie? Let's play a game while your sister talks more boring business."

Tezra couldn't believe how much Patrico had aided her sister. Some of the animosity she had felt for him leaving her to fight Krustalus alone dissolved.

Daemon helped Tezra on with her leather jacket, then escorted her outside.

Two wolves sitting on the wooden porch swiveled around to look at Daemon and Tezra. Both bowed their heads slightly. Five more stood on the beach watching them.

"They look out of place here," Tezra said.

"They're meant to be a deterrent. No need to be subtle."

He walked her along the shore, and she shivered against the breezy cold. Gray clouds blocked any hint of the sun. Waves roared against the beach, splashing white spray on top of boulders the color of the sky. The cold air thick with the smell of fish and seawater made her think of more pleasant trips to the beach with their parents when Katie and she were little.

Daemon's hand tightened on hers. "No more secrets, Tezra."

"Krustalus hasn't contacted me yet."

"When he does, we go together."

"He says for me to come alone."

Daemon gave her a sinister look. "He will expect me to come too. He knows I'm protecting you. He also knows I won't let you out of my sight to see him, or out of my guards' sights either."

"He said he wants to give me his side of the story."

"Which means he wants to end the game."

Her blood chilling, she drew into Daemon's side and cherished his warmth. He wrapped his arm around her shoulder.

"I guess I always knew it would come to this," she said, half of her resigned, the other half ready to fight him to the end. "Some part of me said I'd be chasing his shadow until I was old and gray, and he'd come and taunt me on my deathbed. But another part of me said he'd face me when I was the right age, more of a challenge than when I was a teen."

"It's more than just you."

Tezra looked up at Daemon and saw the darkness in his features.

"He wants to replace me. I've learned he's been stirring up a rebel force for some time. I don't believe he expected me to take you under my wing, and that's complicated matters for him a bit, but he's definitely interested in overthrowing my rule."

"Because of me?" She'd already triggered so much hurt, the notion she'd caused Daemon more strife...

Daemon kissed her cheek. "Dear Tezra, you are not the reason for Krustalus's madness."

"I pushed him over the brink when I threatened him."

"Like most serial killers, he's a master at deception and manipulation. He could have been your best friend growing up, and you'd never have suspected he'd murdered hundreds of innocents."

Tezra couldn't stop the shiver trailing down her spine.

Daemon rubbed her arm and kissed her cold nose, then headed back to the house. "You didn't make him the monster he is."

"But if I hadn't—"

Daemon kissed her mouth and when he let her up for air, he said, "He kills, Tezra. That's what he does best. You have to let go of your self-loathing. It'll eat you up inside, leaving nothing but an empty shell. You have so much more to offer, but you'll turn into a full-fledged renegade if you don't let go of the hurt."

"I..." She shook her head. No matter how much she wanted to believe otherwise, she knew Krustalus would never have murdered her parents if she hadn't taunted him.

Daemon sighed deeply and pressed her tighter against his warm body. "I didn't want to get your hopes up prematurely, but I don't believe your threatening him pushed him to kill your parents."

"Why?"

"It's not in character."

She frowned. "Like hell it isn't. He kills. It's a game to him."

"No. He's methodical. I believe there was another reason he targeted them."

"Why?"

"Because you were never a threat to him. You're not the kind of woman he's interested in killing. He taunts you because it gives him some kind of sick pleasure."

When they reached the back door of Patrico's house, a telepathic voice said, *"Return to the warehouse district, sweet Tezra. You'll find the answers to your questions there."*

Her heartbeat quickened. *"Where, Krustalus?"*

But he didn't reply.

She squeezed Daemon's hand. "Krustalus says I'll find the truth in the warehouse district."

His eyes darkened, then he bowed his head. "So be it." He yanked open the door to the house and said to Atreides, "Ready fifteen men. We return to the warehouse district. Tezra and I will take the slower way to get there."

Atreides's brows furrowed. "Meaning?"

Daemon said to Patrico, "I need to borrow your car."

"Car?" Atreides said.

Daemon gave him a hard look, silencing his questions.

"I can manage," Tezra said.

"We'll drive." He held out his hand. "Keys, Patrico."

Patrico yanked them out of his pocket. "I want to go with you also."

"No, you stay here with Katie and Voltan." Daemon grabbed the keys Patrico handed him and led Tezra to the door.

She got the distinct impression from the scowling expression on Patrico's face that he wanted to confront Krustalus as much as he wanted to protect his car, and he did *not* like a vampire telling him what to do either.

"We'll meet you there?" Humor edged Atreides's words.

Daemon ignored him and walked outside to the blue Corvette. His lips lifted.

"You do know how to drive, don't you?" Tezra said, while

Patrico, looking uneasy, hovered in the doorway.

"I'm an ancient." Daemon opened the car door for her. "I know how to do everything."

"Right. Being conceited tops the list."

Once they were in the car, Daemon peeled out of the driveway, and Tezra was certain he gave Patrico a heart attack. At least Daemon nearly gave her one while she clung to the seat. "Jeez, Daemon, who taught you to drive?"

"I said I know how to drive, but I don't like to go slowly."

"Slowly? Hell, you're twenty miles over the speed limit already."

They barely made a narrow, twisting curve, and Tezra grabbed the dashboard. "Believe me, if you don't slow down, I'm going to throw up. This is not making me feel any better than vampire transportation."

Daemon eased around the next curve in the coast road much more slowly, his neck straining with tension. "I move quickly. I don't like being confined to human limits."

She managed a brief, albeit hysterical, laugh. "I'll remember that the next time you offer to drive me somewhere."

With closed eyes, she managed to survive Daemon's driving though every time he took a curve, the brakes and tires squealing, she clenched her teeth. When he parked the car, she opened her eyes and tried to settle her stomach, but the old feeling of being in Krustalus's killing field snowed her over.

At midmorning, the old red brick warehouses were bustling with activity, and if her stomach would settle she would feel a little less apprehensive about meeting Krustalus. Men were loading and unloading trucks, some were pulling out with full loads, and though it was a gray day, at least she could see what they were up against.

Then Atreides contacted Daemon. *"We're in the warehouse district."*

"We're parked near the west side of the Storm Tire Company. Meet us here."

Daemon rubbed Tezra's shoulder, thinking she looked a little green, but he hadn't wanted to waste any time delaying their arrival here and hoped she'd feel better soon. He approached three men taking a smoking break while Tezra hung close by his side. "Are any of these warehouses vacant?" he asked.

One of the men shook his head, and the beanpole of a man reminded Daemon of a scarecrow in jeans, checkered shirt, cowboy boots and baseball cap, only he'd lost most of his straw stuffing.

A shorter, stouter man tilted his beak of a nose up and asked, "Why do you want to know?"

Daemon grabbed the man's throat, not in the mood for games, his canines instantly extending. "Answer the question."

"Yeah, yeah," the third man said, his teeth stained yellow, matching the color of his hair. "Over there!" He pointed to a dark warehouse, absent of any activity, two stories tall. "Never see no one—well, rarely—go in or out. Me and my buddies figure bloodsuckers..." He paused, his green eyes shifted to Daemon's canines, and his Adam's apple bobbed up and down.

"Go on," Daemon growled.

"Vampires own it and drop in whenever they like. They don't use no front door."

Daemon released the man, who coughed, holding onto his throat, and backed away.

Atreides and fifteen men appeared, and to Daemon's surprise, Bernard was with them.

"He wanted to come and protect Tezra. He's her bodyguard," Atreides said.

The more backup, the better, Daemon felt.

"Damn right," Bernard growled, giving Tezra a harsh look.

She took his reaction in stride and motioned to the dark warehouse. "Let's learn Krustalus's secrets, shall we?"

Daemon moved her vampirically to the warehouse, hoping the short distance wouldn't bother her this time, but he wasn't willing to delay finding out what Krustalus had in mind to share with them. Then he'd finally eliminate the rogue.

Bernard broke the window and after clearing the jagged glass, helped Tezra in, which didn't sit well with Daemon. He realized then how much he needed to curb his possessive streak when it came to her. Bernard quickly invited the vampires inside.

Atreides found a light switch and illuminated a building filled to the ceiling with crates.

"Over here," one of Daemon's men called, having moved deeper into the warehouse through the maze of crate-bordered paths.

They reached the site of a strange memorial—a woman's skeletal remains dressed in a police uniform, laid out on a table. Tezra took a deep breath, trying to settle her raw nerves.

Atreides motioned to the remains. "The reason for the police killings a decade ago?"

Fresh yellow roses sat in crystal vases beside the remains, the scent filling the air with a sweet tea fragrance. With a trembling hand, Tezra removed one of the cards tied to the vase. *"To my love, Jane. Krustalus."* The words were written in the elegant writing of a bygone era. Eyes misting, Tezra looked up at Daemon. "His lover, but apparently he hadn't turned her."

"All the cards read the same," Atreides said, holding several up for them to see.

Daemon unbuttoned the woman's police jacket and revealed the bullets beneath the shattered ribs. "Whatever she was wearing when she was murdered was replaced by a new uniform. Run her badge number by the police and see what name they give."

"Maison's on it," Atreides said.

Tezra crouched next to the table and opened a wooden box. Inside, she found a yellowed newspaper clipping and brought it out. "It's Jane Cramer. She's...she's Chief O'Malley's sister. The police officer who had problems with depression and committed suicide a year after the police killings."

"How much do you want to bet she died before the police killings began?" Daemon asked.

Tezra's eyes widened. "You mean the police killed her?"

"If she and Krustalus had a thing going." Daemon shrugged. "You said her husband is with the force also."

"He ordered the hit on her? And the chief? Had he known too?" Not in a millennium would she have guessed the chief had been involved in his sister's death. But it made sense. What had Mandy said? *The chief wasn't the same, not his old jolly self for months, way before the police officers were killed.* And the business about the police officers and their private meeting in the coffee room that Mandy had witnessed? Now she wondered if the meeting had taken place before they killed Jane Cramer or afterwards.

Maison relayed, *"The police department says there's no record of this badge number. Must be a fake."*

"Speak with the chief," Daemon ordered. *"We've just learned the woman is his sister. Tell him we know how she died. Find out if he was involved in the killing or just the cover-up."*

With tenderness, Daemon rebuttoned Jane's blouse and shook his head.

Tezra found a diary in the box and flipped to the final pages. *William knows about me and Krustalus. He said he wouldn't allow it. He said I'd hurt his reputation, his good name. That I didn't deserve to live after what I'd done. I have to get in touch with Krustalus, but I haven't been able to get word to him.*

Two days later, the final entry said: *Krustalus has made arrangements to meet me in the warehouse district after my shift ends Friday night. He insists I have to agree to being changed or he can't protect me from my husband. He's certain William will kill me if we don't take the next step in our relationship. I love Krustalus more than I have ever loved anyone, but the idea of becoming a vampire...well, I just can't see myself as one, and I'm still not sure I can handle what Krustalus expects of me. I swear he's ready to get on bended knee and beg if I don't agree readily enough. I've never known anyone who cares so much about me.*

Tezra could sympathize with the woman not wanting to be changed, but she couldn't imagine Krustalus being capable of loving anyone that much. "Something must have delayed him in meeting with her. No further entries were written after this."

"Here are three police officer badges," Atreides said, pulling them out of another box near the table.

Daemon considered the numbers. "Have Maison identify who they belonged to and verify with the chief that these were the hit men. Also, have Maison find out if her husband ordered the hit."

"Why would Krustalus not kill her husband and the chief if they were involved?" Tezra asked.

"Sometimes letting the rabbits run scared gives more satisfaction than terminating them. The game is ended too quickly then," Daemon said.

Atreides handed him a file. "Yeah, well, here's all about the woman who wasn't in their records. Jane Cramer, twenty-five, special investigations. Here's a note in police records about her disappearance. 'After searching for the whereabouts of missing police officer Jane Cramer, and no new leads, the case was closed.' If you notice, it was signed by Chief O'Malley, who ten years later denies she ever *was* a police officer."

"Then a year later, they said she committed suicide." Sickened by what the police had done, Tezra took a deep breath.

"Have you seen enough here, Tezra?" Daemon asked.

She nodded, but Daemon seemed even more disturbed than she was, and she couldn't imagine anyone being more upset than her.

"Take Tezra back to Patrico's," Daemon suddenly said, his voice hard. "Now, Atreides."

Atreides seized Tezra by the waist, but before she could ask what was going on—though she assumed Krustalus had arrived nearby and she just hadn't sensed him yet—she found herself in the black void of vampiric travel.

As soon as they reached Patrico's beach house, the overturned sofas and sword slashes in the walls and furniture warned her of a vampire struggle. Her heart filled with panic, Tezra screamed, "Katie!"

Patrico groaned from behind one of the sofas, and she dashed to him while Atreides vanished. "Patrico!" His head sported a bloody gash, and he was favoring his left arm, his face grimacing with pain. "Where's Katie?" she asked, then heard someone in one of the bedrooms.

Unsheathing her wrist blades, she dashed down the hall only to find Atreides searching the rooms. "They're not here."

"Voltan? The guards out back?"

Atreides shook his head. "No sign of anyone."

She knew as well as he did that if the men were killed outside, their ashes would have scattered in the wind. Her heart beat so hard, but the blood seemed to drain from her brain, and feeling lightheaded, she grabbed Atreides's arm. "Did Daemon know about this?"

"No." Atreides led her back into the living room. "Take care of Patrico. I've got to get some other men here at once."

"But...why did Daemon send us here?"

"Krustalus sent him word he was meeting him there for a final showdown. He wants you, and he came to fight Daemon for you."

"It was a ruse, dammit."

"No. He was there, maybe beyond your range, but there

nonetheless."

"He's got Katie!"

"We'll deal with it when we can. For now, you take care of—" Atreides turned his attention to the back porch. "Dammit. Stay here!" He vanished.

Tezra nearly quit breathing. She could deal with this. Racing into the kitchen, she grabbed a roll of paper towels, then hurried back into the living room. Patrico was mumbling something but barely making any sense.

"Voltan went with them. The traitorous bastard," Patrico suddenly said, sounding more lucid.

"Voltan?"

As loyal as he was to Daemon, she didn't believe it for a minute. To keep Katie safe? To play along?

"Why didn't they kill you?"

Patrico's eyes drifted.

"Patrico!" She pressed the towels against his forehead. "Why didn't they kill you?"

"Krustalus's people told me to tell you if you want Katie back, you'll have to go to Krustalus alone," he blurted.

Swords clashed outside, and she said, "Hold this against your head, Patrico. Hold on. We'll get help soon." Then she ran to the window, and her heart took a dive. Four vampires targeted Atreides, two slashing at him with swords, the other two waiting in reserve. He'd never make it. *Dammit.*

"Bernard!" she called telepathically. *"We need help. Don't distract Daemon if he's fighting Krustalus. Krustalus's minions have taken Katie and Voltan. The others must be dead. Patrico's severely injured. Atreides is outnumbered. Have someone send help to Patrico's place—four-oh-five Seabreeze, Seaside!"*

Without waiting for a response, she grabbed a sword out of a stand near the back door and ran outside. One of the vampires turned and hissed at her. Atreides jabbed his sword into him, turning him into ashes that blew away in the stiff breeze, his clothes remaining behind in a pile on top of the sand. A redheaded vampire appeared next to her. Tezra sliced at his shoulder, and he cursed but seized her sword hand and teleported her away from the house. She swore at him, at Krustalus and the world for her mistake.

৵

When her senses stopped swirling, Tezra found herself in a lighted cellar. The vampire who'd moved her here yanked the sword from her hand. Two others appeared, and when she attempted to use her wrist blade on the redhead, another came up behind her and grabbed her wrists and *tsked*. The smell of her father's cologne assaulted her. *Krustalus.*

Sliding around her, the vampire was tall like Daemon, dark-haired and eyed, only his eyes appeared fathomless, daunting. She didn't think any vampire could mesmerize her, yet he stole her thoughts, her speech. Krustalus wore blue jeans and a simple shirt. He'd blend in with the ordinary Joe on the street, except for the cleft in his chin the size of the Grand Canyon, and didn't look like the devil incarnate.

"Krustalus," she breathed, her heart racing, irritating her. She didn't want the monster to know how scared she truly was of him.

"Tezra, sweet. You have come to me as I knew you would."

He released her, and she lunged at him, her wrist blade aimed at his heart. He vanished. Unable to stop her forward motion, she slammed into a rack of wine. A sharp pain radiated through her left wrist.

A scrawny young male vampire laughed—his eyes as blue as Bernard's and hair straw blond like Maison's. "Krustalus has other business to take care of before he can have you, but know this, your actions are seen as sexual foreplay to the ancients. He's the most controlled vampire I've ever known, but you nearly made him lose that restraint. That's why he left instead of playing with you further. It's nice to know he's kind of human sometimes. Next time you attack him, if he's done with his other business, he'll not hesitate to make you his."

Before she could respond with a huntress's fatal retort, he and the others slammed her against the floor, nearly jarring her teeth loose from her head when it smacked against the concrete. Dazed, she couldn't fight them when they grabbed her wrists and removed her blades, then just as quickly they vanished.

Sitting up, she rubbed the back of her head where a lump had already risen and pain streaked through her skull. Rising unsteadily to her feet, she considered her prison. The concrete block cellar was filled with several racks of wine bottles, similar to the one beneath Daemon's home, except there was no bed.

Torn between feeling trapped and not allowing herself the emotion, she listened for any telepathic voices or any other communication, but heard none. She crossed the small room to the barred window and stared out at the ocean waves crashing endlessly against the rocky beach. Against one wall behind a row of wine bottles, she saw crates stamped with the name *Clam Diggers*.

If she could reach Bernard without distracting Daemon... *"Bernard, I've been taken prisoner by Krustalus's people, and I'm being held at..."*

The door squeaked open, and she quietly waited for the next vampiric confrontation she was sure she'd have, her heart beating at twice its normal tempo.

"Join your sister," a blonde-haired vampiress said with a sharp tongue, then whipped around and slammed the door shut, the lock clicking afterwards.

Tezra rushed forward and ran up the stairs to greet Katie. "Oh, Katie honey, are you all right?" Wrapping her arm around her trembling sister, Tezra led her downstairs and hugged her close, thankful she was unharmed for the moment.

Katie's face was ghostly pale, but she looked like she was holding up otherwise.

But suddenly Katie squirmed free, reached under her sweater and pulled out a sheathed dagger.

Tezra couldn't believe it. "Where the hell did you get that?" Shaking her head, she took the dagger and attached it to her own belt, the weapon giving her a modicum of hope. "Stay right here." She moved Katie between the row of wine bottles and the crates.

Tezra seized one of the bottles and slammed it against the window, shattering the glass and the wine bottle. The noise was sure to alert the rogue vampires, but she had to do something to get her sister out of here.

Reaching through the shards of glass dripping with burgundy wine, she desperately attempted to move the bars cemented across the window, hoping that at least one of them was loose, but they didn't budge.

Katie gasped and Tezra whipped around. Her heart dropped

when she saw the tall, thin, black-haired vamp dressed in ebony leather standing near Katie, who was wearing a white sweater and jeans. The contrast made Tezra think of an angel and the devil.

"Lichorus." Tezra barely breathed, assuming that's who the vamp was. Tezra dashed between her and Katie, shielding her sister.

The vamp's ebony eyes flashed in irritation. "Lichorus? Ha! She has *Mustaphus* for her lover though she still wants Daemon. I am Ionia, and *I* will have Krustalus."

"Good for you. Release us, and you can have every bit of him."

The vampire bared her wicked teeth. "For years he's stalked you, wanting nothing more than to have you. A test of wills. The perfect conquest, so he has often related. Only I will kill you first."

Tezra held the blade behind her back, waiting for the vampiress to draw closer, trying to reason with her. Diplomacy worked sometimes, but she doubted anything she said would convince this vamp not to touch her or Katie. "He'll know you murdered me. Then he'll finish you off."

Ionia smiled, the look pure evil. "I will make sure Krustalus believes it was Lichorus who did the deed. Easy enough to do. She truly lusts for Daemon, and she hates you for stealing his heart." She ran her tongue over her sharp fangs. "The only reason she hasn't killed you before now is she fears Krustalus's retribution. He's not one to betray." Ionia took a step forward.

"But Krustalus can read your mind. He can find out what truly happened." At least Tezra assumed he could if the vamp let down her defenses.

The vamp stopped, twisted her head as if considering the notion, then gave a wicked smile. "I'm leaving evidence incriminating Lichorus, and he won't bother to read my mind."

Enough of diplomacy. "As if he'd trust you."

Hissing, Ionia flew through the air at her.

Tezra pulled out the concealed dagger and for an instant, the vampiress looked surprised. Tezra thrust the blade at the vampiress's chest, but it glanced off a rib.

Ionia screamed and retaliated, giving Tezra a vampiric shove, knocking her onto her back against the unforgiving concrete. Tezra dropped the dagger while pain radiated through her spine. Ionia gloated.

Feeling the bottom half of the broken bottle where she'd dropped it, Tezra grabbed it. She jumped to her feet and shoved it into the woman's chest, desperate to kill her before the other vampires could come to her aid.

Clutching her bloodied chest, the vampiress howled. Tezra dove for the dagger on the floor nearby, her fingers gripping the blade's leather handle. As soon as she had it in her grasp, she stood, but Ionia seized Tezra's hair and yanked her backwards. Twisting around, Tezra jammed the hunter's weapon between the vampiress's ribs and into her heart before Ionia could react.

Ionia shrieked, then her body dissolved into ashes. Before Tezra could breathe a sigh of relief, four vampires appeared in front of her, all males bearing fangs, and all looking famished, especially the blue-eyed blond.

"*You*, we're supposed to keep alive, but *her*," he said, motioning to Katie, "she's of no consequence."

"No!" Tezra screamed and thrust her blade at the blond.

Chapter Thirteen

In the middle of the battle with Krustalus's minions at the warehouse, Tezra's telepathic voice reached out to Daemon.

"Dae...mon." Her voice sounded weak, broken, desperate.

Tezra. His heart nearly stopped as his thoughts shifted to where she was supposed to be, safe with Atreides and Voltan at Patrico's place with her sister. *"Tezra, what's happened?"*

Silence.

Shit! Daemon's blood pressure elevated, and he wanted to leave for Patrico's house at once, but couldn't abandon his people to fend for themselves without putting another ancient in charge.

"Bernard," Tezra called out, not focusing her message.

Daemon glanced at the bulldog of a man who was fighting a vampire, their swords striking at each other, but Tezra's communication distracted him. Daemon finished off the vampire he was fighting, then went to Bernard's aid.

"What did you say to her, Bernard?" Daemon growled through clenched teeth.

"Nothing. Hell, she's supposed to be safely at Patrico's house, isn't she?"

Daemon sent a message to Atreides. *"Where the hell is Tezra?"*

When his brother didn't respond, Daemon forced himself to remain focused on the vampire danger in front of him. After getting the best of Krustalus with two wicked slices to his sword arm, but not terminating him like Daemon would have liked, the vampire had made a hasty retreat to lick his wounds somewhere else. But several of his minions, though not turned by the earlier plague, were well over hundred years old and formidable enough.

"She's all right, isn't she?" Bernard asked, his tone murderous, and he sounded like he was ready to kill anyone, including Daemon, if he found Tezra was in danger.

"Maison, I need your assistance in the warehouse district, now," Daemon transmitted to his friend. *"Voltan, what the hell's going on?"*

No one responded, and Daemon felt he'd been dropped into a black void where none of his telepathic communication could be heard.

"Where are you, Tezra?" he asked again, trying not to sound as panicked as he felt.

"Daemon, I'm here at the warehouse now, but someone needs to invite me in," Maison said, sounding frustrated.

"Come in, Maison."

In a split second, Maison was swinging his sword at the dwindling number of renegade vampires. "What the hell's happened?" he asked from between clenched teeth while he struck another vampire down.

Daemon fought one at his back. "Tezra's supposed to be with Atreides and Voltan at Patrico's home, but she called me and she sounded like she was in pain. I can't get any response from either my brother or Voltan."

"Hell, I'll take care of this rabble and—"

"Daemon, your...your trust was misplaced."

Daemon didn't recognize the telepathic message and glanced at Maison to see if he did. He raised a brow, evidently not knowing who had spoken either.

"Musta—Mustaphus t-took Katie. And..." The man grew silent.

"Who the hell is this?" Daemon asked, thrusting his sword at one of the last of the vampires.

"Pat-rico. Voltan not—not only let him—him have her, he went with him."

Shit! *"What about Tezra? Atreides?"*

Patrico didn't respond.

Daemon stabbed the last of the vampires in the heart, then said, "We go to Patrico's house, now."

When they reached Patrico's house, they found the place in a shambles, no sign of anyone except Patrico passed out on the floor, his head bleeding.

Daemon quickly roused him while one of the vampires wrapped a towel around his head. "How many were with Mustaphus?"

"Ten, in-cluding a scrawny woman."

"Lichorus." It had to be her—she'd sealed her fate this time. Daemon's blood boiled. "Why did they let you live?"

"I had no weapons, no way to defend myself, no way to save Katie."

Daemon paced. "But Voltan knew you were telepathic and could warn me. It doesn't make any sense that he wouldn't have killed you."

"Mustaphus was...running the show. I'm certain he recognized me as the hunter who couldn't kill him ten...years ago. I-I think it amused him that I couldn't fight him now any more...than I could then. I've been in contact with Tez-Tezra, however."

Hell, no wonder she couldn't contact Daemon. She was too busy communicating with the damned hunters. He ran his hand over his unbound hair. "Where the hell is she?"

"She said something...I think I passed out, then she cryptically said, 'the ocean.' I assume she's got to be someplace...nearby."

"Do you believe him?" Maison asked.

Daemon rubbed his chin while he considered Patrico's words. He nodded. "Yeah, I do."

"What about Voltan?"

Daemon was certain his smile looked purely evil. "They've let the wolf into the sheep's pen."

"Hopefully he won't get himself killed."

"If I'm not wrong, he's playing a twist on the situation we had in the Americas during the Revolution. Remember when one of Sir William Howe's men captured Missy Temple, saying she was a rebel spy?"

Maison nodded. "Somewhere Voltan got a Brit's uniform that was lanky enough to fit his tall frame and sneaked in to interrogate her."

"Right, and took her safely from her cell."

"And nearly got himself killed—shot three times and lanced once, the blade just missing his heart," Maison reminded him wryly.

Daemon didn't want to consider that part of the equation.

"Come to Clam Diggers, my lord," Voltan suddenly relayed.

"Tezra and Katie are there?" Daemon asked.

"Yes, yes, hurry."

Minutes later, Daemon and his army stormed the seafood restaurant just a mile down the road from Patrico's place, praying he wasn't too late to rescue Tezra and her sister. Inside the darkened building, they found Voltan fighting six vampires at once, his face red, his arm cut and bleeding, sweat dribbling down his iron jaw. They'd knocked over tables and chairs, some in splinters. Broken glass from the lobster tank and water covered the wooden floors. No sign of Tezra or Katie.

Jumping into the fray, Daemon unsheathed his sword and beheaded a blond male, while his men quickly took care of the rest. "Where is Tezra?" he hollered at Voltan.

"Fighting a vampiress in the cellar. I think she's your former lover, Lichorus—and from the scream I heard coming from there, I believe the vampiress is dead."

"And Atreides?"

Voltan shook his head.

Daemon and Bernard barged down the stairs, only to find the dusty remains of the vampiress and her leather clothes and Tezra fighting four vampires who were attempting to stay out of her dagger's reach. Katie was cowering behind her between the wine rack and wooden crates stacked against the wall.

Seeing the spirited huntress at such a disadvantage, his heart reached out to Tezra. In that instant, he made the decision to turn her for her own protection now and forever. Until Krustalus was dispatched, she'd be safer as a vampiress and maybe Katie's only chance to have a life. With his sword poised, Daemon dispensed with two of the vampires while Bernard finished off the other two. Tezra hugged Katie to her chest.

Tezra was way too vulnerable as a huntress. He wouldn't take her for his mate and go down that dark path, but he couldn't lose her to Krustalus or to any other ancient who might wish to lay claim to the enchantress. He would make her his ward, under his protection for as long as he ruled. And rule her with an iron hand to ensure she didn't turn rogue.

Maison appeared suddenly in the cellar and lifted a broken

necklace from the vampiress's remains. "Lichorus's."

Daemon stared at the necklace, recognizing it as the ruby heart he'd given her many centuries ago when he thought her sweet and innocent.

"Ionia," Tezra said, finally able to get a word out.

"Sorry, my prince," Voltan said from the top of the stairs. "I thought it was Lichorus. She and Ionia played tricks pretending to be each other because of their similar looks."

"Mixed them up once at a bash Maison had given. Lichorus thought it was funny as hell until I kissed Ionia pretending I still thought she was Lichorus." Daemon let out his breath in exasperation when he realized he hadn't seen his brother yet, but wouldn't give in to the concern he had that Atreides might not have made it. "Where's Atreides?"

"He, he was fighting several vampires on the beach," Tezra said, tears filling her eyes.

"Here." Atreides poked his head through the doorway. His bloodied arm dangled at his side. "Sorry I was late again. The buggers wouldn't tell me where they'd taken the women hostage. And when they teleported to the warehouse district, I tagged along. I convinced the last one to tell me where the ladies were, though he was pretty reluctant."

More than relieved his brother, his last living blood relative, was fine, Daemon glanced at Tezra, knowing he had to do this now. "We have to talk."

Tezra stared at Daemon, wondering what this was all about. A darkness seemed to fill his spirit, and she didn't like it.

He walked her outside and to her surprise, the Corvette sat in the parking lot. "Maison drove it here so I could get to you more quickly, but I'm not chancing having you get sick from transporting all over again." He said to Atreides, "Take Katie back to Patrico's place. Double the guard. We'll return there soon."

She gave Katie another hug, not wanting to leave her alone again, but Daemon's tone of voice made her think better of questioning him. Atreides held Katie close, irritating Tezra that he didn't put more distance between them, then he and several of the others, including Voltan, vanished.

Tezra didn't like that Daemon was planning to drive the car again. She rubbed her arms. "Can I—"

He shook his head and ushered her to the car, then opened

the passenger's door. "We should get back to Patrico's place soon."

"In one piece, Daemon." She gave him the evil eye, meant to quell his lead foot.

He climbed into the driver's seat, but before she could brace herself, he zipped out of the restaurant's parking lot.

"If you still want me to turn you, I will."

Her heart barely beat. "I thought—"

"You'll be my ward. I won't take another mate."

"But you said—"

"If you turn rogue, I won't terminate you. I...couldn't, Tezra. So understand this, if—"

"So, there *was* another option for turning me other than my becoming an outsider." She touched his lips, silencing him when he opened his mouth to speak again. "What exactly does being your ward entail?"

"You abide by *my* rules. If I so choose, I can give you to one of my loyal vampires as a mate in payment for their service to me, just like the royals did with the women who were wards of their courts during their reigns."

She stifled a sarcastic laugh. He was way too controlling to give her to one of his friends. "Would you really?" she asked, though she didn't believe him for a minute.

"It is always an option, and I wanted you to know what being my ward truly means."

He sounded totally serious, but she knew he was only trying to get her to change her mind about being turned and wouldn't give her up to anyone. Beyond that, no way would she allow it anyway. "All right, well, I promise I won't turn renegade on you, and being your ward is acceptable."

Yet she couldn't help feeling hurt that he didn't want her like he did the other women. She wasn't like the others. She was committed to being turned, and she could love Daemon without reservation. So why did it distress her so much?

"Why did you change your mind, Daemon?"

"Krustalus will always come after you." He glanced at her. "I intend to kill him, Tezra, but I can't be certain I will always be there for you. He separated us, and I cut him a couple of times before he vanished." He let out his breath. "I couldn't see it before, or maybe I didn't want to believe it. You were right.

Krustalus was waiting until you were older. But not because you could fight him better. He wants you for his lover. He's lost his chosen mate, and he's staked his claim on you. It's too great a risk with you being so defenseless. If I turn you, you'll be a fledgling. But you'll have speed, the ability to see in the dark, a heightened sense of hearing and—"

"I can bite him."

He gave her a dark smile. "I'm thinking more in defensive terms. You'll never have his strength, but vampiric abilities will give you a better chance at detecting danger and avoiding it until I can reach you and terminate him. The heightened senses will be immediate. Teleporting is different for everyone. Some catch on quickly. For others, it takes longer to master."

"But I can control a human's mind."

"Also limited to a degree. Early on you should curb your use of it or you'll experience debilitating headaches."

"But for Katie's sake—"

He nodded. "If she doesn't resist your suggestion, it should work."

Not expecting Daemon's sudden change of heart, Tezra didn't say anything for a moment.

"It's up to you, Tezra. It has to be your choice, but I will do it if you desire."

What she desired was to set Katie free from her nightmare.

Convinced Tezra would be safer if he turned her, Daemon couldn't let Krustalus get hold of her no matter what. Instead of taking her to Patrico's home, he drove her to the privacy of his.

As soon as they were inside his home, Daemon grabbed her up in his arms and carried her to his bedroom, then dispensed with their clothes and lifted her onto the high bed. The sound of her sweet murmur, the smell of her heavenly floral scent and touch of her silky skin against his instantly aroused him.

"Daemon," she mouthed against his lips as he kissed her into submission.

He leaned against her, and her fingers skimmed his back. Her pink tongue flicked at his, teasing him. His need for fulfillment roared through him. He prodded her parted lips with his tongue, simulating what he wanted to do with his hard erection between her legs. He licked the tender skin at her throat, and her pulse beckoned him.

If she wasn't so close to being a huntress rogue, he might have considered taking her for his own mate. She was perfect in every way otherwise—if it hadn't been for his past failures when he attempted to take a mate.

His eyes feasted on her soft, rounded curves. Her long dark hair screened his view of her rosy nipples peeking out shyly between the strands, and the length draped down to the top of her short curly hairs.

Breathtaking. A vision in one luscious body.

Trailing kisses down her abdomen, he stroked her nipples, drawing them upwards into cherry-colored, twin peaks. She touched his unbound hair, and her lips curved up, her eyes heavily lidded. Her smile was contagious.

"Do you still want this?" he asked, needing to be sure.

She took a deep breath and nodded. "For Katie, and so that I'll have more defenses against Krustalus."

"I'm not pushing you into this."

"Do you want me to bite you first?"

He chuckled and licked her neck. "I'll drink as before, then it's your turn." With the gentlest of pricks, he tasted her sweet blood, taking enough this time to ensure she needed his to complete the transformation. But as soon as he did, he felt the urge to make her his for all eternity. The spitfire and sensual sweetness that was all Tezra drew him in, captured him, held him prisoner. When he sealed the wound, she closed her eyes, her pulse slowed.

Using his teeth, Daemon cut his arm and touched it to her lips, ready to fulfill his promise to her. "Drink."

She swallowed, then choked, her eyelids fluttering.

"More," he coaxed, his brow wet with perspiration.

Her dark, dampened curls rested against the satin pillow. Her breathing was shallow, her skin deathly pale. Even her lips were colorless except for the light stain on the bottom where his blood had touched her.

"Come on, Tezra. Drink." He continued to drip blood into her mouth, hoping the nourishment would entice her to feed soon. "We need to see Katie." And the sooner Tezra was turned, the sooner her defensive abilities would kick in.

Tezra's lips moved as if she was trying to say her sister's name. She swallowed hard, then licked his arm with a tentative touch. His heart soared.

She licked again, and the velvety tip of her tongue caressing his wound stirred him.

She ran her tongue over her lips.

"Tezra, feed." His husky words sounded desperate. He wanted to force her compliance like any other human, but he couldn't compel Tezra. Maybe that's why she appealed to him so much. He couldn't control her, though in this instance he wished he could. "You will obey me in this."

She opened one eye lazily and pursed her lips.

He touched her throat, feeling the slow pulse. Brushing away her hair, he exposed her breasts, then ran his tongue over the tip of one.

She weakly grasped handfuls of his hair, but her gaze wasn't focused on anything in particular. Her tongue slipped out of her mouth, moistening her lips. Her action mesmerized him, and he hoped the bloodlust was beginning to stir her.

His tongue tangled with hers again. She grasped it between her lips and sucked, nearly making him spill his seed. Groaning, he managed to sputter, "Tezra, honey, you're killing me."

Her mouth curved up, and she licked his chin, her eyes barely open, her teeth still human-sized. Regretfully, it didn't appear she could extend them yet.

A shudder of need ripped through him, and he bit into his arm, then offered her the sustenance again. When she didn't react, he pulled away to kiss her, but she tried to rise, to follow the blood on his arm. His heart rate increased. God, how he wanted the sexual pleasure of feeling her canines sink into his vein.

Her eyes widened when he pulled his arm farther from her mouth, her gaze focused on his blood. A small growl rumbled in her throat. He smiled, but her fangs still hadn't extended.

None of the other women had been a problem, but then he reminded himself Tezra wasn't like the other women he'd mated. A huntress telepath, she would never be quite like them or anyone else he'd ever known. On top of that, he was certain she truly didn't want to be turned, only wanted to save her sister.

He moved onto his back. Her eyes remained fixed on his arm, two droplets of blood still rising atop the pinprick punctures. She closed her eyes, and he took an exasperated breath.

The wound on his arm sealed. He bit his finger and inserted it in her mouth. Taking hold of his hand, she sucked on his finger. His libido surged with renewed gusto.

She licked and sucked until he could barely last. Moving between her legs, he lined up for maximum penetration when she bit his finger hard.

A jolt of pain shot through his finger all the way up his arm. Yanking it free, he squelched a curse. "Gently," he said, his eyes watering. He rolled onto his back, then pulled her on top of him. Her soft body pressing against his very hard erection nearly killed him. Tilting his chin to the side, he offered his throat to her, pleading silently that she'd bite him more tenderly.

At first, she snuggled against him, ignoring his offer, her satiny hair tickling his skin, his heart beating rapidly. Her tongue flicked over his nipple. Heat poured through his veins with the tickling, teasing touch.

He'd never been with a woman he'd wanted this much. He swept his hands down her back and cupped her soft ass. After spreading her legs apart, he moved his fingers into the drenched curls.

Stroking into her honeyed sheath, he felt her stir. Her head rose from his nipple, and she eyed the pulse in his neck. *"Bite me, gently."*

Licking her lips again, she shifted her hungry gaze from his throat to his eyes. She drew closer to his neck, pressing her body against his painful arousal.

He groaned, but she ignored his complaint, her attention riveted to his pulse. Frozen in anticipation, he waited for her to hunt him down, to sink her fangs into his neck and suck his life force, to replenish the blood she needed, to send him hurtling toward the heavens.

Her teeth scraped at the skin of his throat, but her canines still hadn't extended, dammit!

He meant to rake her long nails across his neck, to draw the blood and let her feed that way, but she pulled her hand away, her gaze still focused on his throat. Not being able to wait any longer, he lifted her hips and entered her.

She bit him on the neck.

Not gently either. Streaks of pain shot all the way from his neck through his shoulder. Yet he chuckled. How he loved every soft, sweet inch of her.

Her sucking began, turning his thermostat up to blazing hot. Shoving his erection into her again, he pumped without reservation, her lapping and soft moans driving him insane.

But the sweetest kind of insanity.

Her body rocked against him, hard, relentless, her tongue stroking the wounds she'd made. Her lips latched on and sucking again, drew out his blood, bringing him to the peak of ecstasy before he could slow the process down.

She arched her back and cried out his name. He groaned again—hot, satiated release.

"Ahhh, Tezra honey." His hands brushed over her hair and skin, wanting the intimacy to last forever.

She touched his wounds with her fingertip and licked the blood off her finger like she was sucking on the sweetest candy cane. His erection stirred deep inside her.

Reaching up, she ran her tongue over the wounds to seal them, dropped back down and closed her eyes. She whispered, "You sure...are bossy...you know?"

Grinning, he wrapped his arms around her and pulled her close, her head resting against his sweaty chest. "You have to learn who's in charge."

"Hmmm," she said, deeply sighing, "say that to me again, when I'm...not so...sleepy."

Then she lifted her head and pressed her chin against his chest, her eyes sparkling.

Now what the hell? She studied him so intensely he swore she was trying to control his thoughts, and him an ancient vampire!

"Vixen, rest," he growled.

She laughed, but foreboding filled him. If she was attempting to control him like the women he'd turned before her, what else would she try to do? The memories of changing the others returned to him with a vengeance. Tezra might not think she could be like them, but her penchant for revenge

191

could push her over the edge if he didn't keep her under his tight control.

Already, he sensed disaster in the form of one hot, sexy SCU investigator/hunter now turned vampire.

After they rested, Daemon drove Tezra back to Patrico's house, though he tried to keep from driving too fast and had to wipe only one traffic cop's mind of the speeding ticket he wanted to give him. Even so, Tezra kept her eyes shut the whole way back. Well, except when she gave Daemon her I-told-you-so glower as the cop tried to write him up.

He couldn't tell how she was feeling about being a fledgling vampire. Maybe worried she wouldn't be able to reach Katie, maybe concerned that Krustalus wanted Tezra for his own. Daemon wished she would talk to him, but then again, perhaps it was just his driving that was getting to her the most.

After shutting off the car's engine, he glanced at Tezra and found her staring at Patrico's house. He reached over and patted her leg. "Are you all right, Tezra?" He tried to settle the worry that the change had turned her into something he'd grow to despise. The silence between them was killing him.

"Yes," she said, but she didn't sound sure of herself at all.

And for once, he felt he had no control over the situation. No way to soothe her fears. No way to reassure her everything would work out the best for all concerned.

Because for the first time in years, he wasn't sure himself.

What if Katie didn't respond to Tezra's trying to help her rejoin the world? What if her attempts did more damage than good? No matter how hard Tezra tried to dismiss her insecurities, they flooded her. Not only that, but she couldn't help worrying that her canines would suddenly extend. Just pop out for no reason. Hell, if that happened when she was trying to talk to Katie, it would probably put her into a coma!

She glanced at Daemon, his look concerned, and she

offered a small smile, but his expression didn't change. He already knew her better than that. Her anxiety must be imprinted all over her face.

He rubbed her shoulder and kissed her cheek. "Come, Tezra. Let's see your sister."

She should be thrilled with the prospect of aiding Katie, but she couldn't help agonizing over the change. So far she didn't feel any different. She didn't crave blood, her teeth were back to their normal-size, she moved like she typically did—maybe a little slower than normal, reluctant to face Katie, fearing failure. But then she smelled the sea, not like she usually did but the more subtle fragrances—the salt and fish, even the wet sand and rain saturating the clouds overhead.

Over the crash of the waves out back, the sounds of birds chirping and singing, but when she listened even closer, the whoosh of the sea breeze stirred the needles of the pines and the sound of voices inside the house carried to her ear.

Tezra glanced at Daemon, and from the expression on his face, he knew. He recognized her insecurities, recognized how the changes in her were throwing her off-kilter. Taking her hand, he squeezed with reassurance, then transported her to the dining room, giving her another minute to brace herself for the next phase in her life.

Surprisingly, she didn't feel dizzy at all, which was definitely something positive.

She tightened her hold on his hand and nodded, ready to take the plunge, or at least she hoped so. Then they joined everyone in the living room. Patrico sat on one sofa, while Voltan stood slightly behind him. Katie sat opposite Patrico, and Atreides reclined next to her. He wasn't interested in her sister, was he? He had better not be.

Everyone eyed Tezra and Daemon and she wondered if they realized Daemon had changed her. Well, everyone but her sister. But she couldn't tell from their facial expressions how they viewed Daemon's decision.

Tezra gave Atreides a look like he should move it or lose it. He glanced at Daemon who nodded.

Atreides smiled darkly. "Anyone want some coffee?" He disappeared into the kitchen and banged around.

It was now or never. Tezra sat next to her sister. Reaching out, she took Katie's hands. Her stomach rolled like the waves curled and crashed on the beach. She gathered her strength to delve into her sister's fractured mind.

Tezra hoped the smell of the salty air and the screeching of seagulls in flight in the seaside setting would bring the cheerful memories back to her sister. "Katie, do you remember a time when we played at the beach? We collected seashells and—"

Pulling her hands away from Tezra, Katie looked away from her.

Tezra tried a different tack and recaptured Katie's hands, rubbing her thumbs gently over them. *"You will listen to me, Katie. Hear my words and don't think about anything else unless I give you permission."*

She wasn't sure she was having any effect on Katie, but it surprised her how easy it was to attempt vampiric mind control, as if she'd been born with it. She could see how seductive having the power could be.

Daemon drew close to Tezra and touched her shoulder. "I want you to quit, Tezra, if your head begins to hurt."

Her gaze shifted to him and she nodded, but she had no intention of stopping, not until she rescued her sister from the darkness.

"I mean it, Tezra."

Not about to allow him or anyone else to control her, not when this was so important, she turned away from him. *"Remember when we spent Christmas with Aunt Ritania? She gave you an amethyst ring, your birthstone, but gave me a Mickey Mouse watch because I could tell time. But I wanted an emerald, my own birthstone, something pretty and feminine. Not a Mickey Mouse watch. It was a boy's watch, for heaven's sake."*

Katie looked away, but Tezra touched her cheek and forced her to face the memories.

"They're dead," Katie said softly.

Tezra stared at her sister in disbelief. To hear her sister's first words spoken in a decade, Tezra's heart ached with joy. Yet bringing up the subject of their parents' murder didn't seem like a good idea now. But another notion concerned her. Had her sister not been as traumatized as everyone thought? Tezra didn't think she'd done anything to reduce her sister's fears enough to bring her out of her silent world.

Katie looked at her, her expression solemn, her eyes barely blinking.

"Uhm, yeah, Katie Bird, Mom and Dad are dead. I'm..." Unable to keep her emotions in check, she pulled Katie into her arms and crushed her against her chest, traitorous tears rolling down her cheeks. "I'm so sorry for everything that happened."

Pulling away, Katie wrung her hands and shifted her eyes to the floor.

The rejection hurt, but Tezra wasn't finished explaining. "I wanted so badly to catch the killer vampire who was murdering police officers, I didn't think of our family's safety."

Katie looked back at Tezra, her eyes filled with tears.

"Can you ever forgive me?"

Katie's jaw tightened. "I-I..." She clamped her mouth shut.

Daemon took Tezra's hand and rubbed it.

With a sinking feeling, Tezra realized she had a long way to go in helping her sister to mend. "What, Katie? Tell me how you feel. I'm so, so sorry."

Katie swallowed hard and fisted her hands in her lap. "I-I..." She shook her head and avoided looking at Tezra.

Shaken, Tezra feared her sister hated her for what happened. "Katie..."

"No!" Katie's green eyes were icy daggers. "I...h-had a fight."

Tezra opened her mouth to speak, but then curbed the urge and tried to hold onto her sanity while she waited impatiently to hear her sister out. She wondered if in some insane way Katie had felt their parents' deaths were her fault. When Katie didn't speak, Tezra tried again. "Katie, none of what happened was your doing, honey."

"I-I...had a fight." Katie struggled to get the words out, as if after not speaking for so long it was difficult now, or was it the grueling emotions that caused the problem?

Trying to calm the blood rushing pell-mell through her veins, Tezra took a deep breath. "Tell me what you remember." No way was her sister responsible for what had happened, and she wanted Katie to understand that right away.

"You..." Katie wiped away tears rolling down her cheeks and stared at her lap. She looked up at Tezra, her eyes reflecting pain and anger. "You got to go to the SCU school early. But I-I was twelve, the same age as you when you...started. They w-wouldn't let me go. Said I wasn't as..." She sobbed, and the woeful sound wrenched at Tezra's soul.

Tezra rubbed her arm. "It's okay, Katie."

"I wasn't as strong or agile or quick as you. W-when he came, I let..." Katie looked at the floor and shook her head.

Sitting back against the sofa cushions, Tezra stared at her in disbelief. "You invited him in." She'd never considered how the murderer had gotten into the house, and she'd never thought her own sister would feel responsible for their parents' murders.

"I was sooo...mad at Mom and Dad, I-I wasn't thinking...straight." Katie's face puckered up in anger, and she wouldn't look at Tezra. "F-first rule t-taught..." She swallowed hard. "To every hunter child, never in...invite a vampire into your home."

Daemon took a deep breath, and Atreides shifted a bit.

"Who was he?"

Katie stared at her, resentment still burning in her eyes. "How...how would I know?"

Oh, God, Tezra had never considered Katie wouldn't know who the murderer was. Of course, she wouldn't know him. How could Tezra have been so deluded to think Katie would?

"Do you recall what he looked like?"

Katie shook her head.

"I have to know for certain. He can't hurt you. You're safe with us. Did you even look at him when you answered the door?"

"I-I was so angry," she admitted. "He a-asked to see Dad. Mom was in the kitchen making..." She brushed away fresh tears. Atreides handed her a box of tissue and she blotted the tears with one. "Chocolate chip cookies, your favorite dessert, b-because you had made honors a-at the school. Dad had been taking a nap. I froze when the man...pulled out a sword and...killed Mom. Dad tried to save us, but the man killed him too. I-I think he looked at me. I was too scared to see, then he vanished."

"He didn't walk away? He vanished like a vampire?"

"He...he walked away, vanished. I don't know. I couldn't look. Then you came home, and I-I don't remember anything after that."

Tezra studied her sister's actions, the way she avoided her look, and she suspected Katie wasn't telling the whole truth

"Was he tall like us?" Atreides asked, motioning to Daemon and him.

Katie shifted her gaze from them to Tezra. "About as tall as Dad," she said to Tezra as if the others weren't in the room.

Tezra nodded, confirming the answer to Atreides's question.

"What color was his hair, his eyes?" Atreides asked.

Fisting her hands in her lap again, Katie scowled at him. "I *don't* remember." She faced Tezra. "We h-have to kill him for what he d-did. We have to."

Tezra patted Katie's hand, having every intention of putting Krustalus out of his misery. "I promise you, he'll pay for his crimes."

"Why...why did you think you were the one that caused our parents' deaths? Because you weren't at...at home at the time and didn't help protect Mom and Dad?"

"No." Tezra sighed heavily, wishing for the millionth time she'd not threatened him with exposure. "I was on his murdering trail, trying to discover who he was."

But a new worry consumed her. Tezra didn't believe for one second that she'd used any vampiric ability to reach Katie.

With her heart in her throat, Tezra asked, "Katie, tell me the truth, have you been able to speak for some time?"

Chapter Fourteen

No one said a word at Patrico's house as they waited for Katie to tell Tezra the truth. Had she been pretending to be wrapped in a bubble of silence for a decade, or not?

Katie didn't respond.

"Katie..." Tezra's head began to pound. *"Katie, tell me, have you pretended not to be able to communicate with us all this time?"*

Fighting Tezra's attempt at persuading her to reveal the truth, Katie clenched her teeth and closed her eyes.

"You will tell me honestly, Katie. Did you understand everything that's gone on the last ten years? Were you able to speak with me all this time, but refused?"

Katie swallowed convulsively as Tezra's head began to ache, and she feared the answer. Why else would Katie resist giving up the truth?

"Katie..."

Her sister shook her head.

Tezra took a settling breath, but the relief was too short-lived.

"Only since yesterday," Katie whispered.

Tezra's heart felt like it was being crushed between collapsing stone walls.

"When...when Patrico took me away from the hospital. I...I was afraid I'd never see you again. S-something inside me snapped. But then I was too afraid to speak. Afraid he'd be mad at me, and then you'd be angry with me...for...for what I'd done."

Tezra closed her eyes to hold the tears in, the knowledge

she'd had Daemon change her when there had been no need washing over her like an icy Arctic wave. She had no idea how much being vampiric would truly affect her, had no idea how to cope with all the changes psychologically and physically, and hell, what if Daemon killed Krustalus before the killer ever got to her again? She wouldn't even need the extra defensive measures.

She'd always hoped once she proved Krustalus was the killer, the SCU would exonerate her—even accept her. That wouldn't happen now that she'd been turned. The cherry on top of the sundae would have been revealing Patrico was alive and well. Now, what did any of it matter?

She was a vampiress, and that couldn't be changed. Worse, Katie was bound to feel responsible for this now too. And what if her sister hated her for being vampiric after what Krustalus had done to their parents?

"Why didn't you tell me, Katie? Why?" Despair filled Tezra's words. Daemon squeezed her hand. She couldn't look at him, but stared at Katie instead, her whole world turned upside down all over again.

Katie shook her head. "I killed our parents. You would have hated me for what I did. I...I couldn't live with it. You...you loved me and treated me kindly and...and even when I wanted to tell you yesterday, I couldn't."

Katie was an emotional wreck. It wasn't an act.

The fact remained Tezra hadn't needed to be changed to reach her. Her whole body trembled. She wanted to scream, to shake the earth, to kill Krustalus with her fangs, ripping him to shreds slowly, painfully, until he begged for mercy, and then she wanted to torture him some more. She could easily be a rogue, as Daemon had feared.

"It was my fault," Tezra said quietly. "*My* fault they died, *not* yours, and for this..." She swallowed hard. Her greatest fear was not ever being accepted by her hunter kind. "For this, I will forever be punished."

Shakily, she stood, wanting to get away from everyone— Daemon's concerned touch, her sister's worried look, the rest of their shocked expressions. She wanted to bury herself in a hole and never come out.

෧

Tezra retired to Patrico's bedroom, unable to be with anyone for the moment. She wished she had some family left who could take Katie in and help her to adjust to the world now that she'd rejoined it. Tezra wished her hearing wasn't so damned acute, wished that when Voltan whispered to Atreides down the hall, she couldn't hear them.

"He has changed the huntress...our prince, has he not?" Voltan asked.

"Didn't you see it coming? As soon as he issued a death threat to any who might consider turning her, he made it clear he was claiming her," Atreides responded.

"What about the last one?"

"Don't *even* bring Lynetta up. For decades, I had to put up with Daemon's foul mood over the mess with the rogue huntress, and I don't *ever* want to have deal with that again."

Daemon had tangled with another problem huntress? Tezra collapsed on the bed and groaned. Atreides and Voltan didn't say another word.

Wanting to get away, Tezra closed her eyes and imagined walking along the beach forever until she left this realm and entered a world where no one knew her, where she could live in isolation for the rest of her life. But no matter how much she tried to shove the concerns from her mind, she couldn't even walk along the beach without the threat of Krustalus hanging over her head.

"Tezra's mad at me, isn't she?" Katie asked someone in the living room.

Tezra covered her ears, wishing you she couldn't hear them talking about her, but it didn't help.

"She's very happy for you, Katie honey," Patrico said. "She's just very concerned about this matter with Krustalus."

"I heard one of the vampires guarding the house talking to another, and he said Krustalus wants Tezra for his mate. Why?" Katie asked.

"He's attracted to her, and he lost his own mate some years ago."

"Oh."

"Tezra," Daemon said softly next to her, and she opened

her eyes, her heart pounding. "I'm sorry. I didn't mean to startle you or intrude on your privacy, but I wanted to see if you were all right."

She hated it when anyone felt sorry for her. The best way for her to deal with all the unwanted emotions slamming into her was to get on with the deadly business at hand. She sat up in bed. "I want to know who wrecked my place and why."

Daemon eye's widened. Was he surprised she was considering the case again? "Maison had some men go over it, looking for clues. They discovered Lichorus had been in your apartment. Whether she did all of the damage or she had help is not certain."

"Lichorus. For what reason?"

"Maison assumes she was looking for your files to see if you had any evidence against Mustaphus, her current lover. But Maison also believes she took great pleasure in trashing your place."

"Because of your interest in me."

Daemon bowed his head in acknowledgement.

"Tell me about Lynetta, the huntress you fell in love with. Atreides mentioned you were...*upset* over her and hoped the same would not happen again with me."

Daemon's face grew stormy. "Atreides should learn to keep his mouth shut."

Tezra folded her arms and waited. If Daemon had had a horrible time with another huntress, why hadn't he told her about it? She feared the worst. It was not that the other women he'd turned had become renegades that had upset him so, but the woman he had really loved—a huntress—had done something awful to him.

She suspected Atreides wouldn't tell her anything about the huntress if she questioned him. "Well, Daemon?"

Daemon took a seat on a chair next to the mahogany dresser. "What do you wish to know?"

"What happened between the two of you?" *For starters.* Who she was, how much he loved her, why he had fallen for her—all piqued her curiosity. Was Tezra just the same as her, or totally the opposite? That's what she wanted to know.

"Quite simply, Lynetta used me to entice a hunter so that he would come to her rescue. She told him I'd tried to turn her against her will. Of course, I wanted her to agree to being turned, and she teased and cajoled me into believing she wanted the same. Until the hunter nearly killed me over it. But somehow he learned the deception of her ways, and he later apologized for his attack on me."

"I don't understand how he could have gotten the upper hand."

"I wouldn't kill him, Tezra. I knew he was being manipulated, but I couldn't terminate him or the SCU would have labeled me a rogue. Lynetta would have made certain they knew I'd targeted a hunter."

"I'm so sorry." Tezra shook loose of her own morbid thoughts, rose from the bed and joined him. She leaned over and kissed his cheek. "What happened?"

He pulled her into his lap and held her tight. She loved his tenderness. "The most unbelievable scenario you could imagine. Despite the fact she nearly had me killed due to her lies to the hunter, he married her apparently because he was much impressed that she'd go to such lengths to catch his interest."

"I hope they both hated each other soon after," Tezra said, her voice angered.

Daemon kissed the top of her head with tenderness. "They stayed together until the end of their years. Whether they were happy, I never wished to know. All I knew was the huntress was not the one for me, and I nearly lost my life for wanting her. I believe I might have been angry about it for a while."

"Several decades?" Tezra wondered if he finally let the hurt go when the woman died.

Daemon's mouth curved up some.

"And here I thought I held long-term grudges."

"You were resting with your eyes closed when I disturbed you." Daemon kissed her ear, making her whole body tingle with expectation. "Did you want to return to bed?"

She raised her brows and that was all she needed to encourage him. The next thing she knew, he'd moved her to the mattress. "When do I get that vampiric speed of yours?"

He chuckled and quickly dispensed with her clothes and his, then joined her in bed, but resting wasn't what he had in mind.

Later that afternoon, Katie took a nap in one of the guest rooms, and Daemon had Maison bring Chief O'Malley to Patrico's home so Tezra could have some resolution in the earlier murders. She'd lightened up some when he'd talked to her about his former huntress lover. And she'd seemed to enjoy their lovemaking. But as soon as they were done, she'd wrapped herself in that damnable cocoon. He felt her pulling away from him, not physically, but emotionally. It was too much like the way his mates had reacted after being changed—first severely depressed and inconsolable, then vicious and uncontrollable.

She wasn't adjusting as he'd hoped, and he assumed a big part of it was because she hadn't needed to be turned. If only Katie had opened up to her sooner... But the situation couldn't be undone and Tezra had to live with it. And somehow he had to get her through the dark period without her turning rogue.

In the living room, Chief O'Malley eyed the vampires in terror and sputtered, "W-what do you want with me?"

Voltan still nursed a torn-up arm, but Atreides's wounds had healed. Patrico looked like a war hero, sporting a bloodied bandage around his head. Yet, as far as Daemon was concerned, Patrico hadn't earned a right to be in the same room with the rest of them.

Daemon wrapped his arm around Tezra's shoulders while they sat on the couch opposite Chief O'Malley. The notion she might want to rip out the chief's throat briefly came to mind. "You owe Tezra some answers."

Tezra glowered at Daemon. "You don't have to restrain me."

"I hadn't thought of it as restraint but more of a loving gesture." He kept his tone lighthearted, not sure how to deal with the feelings she'd bottled up. He still felt she was safer with her new abilities, as long as she didn't use them as a vampire rogue would.

"It's called restraint from where I'm from." She turned her aggravation on the chief next. "Tell me the truth about Jane Cramer."

The chief looked at Daemon, but this was Tezra's show, and he waited for her cue.

Tezra turned her head slightly in a menacing vampiric way, not willing to play any word games with the chief. But she was thankful Daemon had Voltan bring O'Malley to the house while

Katie slept—just in case Tezra's abilities got out of hand. "I can force you to reveal the truth, but I'd rather you cooperate. I might not be able to keep my new fangs under control."

Unaware she'd been turned, the chief looked startled. His eyes widened and his skin paled. "I'm sure you know Jane was my sister," he quickly said.

"Yes, and she was having an affair with Krustalus."

The chief narrowed his eyes. "Yeah, the bastard."

"So you had some of your officers murder her." The image of Jane's skeletal remains came back to her, and a tingling sensation centered around Tezra's canines. She clenched her teeth against unsheathing them. "What was her husband's involvement?"

"He planned it. The three officers were in debt up to their eyeballs, and William offered to pay off their bills. No one liked that she was screwing around with the vampire."

"But you knew about it and sanctioned it?"

"I didn't stop it." The chief stared blankly at the floor. "My brother-in-law and I expected all along Krustalus would come after us. We're always watching our backs, but it won't do us any good when Krustalus finally decides to take revenge."

She ground her teeth, trying to keep them under control. "Did you know all along that he murdered my parents?"

"No. You have to believe me. I didn't know until he told me to tell you so."

Unable to comprehend how the chief would allow his sister to be murdered like that, Tezra glared at him, but didn't say anything more. If Krustalus didn't finish him off, she knew the police would deal with the chief and his brother-in-law soon. She'd make sure of it.

Daemon asked, "Are you through questioning him?"

"What would it have hurt if she'd loved the vampire?" Tezra asked sadly. "Why did she have to die?"

"She loved a renegade, a murdering bastard," O'Malley said, his words cold-blooded.

Tezra sat taller, wanting to give him the benefit of the doubt. Wanting to believe the chief couldn't be that evil. "Did you know that then? That Krustalus was a rogue?"

The chief dropped his gaze to the floor and shook his head.

"What if Jane didn't know either? What if he'd manipulated

her like he had so many others?" Tezra rose from the couch. "I'm through with the chief, Daemon."

He motioned to Atreides, who took Chief O'Malley by the arm and disappeared. To Maison, Daemon said, "Put out the word there's to be a celebration at my home, open to all vampires."

Maison frowned. "Are you certain..."

"I'm certain Krustalus and Mustaphus will come. Lichorus too. I want them and anyone else they've recruited. Time to end this."

"I agree." Maison motioned with his shoulder in Bernard's direction. "What about him?"

"He comes with us. He's still Tezra's bodyguard." Daemon swore the hunter's chest puffed up a bit, and his hard scowl softened.

"I don't want to be shown off at a vampire bash," Tezra growled between clenched teeth.

"I thought you were willing to be bait for Krustalus. Now is your chance." Daemon figured she was worried how his clans would accept her, maybe afraid how'd she react around others of her kind now. But she had to get used to them, and he had to get rid of the rebels in his midst.

"I want to be at the bash too," Patrico said.

"Count on it," Daemon responded, his tone icy, not satisfied that the hunter had made up for his past transgressions where Tezra was concerned.

"I don't want Katie or Patrico there," Tezra said, her voice firm.

Katie suddenly appeared from the hallway. "No, no, I want to be there, Tezra. You can't shut me out of your life now." She sounded like Tezra—stubborn and unmoving.

If Atreides was even considering pursuing the redheaded wench, he had a real battle on his hands, Daemon thought, watching the two women. He could see now how similar they were when they pinched their brows and narrowed their eyes, their spines rigid with determination.

Tezra had to deal with her own insecurities of being a vampire among vampires and didn't want her sister to see her like that. "You might not be safe. I'd be distracted, concerned for your welfare. We can't risk it."

Katie's green eyes were hard and her words harsh. "They already grabbed us at Patrico's home. Where am I supposed to safely stay?"

Tezra considered the SCU, but she wasn't really on good terms with them at the moment, so no, that wouldn't work.

"Let me go with you too. Daemon already said I could," Patrico insisted. "It's time I did something worthy of my former position."

Tezra looked at Daemon for his support, but he only shrugged. "It's up to you. This is your show."

Tezra could have socked him. Not that she didn't mind being in charge, but this was one time she could use his help in changing her sister's mind. "All right, but I want Voltan to guard Katie, and this time he's not to join the rebels and turn her over to them." Though she knew he had done it so that he could inform Daemon of their whereabouts once they were taken.

Voltan bowed, a small smile touching his lips.

"And, Patrico, you're to be at Katie's side constantly. Let no one get near her." Tezra's voice brooked no argument, yet she still didn't feel right about it.

Patrico nodded.

"Katie?" Tezra said, soliciting her agreement.

Katie relaxed. "I'll be happy to stay in the background."

Atreides cleared his throat. "I'll watch over her too."

"You'll be looking for anyone who's there to disrupt the party," Daemon countered, his tone stern, and Tezra was glad he at least was in her court on that issue.

Atreides winked at Katie, then bowed to Daemon.

"I'll be keeping a close eye on Tezra." Bernard tilted his chin up.

Daemon gave him a disgruntled look, and she swore he thought Bernard might be competition for her affections. He ought to have known better.

Daemon turned his attention to Maison. "You know how I like the bashes, only slightly modified."

"As you wish, my prince." Maison bowed, then vanished.

Tezra shuddered internally, ready or not to be the bait.

Daemon wished he could help her through her internal struggles, but for now he had to defeat Krustalus's rebellion and terminate the bastard and his cohorts before he could deal with Tezra's troubles. Her green eyes reflected anxiousness, and when she caught his gaze, she looked away from him, shutting him out like she'd done ever since speaking to Katie.

He caught Atreides's eye. His brother raised a brow, but his expression remained thoughtful. Daemon had expected his brother's condemnation for turning the huntress. Despite the SCU calling her an investigator, she had killed the ancient vampiress Ionia, and that proved she was a born huntress. A mere investigator could not have handled the vamp.

Maison didn't let on that he was disappointed that Daemon had given up his vow and turned Tezra, either. Maybe they'd finally come to the conclusion Daemon had no control when it came to some women.

Even Katie kept her distance from Tezra as if the woman had suddenly erected a barbed wire barrier covered with charges that screamed, "Stay away!"

Her skin clammy, Tezra walked over to the window and stared out at the clouds billowing into mountains of white. Behind the innocent looking puffs, electrical energy gathered, building into a massive thunderstorm.

She worried not only about meeting Krustalus and fighting the urge to kill him outright, but about how Daemon's people would receive her. Would they back him or side with Krustalus? More than that, how was she to explain to Katie what she'd become? Could she accept her? Worse, Tezra had to ensure her sister never learned the truth, that Daemon had turned Tezra so she could help her sister see the light. The reality would damage Katie's fragile emotional state.

Blinking away tears, she knew she had to tell Katie the truth before she learned it on her own. Tezra felt the cold return to her bones. Taking a deep breath, she joined her sister and led her to the sofa. "Please sit. I have something to tell you."

Katie's back was as stiff as a rigid oak, but she acquiesced.

Tezra sat beside her and forced herself to gaze into Katie's eyes, to not look away with shame. "I'm..." The words stuck in her throat, and she avoided looking at Daemon, knowing how much he must hate her for still being so troubled over having been turned. She swallowed hard and took her sister's hands. "I asked Daemon to change me so I..."

Katie's eyes widened, and she yanked her hands away from

her. "You're one of them?" She jumped from the couch. "Daemon forced you against your will! He had to have! One of them cold-bloodedly killed our parents! How could you?"

Tezra gritted her teeth, angered that her sister's silence was the reason she'd made the choice. "No, Katie. He didn't force me."

"Why?" She turned her gaze to Daemon and glowered at him.

"To...to help fight Krustalus. I couldn't fight him on my own, and he's not going to let me go until he's dead," Tezra said.

Katie brushed away tears dribbling down her cheeks. When Tezra stood and tried to console her, Katie pulled away from her. "You're...you're one of them!" She stalked down the hall.

Tezra watched her retreating backside and let out her breath. Krustalus would pay. If she had her way, he would die tonight. But it would do nothing to bring Katie and her close to each other again.

Before they went to Daemon's bash later that evening, Tezra paced in the living room. No matter how he tried to ease her concern about the party, he couldn't distract her. Katie retired to Patrico's den to watch Vampire Crime Stoppers on television while Atreides, Voltan and Patrico shared tales of momentous battles they'd been in.

Finally, Tezra approached Daemon and motioned to the hall with her head. "We need to talk." Once they were sequestered in the master bedroom, she folded her arms and furrowed her brows. "I want to know what I'll be capable of doing tonight."

Daemon sat on the bed, stretched his legs out and leaned against the pillows stacked against the headboard. "I've told you what you'll be able to do." And he sure as hell didn't want her fighting. Looking beautiful and staying safe were the only missions he wanted her to focus on at the party.

"What about shape-shifting into another animal form?"

"No." He shook his head. "That can take years." Though it depended on the individual. But he didn't want to get her hopes up about something she couldn't rely on this early after being changed.

She pursed her lips. "What about moving with that vampiric speed you use to undress and teleporting to get around faster than the human eye can detect?"

"Some are able to move quickly early on. Think of it this way—everyone is different. Some individuals walk when they are nine months old, some a year, some speak earlier, some learn to read faster. With vampiric abilities, some take centuries to learn certain skills, some can learn them quickly."

She frowned. "Can you teach me how to vanish?"

"Again, that usually only occurs after years of being a vampire. It's been so long ago for me—"

"How did it happen when you first did it? Did you wish it?"

He was sure as jealous as she seemed over Lichorus, she wouldn't care to hear about his misadventure with the knight's daughter. Yet he wanted to keep their relationship open and honest, and if it took her mind off the party scheduled for later...

Her eyes narrowed. "What?"

"I..." He shrugged. "It was a long time ago, Tezra. I was kissing a knight's daughter and—"

"Only kissing?" Tezra raised a brow in question. "Seems the tips of your ears are too red for just having kissed the girl."

He grinned, amused every time Tezra showed a jealous streak over him, despite her denial.

"Dressed or undressed?" She tilted her head slightly to the side, her tone amused.

"I don't remember." He rested his hands behind his head.

This time both brows rose. "If you can't remember, I venture to say you weren't dressed. So what happened?"

"She was, well, an amorous type. She wouldn't take no for an answer. Mary had been with several before me. She was just very..."

"Promiscuous?"

"You could say that. Anyway, I was kissing her—"

"Among other things."

He couldn't help smiling, amused at Tezra's take on the story, though her perceived version was closer to the truth than he was willing to admit. "Her father arrived home from a tourney and heard us—"

"Just kissing?" Dimples punctuated her cheeks, and her

eyes sparkled with mirth.

He cleared his throat. "And—"

"You were doing it in her home?"

"The stables," he admitted. "Anyway, he stormed into the stall, and I knew my life was at an immediate end, particularly when I saw the bastard sword he was carrying."

"But you shape-shifted?"

"Vanished. One minute I was with her, and the next I was in Maison's father's castle. I had wished I could be in..." He paused, figuring he'd get himself into more hot water. "Anyway, so I got out of the knight's path and his sword with just a very fervent wish."

"What place had you been thinking of? Where did you end up?"

"I told you. Maison's father's castle." He knew that wasn't going to satisfy her from the look of curiosity on her face.

"Where, *exactly*?"

Daemon shook his head. So much for protecting her fine sensibilities. "His sister's bedchamber. I thought I'd so much rather be there than in the stall where the knight was about to cut off my head. Maison's sister was betrothed to a duke, and despite all my romantic notions to the contrary, she harbored no interest in me."

"But you were a prince."

"Seems that wasn't enough. Though, I believe it had something to do with my vampiric abilities."

"But Maison had been changed too."

"Which is probably another reason why his sister didn't want much to do with me. She knew better. Anyway, I'd never appeared out of thin air like that, though both Maison and I'd been affected by the plague a good two years earlier when we were prisoners of the Turks."

"And her reaction?"

"She was taking a bath, and I was—"

"Naked."

"Ahem. So she screamed and I vanished again, this time reappearing in Maison's bedchamber. He was astounded to see what I could do. And even more so when he discovered he had the same ability. That night we both visited several different places to explore our newfound gift and much later, exhausted, we returned to his castle."

Tezra took a seat on the chair. "Had you been in any situation where you wished to go someplace before this?"

"Not that I specifically recall, but I'm sure at some time or another in the two years since I'd been changed and before I'd actually shifted I might have wished it, but nothing came of it."

Her brow furrowed, and she stared at the floor.

"Tezra?"

She waved a hand to silence him. He ground his teeth and fought pulling her into the bed and showing her what else she could do with her newfound talents.

She stared at the wall and spoke silently to herself. Was she trying to vanish?

Finally she looked up at him and shook her head. "I guess you're right. I can't do it right away. Or maybe it has to be a death-defying situation first."

Tezra seemed more hopeful than she'd had since she'd been turned, and he relaxed a little, thinking she might be all right after all. But when he saw her pinching her brows together in concentration again, he reconsidered.

❧

Half an hour before Daemon's vampire bash was to begin, he left Patrico's house to check on the final arrangements. Katie was busy getting dressed for the big occasion, after one of the female vampires loyal to Daemon had gone shopping for the ladies and bought them new gowns.

Patrico and Voltan were talking on the back porch about—fishing?—while Atreides was serving himself a cup of hot chocolate. "Want one?" he asked, raising the steaming mug to Tezra.

"No, thank you." She didn't believe for one minute that Daemon would give her away to some other vampire now that she was his ward, yet the notion kept nagging at her. Surely, Atreides knew his twin brother better than anyone. Wouldn't he know?

She sat at the bar's counter and watched Atreides pull out a container of fudge sticks. "So, Atreides, what does a vampire expect of his ward?"

Atreides stared at her for a minute, then frowned. "Where did you hear that term?"

So, Daemon hadn't told his own brother that he'd taken her as his ward?

"I...I just wondered." And wished like hell she hadn't mentioned it.

Atreides dipped his fudge stick in his hot chocolate. "Years ago, and I mean when we were the ruling class in Scotland, those who had vassal lords could take any number of their daughters as their wards, then offer them to one of their loyal lords in payment for services rendered. It hasn't been done in centuries."

"Oh."

"Why do you ask?"

Atreides was too smart and too inquisitive for his own good.

"I was just curious."

Atreides's eyes sparkled with dark humor.

"What?"

He lifted a shoulder. "If you wished to be honest with me..." He let his conversation trail without end, waiting for her to come out with the whole story.

Then it would get straight back to Daemon. But now she wondered what was going on. Thinking it over, she figured Daemon probably *hadn't* taken a ward in centuries, so no mystery there. Though the way Atreides responded to her mystified her thoroughly. She was certain Daemon would have told his brother what arrangements he'd made with her.

When she didn't enlighten him further, Atreides's finally set his mug on the countertop and asked, "He's made you his ward?"

Well, it was either that or she was an outsider, since she wasn't Daemon's mate. This time she shrugged, noncommittal-like.

He smiled, his look pure wickedness.

"What?" she asked, annoyed.

"I wonder if he's told anyone else, or he's keeping the news a secret."

"Why the hell would he?" Wouldn't they think she was an outsider then?

"Well, if he decides to give you up, unless I'm mated by

then, I'm the first in line to receive the generosity of our prince. Putting it plainly, you'd be mine. But you would be my mate, not my ward."

"Daemon won't give me away to anyone."

"I'm sure you're right about that."

"I *mean,* I wouldn't permit it."

Atreides gave her another conceited smile. "I warned him not to turn you."

Tezra opened her mouth to retort but heard her name spoken in a conversation nearby and she looked at the floor and tried to pick up more of the exchange.

"She's at four-oh-five Seabreeze, Seaside? Are you sure?" Bernard asked.

Someone knew they were staying at Patrico's house. Atreides must have overheard Bernard speaking and suddenly vanished. Tezra dashed down the hall to the guest room Bernard was in and yanked the door open. He was speaking on the phone and waved for her to be silent.

Atreides was standing beside him, listening in on the dialogue.

"We're on our way there, just about a mile south now. Meet us there. She'll probably be more cooperative if you come for her once we have her in custody," the man said over the phone.

"Yes, yes, all right. I'll get there as quickly as I can." Bernard closed up the cell phone and swore under his breath. "The hunter says you're dangerous and must be apprehended at all costs. The word has gone out that you've been turned and you, Patrico and Katie are here."

Damn them!

Three black SUVs skidded to a stop outside of Patrico's house, and several men dashed toward the house, their swords raised.

"Their grim faces look like some of the warriors of opposing clans we faced in Scotland long ago," Atreides remarked, while Voltan secured Katie and Maison took hold of Patrico. Three other vampires who were guarding out back ran into the house and one grabbed Bernard's arm.

Atreides wrapped his arm around Tezra's waist, and she felt in that instant he was more interested in her than he was in Katie. Why? Because Daemon may tire of her and give her to

Atreides as his ward—pardon, to be his mate?

"Daemon's ward, eh?" he said, humor coating his words.

And then the hunters crashed through the front door.

Daemon hurried to greet Tezra and the others narrowly escaping from the SCU hunters. He quickly took hold of Tezra's hand as if to assure himself she was safe.

Atreides gave him a bigheaded smirk. "I will be happy to take the huntress as my mate, if you so choose."

Daemon glanced at Tezra, and she folded her arms. It wasn't her fault he hadn't wanted the vampire world to know she was his ward.

"We'll speak later about the matter," he told Atreides, and he didn't seem happy about it.

Atreides bowed, but the smile remained fixed on his face as he vanished.

"When were you going to tell everyone that I'm your ward?" she asked Daemon, irritated to the nth degree. "Or did you want them to think I'm an outsider?"

"Later," he growled.

She scowled back at him, every muscle tense in anticipation of the bash—the worry Katie would be safe, concern for Daemon if Krustalus got the best of him, that his people would not accept her because she was a huntress.

She forced herself to concentrate on the partygoers, to keep her senses attuned to danger. Daemon's house looked like a Christmas open house with every light on in the place, and Tezra figured though the vampires could see in the dark, he wanted to ensure Patrico and Katie could see well enough too.

Daemon opened his mouth to speak to her, but before he could have a private word with her, vampires began to appear.

Bloody cocktails flowed in abundance while the vamps in their designer black satin or sequined gowns floated through the greatroom like black winged butterflies, simpering smiles pasted across their faces.

When Tezra disdainfully considered the crystal wine glasses filled with blood, Daemon pulled her into the kitchen and motioned for several lingering there to leave. Kissing her cheek,

Daemon explained, "At normal bashes some vampires get...frisky with one another, and the next thing you know, they're finding secluded places and sometimes not-so-private places to fulfill their blood and sexual lust. There's to be none of that here tonight. That's the reason for the bloody cocktails."

Tezra made a face. "Your people will despise me because you're changing the rules."

"I wouldn't do it any other way, not for your first time, nor while your sister and Patrico are here."

"Will that satisfy your guests?"

He kissed her throat and took her hand in his. "It will have to."

But Tezra imagined his people wouldn't like it, just like she figured they wouldn't be pleased that he'd turned a huntress and made her his ward—if he ever planned to tell them.

"Atreides warned me the hunters had found Patrico's place and wished to put you under arrest."

"Yeah, for taking my sister hostage." She *hmpfed* under her breath. "Even if I told them the truth, they wouldn't believe me because of the *condition* I'm now in. They'll assume they were right all along—that you influenced me to be turned."

Daemon shook his head.

Atreides announced aloud to everyone in the greatroom, "Adrik, leader of Texas, and Ruric, leader of Idaho, are here."

"Come, we must meet our guests." Daemon pulled Tezra into the greatroom where elegant fluted glasses filled with blood sat on white cloth-covered tables along one wall. Overhead soft classical musical played.

So many fragrant perfumes and men's colognes scented the air, she felt she was in a garden filled with flowers. Unfortunately because of it, she couldn't recognize Krustalus's scent unless he was close enough for his teeth to graze her neck.

Male vampires dressed in tuxes, some with ladies clinging to their arms, others single, drifted in from the back patio to pay their respects to Daemon. Except for cursory glances at Tezra, most ignored her.

She imagined Daemon would need a good neck rub later with all the bowing he had to endure. While he talked with some of his people, Tezra moved away from him, intent on locating Krustalus. Staying beside Daemon took too much of her concentration, the impolite stares, the condescending slights. His people for the most part did not like her and had no intention of welcoming her.

Bernard, dressed uncharacteristically in a tux that looked a size too small, probably worn at the last SCU ball he was required to attend four years ago, lifted a couple of fingers to acknowledge he was watching her. He'd worn the suit to appease her, to blend in with the others as much as possible. She smiled, and he immediately tugged at the bowtie strangling his thick neck and glowered at her.

Tezra heard a vampiress announce telepathically, *"Lichorus, I didn't think you'd be here since Daemon sent out word he wanted you in custody."*

Tezra strode toward the open patio doors where she sensed the communication was coming from. She wished she could have worn her leather pants and turtleneck, easier to fight in than a silky gown split up the side. But Daemon had insisted she wear the gown...to fit in. He wouldn't permit her to attach wrist blades either—too offensive to the vampires. Though she had stashed her swords for easy retrieval—one on the patio and one in the greatroom.

Several females stood on the patio in the soft light, all dressed in their best finery, some cocktail length, one wore a mini-skirt. Some of their gowns fluttered in the night breeze, wisps of black sheers, while others wore clinging satin. Which was Lichorus?

Moving outside, Tezra drew closer to where an evergreen shrub bordering the patio concealed her sword. She remembered Daemon had said Lichorus looked remarkably like Ionia and that he'd almost mixed them up before. Tezra stopped next to the shrubs. Her gaze searched for an ebony-haired, tall, thin woman, while she listened for Lichorus's response to the other vampiress.

"Why, dear Anatola, Daemon invited me," Lichorus finally remarked. *"The rumor he wanted to take me into custody is a mistake. He wanted me to be his lover again. A huntress could never sate his sexual prowess like a centuries-old vamp."* Lichorus laughed at her own words and the other vampiress followed suit. *"Besides, he knows the trouble he got into the last time he mixed it up with a huntress—almost cost him his life."*

Tezra turned her head toward the southeastern part of the

patio where Lichorus was telepathically speaking with Anatola.

"Tezra?" Daemon called out, alarm in his communication.

Her stomach clenched, and she felt she was a cat trying to sneak up on a blackbird, and her master caught her in the act. *"I am fine. Enjoy your party,"* she replied, trying to sound as though she hadn't a care in the world. This battle was hers, and if she were ever to fit into Daemon's world, she had to face the vamp herself.

She leaned down and pulled her sword from the shrubs, then belted it, twisting the leather until the sword rested at her back, a little less obtrusive.

"I want you by my side. Now," Daemon communicated to her, his tone a command.

"Demanding, aren't we?" He had to know ordering her about would not work. Tezra drifted farther into the crowd of vampires, sensing the women nearby. Why didn't anyone arrest the vamp? Surely if they backed their prince, they would take Lichorus into custody like he had ordered. Though she tried to maintain her calm composure, her heart hammered against her ribs. She stretched her fingers, preparing to unsheathe her sword.

"She is coming," Lichorus hissed.

Sure it was a trap, Tezra fought extending her fangs, the teeth itching to appear. But the vamp's goading wasn't the only reason for Tezra's rising temper. Daemon's people's complicity added to the anger she attempted to keep under control. Her teachers' words came back to haunt her. *"Keep your emotions in check,"* they had invariably warned her. *"When facing a vampire threat, if you give in to your feelings, you set yourself up to die."*

Anatola sighed. *"You play with fire, Lichorus. Kill her if you must, but I stand by Daemon, no matter the outcome."*

A woman moved out of the shadows, platinum-blonde, curvaceous. She brushed into Tezra, her icy blue eyes trailing over her, then she headed for the house.

"He will not like that you set me up so that Lichorus could murder me," Tezra calmly threatened.

The blonde glanced back at Tezra, her eyes wide.

Pleased at the vamp's reaction, Tezra smiled.

"You will not live long enough to tell him." Anatola offered a haughty smile of her own.

"He already knows." Tezra got the distinct impression no one else knew Daemon had turned her. If she was to be the bait, she wanted to be the best damned bait she could be. She was certain Lichorus's actions were not part of Krustalus's plan, however.

Tezra moved again, her high heels clicking against the stone patio, the cool breeze tickling a strand that had loosened from the mass of curls piled atop her head. The women and a few men glanced her way. Then she saw Lichorus—bewitchingly beautiful, extremely anorexic, runway model material—but her dark eyes were absolutely entrancing while she stood in the shadows several feet from the house near the end of the patio. She did look like Ionia. And like Tezra, the vamp was armed with a sword.

The vampiress hissed. "Tezra." Which confirmed she was indeed Lichorus.

"Thought I'd killed you at the seafood restaurant," Tezra said, her tone intentionally cocky.

Several vampires moved out of their path as if clearing the way for a western gunfight. Again, the distasteful notion that no one would help her, or warn Daemon the vamp intended to fight her forced her temperature to elevate and her skin to prickle with anger.

"Didn't Daemon tell you Ionia was my cousin?"

"Your nicer half, I take it. Though she left your ruby necklace with her ashes, intending to kill me and blame you for my death." Tezra smiled with satisfaction as Lichorus cursed under her breath.

Reaching behind her back, Tezra pulled out her sword.

"Tezra, where the hell are you?" Daemon asked.

She assumed he was being bombarded by telepathic communications, and he couldn't sense her. Were the vampires doing it purposefully to stop him from helping her?

"Find her, Atreides, Bernard, Maison. Locate her at once and bring her to me," he ordered.

Too late.

Instead of unsheathing her sword, Lichorus exposed her teeth and dove at Tezra.

Chapter Fifteen

Tezra jumped aside, avoiding Lichorus's razor sharp teeth. She could move faster now, though not as fast as ancients like Lichorus, but her action thoroughly confounded the vamp.

Lichorus eyed Tezra in surprise. *"He turned you?"*

Pretending not to hear her telepathic communication, Tezra didn't respond.

Lichorus lunged again, her teeth bared.

Part of Tezra warned her not to kill Lichorus, to leave her to Daemon, but part of her said to hell with that. The bitch threatened to kill her, and that was all she needed to excuse her actions.

Wielding the sword, Tezra sliced at the woman as the crowd grew in size to watch. Barely escaping the blade's sharp point, Lichorus vanished.

Tezra couldn't tell from the vampires' somber expressions whether they wanted Lichorus to win or not. All remained silent, or channeled their communications solely to each other. And she assumed they didn't want Daemon to know the huntress was fighting for her life against one of their own.

Gazes shifted to a location behind her, and Tezra pivoted to face the threat. With teeth bared, Lichorus yanked out her sword and swung at Tezra. Lichorus didn't have the luxury of a long game. She hurried to finish the job before Daemon caught her.

"Tezra's fighting Lichorus!" Atreides communicated to Daemon, sounding panicked.

Then the clatter of sword fighting broke out inside the house, and Tezra figured she had to do this on her own, just as she'd planned from the beginning.

"*Atreides, grab Lichorus! Where are they?*"

"*Damn, Daemon, Mustaphus is here!*" Atreides warned. "*And several of his followers.*"

Daemon should have known Tezra would go after Lichorus to reduce the number of rebels in their midst. Hadn't he told her he wanted her to stay in a defensive mode, safe from harm? "SCU investigator, my ass," he mumbled under his breath while trying to locate Tezra. She was a bona fide huntress whether the SCU wanted to recognize it or not.

As soon as he moved toward the patio doors, four rogue vampires appeared in front of him, all with swords drawn, all trying to keep him from protecting his ward. Nearby, he glimpsed Atreides parrying against the thrust of Mustaphus's sword, and Bernard and Patrico fought their own battles against rebel vampires. Voltan towered over everyone, backing two vampires into a corner near the fireplace. Maison let out a war whoop from the dining area and the swords began to clank with a vengeance. As if the fight had become a free-for-all, Daemon's people joined in the battle, the lines clearly drawn.

"You still have a choice." Daemon waved his sword from the redheaded vampire on one end to the brunette at the other. "Join me, or die."

"Krustalus and Mustaphus will win this day," the redhead said. "There needs to be a radical change in the way of doing business. You have lived long past your prime, old man."

Old man? "Let me show you what this old man can do." Daemon moved so quickly, the blond standing in the middle of the four didn't have time to react to the swing of Daemon's blade. The blond's severed head fell to the floor, and then his body collapsed. "A fledgling?" Daemon asked, knowing he had to be or his body would have dissolved into dust.

The redhead and brunette tried to take him on, but Daemon vanished, then reappeared behind the last three. After beheading the brunette, he vanished again before the redhead and the other man could turn to fight him.

"You don't fight fair!" The redhead screamed like a man who was used to getting his way.

"I'm an old man, as you so aptly put it, Red. Through the ages, I have learned to win my battles any way that I can. If you find my methods unfair, I wonder what you think of Krustalus's and Mustaphus's deeds."

The other man backed away and quickly bowed. "I will serve you, Prince Daemon."

"Your name?"

The man's electric blue eyes shown like ice, but he turned his sword on Red. "Krouse, the Avenger."

"Damn you, you traitor," Red said, and jabbed his blade at Krouse. But Krouse lived up to his word and with a wicked slice, cut Red's sword arm. He promptly dropped his weapon, but extended his fangs.

Without hesitation, Krouse ran him through, then looked to Daemon when Red collapsed dead on the floor—another damned fledgling, arrogant to the hilt.

"Help Maison in the dining room," he commanded, and Krouse bowed, then vanished. Daemon tried to locate Tezra again, swearing he'd lock her up for her own safety until this was over.

If he could find her in time.

As soon as Tezra heard Atreides say Mustaphus was here, she knew he would jump in to protect his lover, Lichorus. No way could Tezra fight two ancients at the same time.

But for now, she had to concentrate on the black-haired menace in front of her.

Tezra stabbed at Lichorus when she came in for another pass. This time her long nails raked Tezra's cheek. The stinging wasn't half as painful as it was for Lichorus, no doubt, when Tezra lopped off her nails to the quick. Lichorus screamed, but a couple of vampires laughed out loud. Tezra didn't figure they thought it funny, but instead tried to cover up Lichorus's cry of distress. To prolong the fight? To ensure Daemon didn't stop the entertainment?

Thrusting with her sword, Lichorus attempted to stab Tezra in the heart. She jumped back out of her reach. But a spectator shoved Tezra toward Lichorus, giving the vamp the advantage.

Tezra's heart sank. It was bad enough that nobody but his brother warned Daemon what was going on, but now to have one of his people aid in her demise was too much.

Lichorus swung her sword at Tezra, but she blocked it with

such force, Lichorus's blade shattered. Slamming the remainder of her sword to the stone patio, Lichorus lunged, her sharp canines aimed at Tezra's throat. Without hesitation, Tezra jammed her blade into the woman's heart.

Lichorus screamed, soulless eyes stared back at her with disbelief, then her body disintegrated into a pile of clothed ashes.

The crowd parted for a second.

"Tezra, sweet."

Krustalus—his thin face exaggerating his large nose, his eyes as dark as a bottomless well and his black hair unbound as if he'd awakened from a long nap—stood tall, imposing, angry.

He stared at Tezra, then looked at Lichorus's remains. "Dear Tezra, the vamp would not have lived a second longer under my rule had you not killed her first."

The memory of her murdered parents flitted across her mind, and the fury boiled inside her. She thrust her sword at his chest. He dodged the blade, seized her wrist and yanked the sword from her hand. Tossing it aside with a clatter to the pavement, he grinned, his chin tilted up, taunting her to try something else.

Before she could struggle free, another vampire, dark-haired and eyed, rushed toward Tezra with murder in his eyes. He looked a lot like the photo of Daemon's Uncle Solomon, and she realized at once how the police could have mistaken his uncle for this man. *Mustaphus.*

Krustalus released her, caught Mustaphus's arm, and shook his head. "She's mine, Mustaphus," he hissed. "None of you will touch her."

The thought flitted across her mind that he was making an enemy of the same people who had already shown her so much animosity, not the thing to do if he was trying to win them over so that he could rule. Or maybe he didn't need to win them over, just rule by brute force.

Not if she had her way. She leapt for her sword, but Krustalus blocked her path.

"Wrong," Daemon said, appearing between Krustalus and Tezra, his sword already unsheathed. "She is *mine*."

She raised a brow, caught off guard by how possessive he sounded, like he owned her and no one would disagree when hell, he didn't even wish her to be his mate.

Before Daemon and Krustalus could fight, Patrico stole the show. Whipping out a sword, he targeted Mustaphus. The two were matched in size, except the ancient vampire had the advantage with his vampiric abilities. Bernard raced in to help, but Patrico waved him away.

What did Patrico have to prove? His head still sported a bloodied bandage—the damned macho hunter was going to get himself killed.

Tezra went for her sword again, but Voltan grabbed her wrist and shook his head. "Let...me...go, Voltan, or you're next!"

He gave her a lopsided grin. "If you do not behave, I will place you in the dungeon for your own safety."

She scowled at him. "I can teleport."

"Try it, if you like."

She attempted to teleport out of his confining grasp. Nothing. *Dammit!*

Not even Daemon would interfere this time, and she wanted to bite him for being so damned...vampiric, leaving the fight to Mustaphus and his challenger—to right the wrongs Mustaphus had committed against Patrico—like a gladiator fight in the days of old. The rest of the vampires watched, fascinated to see the outcome.

Patrico thrust his sword at Mustaphus, the vampire's dark brown eyes now coal black. He easily glided out of the blade's path.

If Tezra couldn't fight the vampire, she would attempt to distract him. *"Murderer!"* she screamed into Mustaphus's head.

Mustaphus glanced in her direction and growled. Enough to give Patrico a decisive jab in the chest, but the vampire suddenly moved and the blade missed his heart.

Mustaphus screamed out in pain. Blood dripped from the wound, the cut hurting his vanity. He retaliated, slicing his sword with a whoosh at Patrico's torso. The hunter dodged out of the wicked blade's path.

Tezra's heart nearly gave out. Krustalus gave Daemon a look confirming they would be next in the fight to the finish.

Again Patrico thrust, but Mustaphus deflected the weapon, the metals clanking in anger.

"You thought Lichorus loved you but she wanted Daemon

back."

Mustaphus's face hardened, but he didn't look in her direction this time. She had to think of something else to distract him!

Everyone seemed to hold their breath, yet the looks on their faces were of morbid curiosity. It didn't seem as though they hoped one would triumph over the other. Instead, they enjoyed the battle, as any might take pleasure in a bloody, violent spectator sport. Except Daemon.

She sensed he was still angry with Patrico for not protecting her earlier on, for hiding and saving his own skin. This fight was a matter of honor. If Patrico defeated his adversary, his prowess would exonerate him. But dammit! Patrico was already badly injured from the earlier fight at the beach house! How could he hope to win?

"Why kill the police officers, Mustaphus?" Tezra communicated solely to him, attempting to save Patrico's life. As far as she was concerned, the fact he'd come to save Katie from Krustalus at his own peril was all she needed to forgive him.

Again Mustaphus glanced in her direction and exposed his canines with a hiss.

For distracting him so thoroughly, she gave him a smug smile. *"You killed Patrico's hunter friend. Before this, you'd murdered several barflies."* She only assumed the woman he'd helped kill in front of Patrico was just one of many, and that he'd still been killing women to this day.

When she felt Voltan's grip loosening a bit, she tried to twist free, but he tightened his hold and she scowled at him.

Patrico sliced at Mustaphus's chest, connecting with the vampire's sword arm. Mustaphus cried out, the blood collecting across his sleeve. He quickly switched the sword to his left hand. Damn, he was ambidextrous?

"The police were on to you, weren't they Mustaphus?" she quickly said, before Patrico wore himself out and made a fatal mistake. *"They planned to take you, except Daemon's Uncle Solomon was at your home. He looked similar to you, despite protesting his innocence, the police officers killed him. He never fought them, did he? He was innocent all right, and your friend. Although, if he'd known the truth about you, he would have turned you in to Daemon. Wouldn't he? You were a master*

manipulator, and you got your best friend killed!"

Mustaphus suddenly teleported, appearing in front of her. He grabbed her throat with lightning speed. Before anyone else could react, Patrico bolted after him and with a thrust, jabbed the hunter's blade into the vampire's back, the metal reaching his heart with single-minded focus.

Mustaphus didn't have time to scream. His hand on Tezra's throat dissolved into ashes, and the remainder of him quickly followed.

Relieved Patrico lived to fight another day, Tezra bowed her head to him. Whatever else he had neglected to do in the past, he was not a coward in her eyes anymore. His chest heaving, he looked like a man exonerated from his past.

But the show wasn't over. As soon as Mustaphus lay in ruins on the stone patio in front of her, Krustalus lunged at Daemon.

"You will die, Krustalus!" Tezra shouted into his brain.

He offered her a sinister smile and struck at Daemon, their swords clanking with the impact. *"Do not think you can distract me like you did Mustaphus, sweet Tezra. That's what you were doing, no? You will be my ultimate challenge."*

Daemon whipped his sword around so quickly it was a blur.

Krustalus again impeded Daemon's progress with a sword block and resulting thunk.

"I promised to kill you, you bastard! I will still do so!"

He raised his brows, but kept his focus on the real threat, Daemon, prince of their people. *"It will be hard to do, if Voltan continues to hold your wrist."*

"It's him." Katie's voice cracked with emotion. "He killed Mom and Dad."

Tezra stared at the gun Katie held, her mind shifting through the ramifications. Bullets wouldn't work on the vampire unless they were silver, though even regular lead bullets could make him weaker for a short while. But she didn't want her sister getting involved. What if the vampires turned on her?

"We'll handle this in our own way," Daemon said, his voice stern. "The vampire way. Put the gun down."

"Katie." The panic rose in her blood as Tezra wriggled

against Voltan's confinement to reach her sister and stop her, but she couldn't free herself from the giant's strong grip. "Katie, honey, lower the gun."

Daemon thrust his sword again at Krustalus, and the vampire defended himself with a whack at Daemon's blade.

For a second, they separated.

A trigger clicked in rapid succession; the explosion deafening to Tezra's sensitive vampiric hearing. The smell of gunpowder discharged in the breeze, and three bullets slammed into Krustalus's chest. Not silver, or Krustalus would have dissolved into ashes.

Tezra glanced back at Katie who immediately turned the gun on Daemon, her face streaked with tears. "You changed Tezra against her will."

Alarmed, Tezra hastily summoned the ability to teleport. Not sure how it happened, but in a blur she slipped out of Voltan's grasp, her molecules shifting so fast, the giant didn't expect it. She didn't have time to think about it. The sensation of being lighter than air changed quickly to feeling pinned down by gravity. Even so, she managed to lunge between Katie and Daemon. If Katie shot Daemon and weakened him, he could die at Krustalus's hand and doom everyone who cared for the prince of the vampire clans.

Katie's eye couldn't fathom Tezra appearing so quickly, and she fired the gun at Daemon. The bullet ricocheted off Tezra's ribs and lodged in her heart before her mind could accept her sister had shot her. Tezra grabbed her chest and collapsed to her knees. Adrenaline flooded her system, preventing her from feeling the pain.

Realizing what she'd done, Katie screamed, "Tezra!" and threw the gun on the patio.

"Jesus," Daemon said, grabbing Tezra's arm.

"Concentrate on Krustalus!" she ordered Daemon, giving him a look that could kill. *"You know I'll live."*

Though she had serious doubts as the warm blood soaked her gown. Then she thought of the irony of the situation. If Daemon hadn't turned her, Katie's bullet would have killed her. If Daemon hadn't turned her, Katie probably wouldn't have shot at him and hit Tezra instead. If Daemon hadn't turned her, she wouldn't have been able to teleport in front of him and wouldn't have been shot no matter what. Such were the strange thoughts swimming through her mind while Katie sobbed next to her, her hand covering Tezra's seeping wound.

A streak of pain jolted her heart. Despite the shock, Tezra's mind drifted and people blurred. She noticed Bernard's left arm was cut when he drew near her. He yanked off his tuxedo jacket and bunched it against her wound while she lay on the hard stone patio. The funniest notion crossed her fuzzy brain— Bernard now had the best excuse in the world to ditch the tuxedo jacket he hated so. Patrico tore his jacket off too, and placed it under her head.

Vaguely, she heard Daemon and Krustalus's swords sweep through the air nearby and crash with clanks and clangs, bringing her attention back to the battle for power. Sweat beaded on Krustalus's brow, but Daemon looked like he hadn't even begun to fight.

Did the bullets help to slow Krustalus a little despite his being an ancient? She couldn't tell if Krustalus was any weaker, though Tezra was glad Katie shot him, for her own peace of mind. But the notion she would try to kill Daemon disturbed her most. Worse, knowing she was the reason for her sister's anguish all over again, Tezra felt sick. How would she ever make things right between them? Another shard of pain ripped through her, and she gritted her teeth.

"*Speak to me, Tezra,*" Daemon ordered.

"*Concentrate on the fight, Daemon,*" she snapped back, not wanting him distracted for an instant over her. He had to kill Krustalus, make him pay for his crimes. And not get himself killed in the process.

Daemon gave her a small smile and slashed again at Krustalus.

Tezra focused on the devil, Krustalus. The blood from the bullet wounds seeped through his shirt now. "*I'm sorry I was not the one to injure you, but as long as the one you hurt most retaliated, I'm glad.*" Tezra broadcast her telepathic communication for all the vampires to hear.

"*Your sister will die when Daemon is dead, but you...you will be my mate and endure many lifetimes with me, Tezra darling. Never fear.*"

"Help me up," she ordered Bernard, finished with the murderer's threats, though she felt so weak she wasn't sure even with his help she could stand.

Bernard's eyes widened. "No, Tezra, lie still until Daemon can take care of you."

"I have business to tend to, dammit, Bernard! Help me up."

Patrico waved his sword at Krustalus. "He was the vampire who was with Mustaphus and who killed the woman in the alley a decade ago."

Several vampires murmured comments.

But Tezra was certain the SCU hunter's words wouldn't influence the vampires much. Certainly, his statement wouldn't affect Krustalus.

Krustalus danced close by, dodging out of the path of Daemon's sword, his black shoes barely making a sound on the patio. She couldn't do much good, she imagined, but she had to strike at him, for her sake, for the sake of her parents, for Katie and because she'd promised the devil himself.

Thrice she tried to teleport to get closer, but her skin grew clammy, her breathing more shallow, her heart rate slower, and she didn't move an inch. Damn that she was so newly turned—well, and that a bullet was lodged in her heart. She felt her body trying to reject the foreign object penetrating the muscle, centimeter by painful centimeter. Having difficulty concentrating, her mind continually drifted, and she knew she needed blood.

Blood. The bloodlust filled her with a sense of urgency, desperation, but not for anyone's blood. Just Krustalus's.

She thought she saw the blonde Anatola smiling at her, but the vamp's face wavered before Tezra, and the expression wasn't sweet. Did she hope Tezra would die? The vamp had to know better. Maybe she sensed Tezra would leave Daemon after this was all over. Or maybe she was amused that Tezra's own sister had shot her.

Tezra gritted her teeth against the physical and emotional pain she felt. How could Katie have tried to shoot Daemon?

In a haze, she heard the sound of swords clanking again. Daemon! Again Tezra tried to teleport. At first, she didn't think anything had happened. Not until Katie screamed, Bernard swore and Patrico attempted to alert Daemon, bringing her back to consciousness. In her weakened condition, Tezra hadn't managed to stand upright, but instead lay on her side, facing Krustalus's ankle.

Good enough.

By the time he noticed her, it was too late. She bit hard into his ankle, through the trousers, sock, everything.

Immediately, Daemon stabbed his sword into Krustalus's heart before he could retaliate.

She hadn't even tasted a drop of the vampire's blood before the pant leg flattened against ashes. Her mind swirled in confusion. Daemon shouted something, peppered with a few choice curses that included her name, then the lights all went out.

೭

Daemon resheathed his sword and lifted Tezra off the floor. "Bring me blood." But before he moved her to his bedroom, Voltan stopped him.

"Six hunters are at the front door, my prince."

Daemon frowned. "They had better not think of arresting Tezra."

"The Chief of Police is with them."

"What?"

"He's told them about Krustalus and Mustaphus."

Patrico joined them. "I'll speak to them. Clear up the whole matter of Tezra's parents' deaths and my speedy resurrection. It's about time I did something right."

Daemon bowed his head, acknowledging the hunter had made his amends tonight. "If you need my help..."

Bernard stepped forward, favoring the wound he'd received when he'd helped Daemon fight the insurrection in the house, his face pinched with pain. "I'll back you up, Patrico. Let's take care of unfinished business."

೭

"Tezra love, stay with me," Daemon coaxed, his heart beating out of bounds. He transported her to his master bedroom suite and laid her in the bed.

Her face pale, she lay deathly still as he removed her bloody gown and pulled the blanket just below the wound. From the bathroom, he retrieved medical gauze, then began issuing orders telepathically while he covered Tezra's wound to stem the bleeding.

"*Maison, where's the doc?*"

"*On his way, Prince Daemon,*" Maison said.

"*The gun—has someone secured it?*"

"*I've put it away, out of Katie's reach,*" Atreides responded.

With all the strife, Daemon had forgotten all about Tezra's sister. "*Katie, who's watching her?*"

"*Mycenia. She's taken her to the guest bedroom and is getting her cleaned up and changed,*" Atreides said.

Dammit. The blood soaked through the gauze and Tezra was growing weaker by the second. Though he tried to stop the flow of blood from Tezra's wound, Daemon found her vampiric abilities were too new to work quickly enough to heal her injuries, and she was still losing way too much blood. "*Where the hell is Doc?*"

Atreides appeared with bagged blood and helped Daemon hook up an I.V. to Tezra's arm. "I'm sorry Doc Hollowell is taking so long. We're not sure what's—"

"I'm here, my prince," Doc Hollowell said, appearing behind them. He added painkiller to the I.V. "I was patching up a couple of your men left to guard the warehouse district who tangled with some of these rebels who hit you earlier." He considered the severity of Tezra's wound and shook his head. "Because she's so newly turned, her system is trying to fight the foreign object in her heart but is incapable of regenerating the broken blood vessels at the same time. If I were to remove the bullet, her body can concentrate on healing."

"Do it."

The doctor worked so quickly, he had the bullet it out in a matter of seconds, while Daemon and Atreides assisted him in the procedure. Then with vampiric precision, Doc Hollowell reconnected some of the larger blood vessels to lessen the bleeding until Tezra's body could take over. "Maison says her sister shot her and appears to be in a mild case of shock."

"If you'll look at Katie, I would be grateful." Daemon held Tezra's hand, rubbing his thumb over her soft, cool skin.

"And the hunters, Patrico and Bernard? Do you wish me to see to their injuries as well?" Doc Hollowell taped fresh gauze over Tezra's wound, then pulled the blanket higher.

"Yes, see to the hunters after you've made certain Katie will be all right."

"I will give you a report as soon as I'm through."

The doctor left Daemon and Atreides alone with Tezra. Daemon continued to touch her and reassure her he was with her and she'd be all right, but he had to make certain everything else was under control.

"Maison, what's going on with the SCU and the police?"

"They've taken Patrico's and Bernard's statements. Chief O'Malley has placed himself under arrest and they're picking up his brother-in-law as we speak."

"Did any rebel vampires escape the bash tonight?"

"Half a dozen, my prince. Fifteen of our men are searching for them now."

"The bodies of the fledglings—"

"Taken care of," Atreides said, a brow raised while he gave Daemon a stern look. "Hell, Daemon, we've lived long enough to know how to deal with a situation like this. Take care of your ward and leave the mundane stuff to us."

"Bernard wants to see Tezra," Maison said.

"No."

Silence.

"He can see her in the morning," Daemon added.

"He's storming up the stairs," Maison warned.

Bernard yanked the door open to a guest room down the hall. Wrong bedroom. He soon found the right one and barged in. "I want to see Tezra. I'm her bodyguard, after all." His gaze shifted to Tezra in the bed. "Is—is she going to be all right?"

"She'll be fine. She's sleeping and the bullet's out."

Bernard frowned at Daemon. "You're keeping her, aren't you? I've heard rumors you wouldn't take another mate again, but you wouldn't turn her and leave her unprotected, would you? Your brother's saying you plan to give her to him, but I want to know that you or your brother is committed to taking care of her. She's been through a damned lot on her own already."

Daemon gave Atreides a scathing look. "My brother speaks out of turn."

Giving Daemon an equally harsh look, Bernard said, "Then you'd better explain to the lady that she's your mate and make it clear to all what the deal is."

Daemon pulled a chair next to the bed, sat and caressed Tezra's cheek. "Not many would be so bold to tell me what to do, hunter."

Bernard gave him a demonic smile. "I'm not just anyone. I've been taking care of Tezra since she was a teen. And now I want your assurance she will always have your protection."

"I think you already know the answer to your concerns."

"I suspect I do."

Daemon considered Bernard's bloodied arm and motioned to the door. "The doctor will take care of your injury. You may see Tezra again in the morning, and you and Patrico are welcome to stay the night."

Bernard bowed his head, surprising Daemon. But then he remembered the hunter's vampiric roots and returned the polite gesture. Bernard quickly retired from the room.

"I have given Katie a mild sedative. She is sleeping in the guest room across from your master suite," Doc Hollowell said from the living room. *"And I've patched up the one hunter named Patrico. But the other has—no, he's returned."*

When no one else bombarded Daemon with messages, he said to Maison and Atreides, *"I do not wish to be disturbed unless the business is most urgent."*

"As you wish," Maison said. *"I will ensure the guards are in place tonight."*

"The rumor has spread that Tezra is your ward," Atreides said, "and I overheard several who are loyal to you saying they hoped you'd consider giving her to them, especially since you are adamant about not making her your mate."

"Atreides—" Daemon growled.

"We can talk later. I'll help the others who are chasing the remaining renegades." Atreides winked and vanished.

Daemon hadn't spoken the last about this matter of giving Tezra up to Atreides. When everything was quiet, Daemon's guards were in place and the injured hunters were both asleep in a guest bedroom, Daemon joined Tezra in bed. "Sweet huntress, will you be the death of me?"

No matter how much he told himself he couldn't do it, no matter how many times he reminded himself of his mistakes of the past, he couldn't let anyone else claim the enchantress.

Which left only one real option, and he hoped he wouldn't be damned for all eternity if he went down that dark path again.

Early the next morning, Daemon considered the way Tezra looked. Her color had returned and the doctor had removed the I.V. several hours earlier. The wound had not totally healed, but she was well on her way to mending.

"Katie's up and is concerned about her sister, but is afraid to see her," Atreides said from the greatroom.

"I'll be right down."

Not wanting to disturb Tezra's peaceful sleep, Daemon carefully slipped out from her soft, warm embrace. After dressing, he appeared in the greatroom to find it filled with people. Katie was sitting on one of the sofas, wringing her hands. Bernard and Patrico were drinking coffee nearby. Maison was dozing in a chair while Voltan stood near Katie like a monolithic statue, his arms folded, his posture wary. Atreides moved into the greatroom from the kitchen, carrying a tray of coffee mugs.

As soon as Katie saw Daemon, she jumped up. Instantly, Voltan seized Katie's arm, stopping her from approaching Daemon, and she cried out.

Daemon motioned for Voltan to release her.

Voltan grunted and did as he was told. *"After what she did last night, the wench should have been thrown in the dungeon."*

"I'm so sorry." Katie choked back tears. "Late last night, Patrico and Atreides told me why you changed Tezra. That it was totally her choice. I—I can't believe I shot her. She—she'll kill me when she's better."

Daemon led Katie back to the couch and encouraged her to sit. "Tezra would do anything to protect you, Katie. As will I and all of my people. She's still sleeping from the trauma, but otherwise she's fine."

Katie shook her head and rubbed her arms. "Physically, maybe. But—but I shot her! How can she be feeling emotionally about that?"

"You shot her by accident. You weren't thinking clearly. The situation was totally understandable." Though Daemon wished Tezra's sister had listened to him in the first place when he commanded her to put down the gun. In that regard, she reminded him eerily of Tezra and how disobedient she could be. Looking her beautiful self, she was supposed to have stayed out of trouble—that's all he'd wanted of Tezra last night.

Well, not any longer.

He'd fought with himself over the matter all night long, and his heart ruled his brain once again. Tezra was his to keep, and he'd hear no objections to the contrary from anyone.

"She's your—your mate now, isn't she?" Katie's eyes glistened with tears.

Everyone watched Daemon to see what he would say, even Maison who had the uncanny ability to wake from sleep when something was going on he wished to be part of.

But Daemon would speak to Tezra first to let her know of his decision before he spread the word to the rest of his people. "I will protect her always," he said evasively.

He could tell by the expressions on Maison and Atreides's faces that they already knew he'd made his decision. Maison seemed resigned. Atreides gave a small smile as if he knew it all along. Voltan muttered something under his breath about Daemon needing a tighter leash on the huntress. Bernard and Patrico looked clueless.

He just hoped Katie could handle the matter well enough in her fragile state.

Tezra found herself in Daemon's bed, naked, the bullet gone, her blood refreshed, but the ugly wound hadn't healed all the way yet. She sat up in bed and listened to the conversation in Daemon's living room, her heart already aching with regret at what she had to do next.

"Katie needs to be with her own kind," Patrico said.

"I have to agree," Bernard said.

Daemon disagreed. "Tezra won't want to live without Katie and—"

"I won't live without her," Katie adamantly added. "I—I'm so sorry about trying to shoot you, Daemon."

"You felt I'd taken advantage of your sister. I've told you

repeatedly, there are no hard feelings." Daemon sounded truthful, yet his voice hinted at concern.

"She will kill me when she wakes," Katie moaned.

"She is awake," Voltan warned.

Tezra dressed in a pale blue sweater and a pair of denims, dreading what she had to do next. Halfway down the stairs, Daemon met her, his face full of concern. He wordlessly wrapped his arm around her waist and transported her to the living room, then sat her on the couch.

Atreides, Maison, Katie, Bernard, Patrico and Voltan stood next to the grouped couches, and everyone's face showed rabid anxiousness.

Once she was sitting on the couch, she fought the emotion that was tearing her up inside, turned to Daemon and said the most difficult thing she ever had. "I can't stay with you. Not for now." She swallowed hard. "After all she's been through, Katie needs me. I have to reintroduce her into our world. We need some time alone."

She sensed his barely controlled anger while he stood next to her, not saying a word.

Katie wrung her hands, her lips parted in surprise, her green eyes wide. But she didn't contradict Tezra. Didn't say it was okay to stay with Daemon. Tezra took a deep breath. "Katie?"

Katie looked at Daemon, then her gaze shifted to the other vampires, and finally the hunters. She nodded.

Tezra clenched her teeth to keep the tears at bay. Her hint of hope that Katie might be all right living amongst the vampires was shattered. But it was selfish for Tezra to want this after all Katie had suffered.

Daemon crouched in front of Tezra, took her hands and opened his mouth to object. But she pulled away from him and pressed her finger against his lips. She didn't want to fight him on this issue because her own feelings of remorse were barely under control, and she feared caving in—which she knew would be disastrous for both of them.

"I have to do this. She's the last of my family and I owe it to her." Because no matter how things had turned out right in the end, Tezra was still to blame for her sister's lost years. She couldn't and wouldn't abandon her at this point in her life. "For now, Katie will enroll in the SCU school, and I'll conduct criminal investigations—what I was trained for. Except I'll be my own boss. No more SCU to tell me what I can or can not do. Katie and I will get an apartment and Bernard will watch out for us."

Daemon stood, his hands fisted at his sides, his eyes darkening to midnight. "But you can do this from my home."

"No. I need..." *To make amends with Katie. To help her readjust to hunter life.* "I need to do this, Daemon. For now."

His jaw ticked. "You'll need blood."

Swallowing hard, she motioned to the kitchen. "I can get hospital blood like you do."

His face remained hard and unyielding. She knew he would fight her on it, but she wasn't backing down.

To her surprise and disappointment, he bowed his head, acquiescing. "So be it, Tezra. Your home is mine when you choose to return."

"No," Maison said, his own voice dark and committed.

Her mouth dropped in astonishment.

Daemon waved his hand to silence his friend without taking his severe gaze off Tezra.

Atreides objected next. "You can't let them—"

Daemon silenced him with a glare.

Atreides glowered back but bowed his head.

Voltan straightened his tall stature. "I'll escort the ladies to where they wish to go."

"Bernard and Patrico can," Tezra countered, wanting to completely cut her ties with the vampires if this was going to work. Tears pricked her eyes, and she was unable to look at Daemon.

"Bernard and Patrico will go with you, but Voltan will take you," Daemon said, then vanished. Not a kiss, a hug or a word of goodbye.

Well, what did she expect? She'd cut him to the quick, but he had all the vampires of America to console him. The notion didn't dissolve the block of ice wedged in her heart.

"Let's go." Tezra's cheeks grew wet before she reached the

front door.

Life without him would be pure hell, but life with him wouldn't be much better, knowing how much she needed to help Katie readapt to her life.

Katie grabbed her hand and squeezed. "Thank you for doing this for me."

Well, that cinched the notion Katie didn't want to stay with the vampires.

Bernard escorted them to the SUV parked in the circular drive. "There's always me. As I vaguely recall, you once said if I hadn't taken you hostage and secured you at Atreides's house, you would have married me."

Tezra raised her brows. "I thought Daemon told Atreides to wipe your mind. And besides, I said, '*If* you hadn't taken me hostage.' After the deed was done it was a little late for backtracking." Tezra glanced back at the house, her heart lost in a quagmire of stinging nettles. No one watched from the windows. It was as if Daemon had cut her loose, and she was already dead to him.

Couldn't he understand how she needed to make amends to Katie? How much harm that needed to be undone? It was the best option, so why did her heart ache as if the bullet was still lodged in the center of it?

"Dammit, Daemon," Atreides said to him later that night while Daemon poured himself another glass of wine. "Other ancients might go after her."

"Why do you think I sent Voltan with them?" Daemon couldn't shake loose the anger he felt that she would decide this and not be open to his suggestion to stay with him at the house. On the other hand, he knew she wouldn't be able to stay away from him for long, and that gave him a sliver of sinister pleasure. She was bound to him, body and soul, and the sooner she learned this, the better for both of them. Yet, he still couldn't censor the irritation running through his blood that she'd leave him. Daemon had every intention of watching her himself most of the time, not trusting that anyone could protect her like he would.

"She expected you to fight more to keep her." Atreides collapsed on the sofa.

Maison poured himself a glass of wine. "I did too, though I knew when you silenced me you had a plan."

"She needs her freedom. And to take care of Katie for the time being. Without my interference." Daemon took a deep breath. "She would have fought me on this until I gave in. But she'll come back to me."

Atreides leaned back against the sofa. "I wouldn't be so sure of that. What if she feels our people won't accept her? That she's better off with Katie for several years? Most of our people slighted her. Ralton even shoved her into Lichorus's path, but I was trying to keep Mustaphus from reaching Tezra at the time."

Daemon's blood heated. "And?"

"Ralton is dead."

Daemon paced, unable to control his feelings. "The same with four others who tried to stop me from interceding on her behalf. Some of Krustalus's rebels. Bernard was on hand to deal with others. And Maison..." He bowed to his friend for his help with more. "What about Anatola? She helped to lure Tezra to Lichorus."

"In custody," Maison said, his voice firm. "Your mate, whether you choose to call her that or not, rules beside you. Any who try to harm her in my jurisdiction will be punished accordingly."

His mate. Daemon couldn't deny Tezra was that for him and much more, a part of his soul that made him whole. "I want Tezra to decide Anatola's fate."

"As you wish, my prince." Maison finished his wine. "I take it you want her watched at all times."

"Always."

"What about when she has a craving for a blood bond?" Atreides asked.

"You heard the lady. She will buy packaged blood." Daemon allowed himself a small smile, the dark side of his nature appearing.

Knowingly, his brother and friend chuckled.

"You didn't tell her bagged blood won't quench some of the bloodlust or sexual craving she'll have after a few days of drinking it, did you?" Atreides asked.

"I'm sure she would have thought it was a ploy to get her to stay with me," Daemon said darkly.

"Three days, a week at the most," Maison said.

Even three days would be the longest time of his life, Daemon thought, hoping like hell the stubborn woman would quickly come to her senses. If not, he'd come up with another plan.

Chapter Sixteen

A week after Tezra had left Daemon, Atreides downed the rest of his glass of wine and clunked the glass on Daemon's bar while Maison, Voltan and Daemon looked on. "I don't understand why you are waiting so damned long to make Tezra yours. If you don't want her—"

Daemon raised his hand to silence his brother. "She will come around. Katie's adjusting as well, making hunter friends, doing great in her training, but Tezra's afraid to leave her alone."

Maison shook his head. "She is as stubborn as you, my prince."

"Do you want me to talk some sense into the huntress?" Voltan asked, his brows raised.

"She will come around," Daemon repeated, annoyed his people didn't trust in his judgment.

"It's been a whole week," Atreides reminded him as if he didn't know, "and she hasn't made any effort to contact you. Even Katie says Tezra has forbidden her to speak of you. The huntress won't capitulate."

Daemon turned to Voltan. "Are you ready to accompany me to the hunter's home for troubled teens?"

Voltan's dark expression took on a lighter, more humorous air. "Most assuredly, my lord."

"Need my help?" Maison asked.

Daemon patted Voltan's shoulder. "I'm certain we'll get the results we want without too much of a fuss."

"I'll be near Tezra's apartment, watching out for her and Katie, if anyone cares," Atreides said, and vanished.

"He wants her for his own, Daemon, and if you don't claim her, he wishes to," Maison said.

"He knows he can't have her. We're to meet Bernard at the home. I'll let you know how it goes later."

Daemon and Voltan teleported to the white brick, sprawling one-story building that looked like a retirement home for senior citizens except bars covered all the windows. Manicured lawns and expertly-trimmed shrubs gave the illusion of a well-ordered and pleasant enough place. Had the running of the home been changed for the better over the years? Daemon hoped so for the sake of the teens currently incarcerated within.

Bernard greeted them at the front door, his look as dark as Daemon felt. As soon as Voltan, the hunter and Daemon entered the administration office, a snippy, officious woman snapped at them. "Visiting hours are from three to four. You'll have to come back then."

"I will see Mr. Worth now," Daemon said, annoyed he'd been unable to reach the administrator over the phone in the past few days.

The woman's green eyes narrowed, and she pursed her already colorless thin lips. "Do you have an appointment?"

"He doesn't need an appointment," Voltan growled.

"Daemon, prince of the American vampire clans is here about human rights violations. As the SCU-appointed hunter bodyguard for the victim who was incarcerated here, I represent both Tezra Campbell and the SCU in this matter. Now kindly tell Mr. Worth we are here to see him, or things could get rather nasty," Bernard said.

The woman's eyes shifted from Bernard to Daemon and her ruddy face took on a gray sheen. "Mr. Worth is in an important meeting. Have a seat and I'll be right back."

She stomped out of the office and down the hall in three-inch heels, and Daemon shook his head. "Things could get rather nasty?" he asked Bernard.

Bernard's spine stiffened. "I don't need to extend fangs to show how angry I can get. If Tezra had ever told me what happened to her here, believe me, I would have straightened this place out years ago."

Within a matter of minutes, two heavily armed security guards arrived, with no sign of Mr. Worth.

"We do not need an escort," Daemon curtly responded to

the show of force, "unless you're here to protect us from your incarcerated teens."

"We're here to show you out, peaceably if we can, or not. Your choice," one of the stony-faced men said.

Bernard took a step forward, but Daemon motioned to Voltan to stop him. "We came here in a civilized manner, but I can see the home and the way the staff manages it hasn't changed. We'll take this to those with more authority. No sense in dealing with peons."

"But—" Bernard objected.

"Bring Bernard," Daemon ordered Voltan. *"We go to the SCU top brass this time."*

Several hours later after wrangling a meeting with an SCU board of inquiry, Daemon, Voltan and Bernard sat before a group of five hunters and five huntresses.

Every one of them appeared as though they were carved from marble, their looks harsh and unyielding, but Daemon sensed they did not feel as self-assured as they pretended.

"These are the human rights violations I had mentioned to you over the phone concerning the home. I believe you have the jurisdiction and ability to right these wrongs, and I will leave it up to you." But only if they did what Daemon expected of them.

Voltan passed out copies of Tezra's journal to the ten-member board.

While the men and women perused the papers, one of the women identified herself as Ingrid and said, "You are aware troubled teens often lie about matters such as these."

"The evidence supports Tezra's allegations. Every time she attempted to see her sister, she was returned to the home and put in the hole, as the home calls it. A woman named Elizabeth Peterson let the rogue vampire Krustalus into the hole and this vampire fed on Tezra several times, claiming her for his own. Tezra writes about the vampire, but didn't know his name at the time. How can you condone the actions of the home's staff?"

"We will conduct a thorough investigation of these allegations," Ingrid said, "but I just wanted to make you aware that juveniles placed there are not the most trusted of our hunter corps."

"You say this, though Tezra's only crime was suspecting that a vampire murdered her parents and trying to prove her allegations. For this 'crime' she was placed in an abusive home when she could have lived with her aunt's friend who pleaded with you to allow her to take her in."

Ingrid's face remained hard. Most of the board members stopped reading the papers and focused their attention on Daemon.

Though he attempted to keep a professional and diplomatic posture, he was certain the reaction of the members meant his tactful persona was slipping.

A couple of the men shifted slightly so they could access their sheathed swords. Bernard glowered at them as if to intimidate them to just try something. Voltan pressed his giant hands against the table, readying himself to leap from his chair.

Daemon's voice grew dark and deadly. "Report to me when you have your findings. You may try to dismiss Tezra as an unstable, troubled teen and not worthy of your concern, but she is now quite the heroine in every SCU circle across the States. I have never been one to rely on the media for support, but try my patience in this matter, and the abuses she suffered will become national knowledge." He gave Ingrid an elusive smile and bowed his head. "Have a nice day."

Voltan seized Bernard's arm, and the three of them transported to Daemon's house. Bernard paced across the floor, scowling while he slammed his fist into the palm of his hand. "Ingrid and her staff better do what's right."

Voltan leaned against the fireplace mantel. "They would not defy Prince Daemon in this matter. That Ingrid woman will see to it that the home is thoroughly cleansed. I'd bet my best sword on it."

Atreides channeled a message to Daemon. *"Carissus, leader of South Carolina, has just arrived, trying to obtain an audience with Tezra. He thinks maybe you might consider giving her to him if Tezra is agreeable. Katie won't let him in the apartment, but she wants to speak to you again about Tezra."*

"She only has to ask." But Daemon sure wished she could influence Tezra to return to him without his interference. *"Voltan will bring Katie here."*

Within the hour, Daemon met with Katie in the greatroom while Bernard excused himself and Voltan checked on the guard detail.

"How is Tezra?" Daemon asked his usual question, and he knew he'd get the same response from Katie.

"You know how she is. She's going mad. Make her come back to you. She's impossible to live with! But she still thinks I need her help. I'm fine, but she refuses to believe me. She thinks if she returns to you, I'll fall apart or something. Tell her I'll be all right. Take her back, Make her return to you."

"I vowed to leave her be until she comes to her senses. I don't want to force my decision on her."

Katie growled. "Force her, already. She can't live without you, and I can't bear to live with her the way she is. Besides, your place is a hundred times nicer and safer, and potential vampire suitors would quit harassing us."

"She can't hold out more than a few days. Though quite frankly, I didn't think she'd make it three." He took a deep breath. "Give it a few more days. If she doesn't see the light, I'll take matters into my own hands."

"You'll have to, Daemon. I don't think there's anyone any more stubborn than she is. As to another matter, Atreides told me you were straightening out the home because of the way they treated Tezra, which affected me horribly too. I have to thank you. Oh, and another thing. This morning while I was in hunter swordsmanship class, I overheard a huntress whisper to another that my dad had been in trouble with the SCU. Could you check into it?"

At once, Daemon feared what he might uncover. In no way did he want to learn that the girls' father had been a rogue. He bowed his head. "I will let you know what I find." And he prayed his findings would not devastate the sisters once he learned the truth.

Two days later, Tezra walked out of the shower in her new apartment and heard the doorbell ringing. Yanking a towel around her, she cursed all the way to the front door, her mood foul, on edge, but no matter how much she tried to improve it, she couldn't find a way.

Looking through the peephole, she saw Katie standing on the porch. Tezra jerked the door open, spun around and headed back through her living room.

"What are you doing home again? Aren't you supposed to

be in school? And where's your apartment key? Lose it again?"

Katie didn't answer her questions, instead started in with a lecture. "For solving the policemen's murders, you're a hero to the police force, Tezra. Not only that, but the SCU has named you their guest of honor at the ball next week."

Tezra studied her, then nodded. She should be happy. She glanced at the stacks of letters from SCU investigators all over the States, piled high on their coffee table, congratulating her for a job well done.

The Chief of Police had stepped down and been arrested for his complicity in his sister's murder. The District Attorney's office had charged Jane Cramer's husband with a murder-for-hire scheme.

Katie seemed to be doing well, but Tezra couldn't shake loose the worry that she'd leave and her sister would return to her shell.

For twelve whole days, she'd been drinking hospital blood when she felt she needed it, but something was the matter with her. Every time she got close to humans, her attention shifted to their damned pulse. The distraction was making it difficult to concentrate on her investigative work. Not only that, but she couldn't stop thinking about the way Daemon made love to her, his tongue tangling with hers, his fingers stroking her nub, the way he sucked hard on her nipples. She barely had enough sleep, just like when she'd tried to chase down Krustalus, and her mood suffered for it.

"Daemon asked when you were going to decide about Anatola's disposition."

Tezra stared at the floor for a minute, then lifted her head. "She wanted me to die, but she stated she'd support Daemon's rule. How many more vampires feel the same way, but he hasn't imprisoned them for their views?"

"Yes, but she led you to Lichorus to be murdered. The others didn't."

Tezra shrugged, figuring she didn't have anything to gain by making the woman hate her more, nor could she afford alienating others who were the woman's friends. "She did me a big favor by letting me know where Lichorus was. Tell Daemon to release her, as long as she still intends to support his rule."

"I think you should tell him yourself."

"I'm sure he's as busy as I am." Tezra knew if she saw him

again, her resolve to stay with Katie would melt away. She headed back down the hall, but when Katie didn't respond, she stopped and turned.

Katie's pink, glossy lips tightened.

"Well, Katie?"

"He keeps asking me how you're doing. If you believe he's going to vanish from your life, think again."

She didn't want him to vanish from her life. Besides, she was just his ward. Her focus had to be on Katie's welfare.

"He went after the staff in charge of the home for troubled teens."

"What?" Tezra couldn't contain the surprise in her voice.

Katie lifted her chin. "Yeah. He registered a complaint against the home—targeted the staff, the fact they wouldn't let you see me when I was in the hospital, and outlined sixty-two other human rights violations based on entries in the diary you kept back then. The SCU has started a big inquiry into the home's procedures, and heads are already rolling."

"My diary?" Tezra shook her head, her knees weak. It must have been mixed in with the investigative files she had hidden in the wall. *Daemon.* She couldn't believe he'd go after them for her. To think she'd filed complaints for the last eight years with any new SCU senior staff member after she'd been released from the home but no one had listened, and one vampire had made all the difference. Well, not any vampire, but Daemon, prince of the American clans. God, she loved him.

She motioned to the open door. "Shut the door, will you, Katie? Our neighbor across the hall is a very uptight old guy. I'm sure he wouldn't like seeing me parading around my living room in a towel."

Katie snorted. "He's probably got his eyeball glued to the peephole."

"I thought you had school today."

"School holiday. Seriously, Tezra, Daemon's worried about you."

Tezra ignored her and headed down the hall to her bedroom, not wanting to think about the seductive vampire. For the twelve days, two hours and thirty-two minutes since she'd left Daemon's house, Katie had abided by Tezra's rules. If Tezra didn't think about him, her heart couldn't ache for him, right?

Right. That's why she couldn't sleep, and why her mind shifted from her work to thinking about him twenty-four, seven. The front door shut with a clunk. "It's not his fault he turned you, but mine. And dammit, Tezra, he's worried about you."

"He needn't be." After all, she wasn't his mate! Tezra whipped around and stalked back into the living room. "And it is *not* your fault he turned me."

"Okay, you're right. If you want to take credit for Dad's screw-up, so be it."

"What?" Tezra tugged the bath towel higher.

"Daemon discovered Dad was a crime investigator too."

Tezra frowned, wondering where Daemon had ever gotten such a ridiculous notion. "Dad wasn't. He worked in accounting at the hospital."

Katie shook her head. "No, well, yes he did do that, as a cover for his real job. He was a deep-cover SCU investigator, but he was also moonlighting for the city police force on the side for extra money-hunting vampires, illegal as hell as far as the SCU was concerned without proper licensing. And, guess what he discovered?"

Knees buckling, Tezra leaned against the back of the sofa, her stomach churning with upset. "He was not looking into the police officer killings."

"He was, Tezra. The Chief of Police knew all about it but since no one had ever thought to question him about Dad, he didn't want to give our father and our family a black eye. He didn't realize you and I have both felt responsible for our parents' deaths."

Katie took a deep breath. "So, because Dad was investigating and apparently getting close to proving Krustalus was the one who had killed the police officers, the renegade vampire targeted him. As for Mom, maybe he assumed since she was a hunter, Dad and she talked about the case he was working on. Or maybe Krustalus figured she'd come after him next for murdering her husband, and that's why he killed both Mom and Dad."

Tezra's thoughts swirled with the implication.

"He didn't figure you were really a threat to him, but he's played with your mind all these years. Not only that, but he wanted you to replace the woman he'd lost, but you were too young yet. And why not want you? You were the perfect challenge. Because I...well, I wasn't in any shape to respond to much of anything, he didn't bother me."

"It wasn't my fault he came after Mom and Dad," Tezra whispered, her mind tackling the twist of events. The moisture in her throat all but evaporated.

"No. And another thing? Dad had a bad gambling habit. That's why he had to sneak around to do the other job. He needed to pay off his debt or lose the house. Anyway, so no reason to carry the guilt around any longer, 'kay?"

Tezra couldn't believe it. But when she studied Katie, her red hair dangling over her shoulders in a fiery mass, her green eyes sincere, Tezra realized something else didn't add up. Katie was wearing the typical training school garb—black martial arts-style pants, black turtleneck, leather boots concealing the hunter's blade, wrist blades. "I thought you said school was out."

Katie's eyes sparkled, and her lips curved up. "Caught me. I took a brief break. You're right. Need to get back to classes."

Tezra scowled at her. "I'm paying good money to have you trained and—"

"Yeah, thanks for everything. See ya later." Katie bounced out the door and slammed it.

Tezra stood staring after the door. Her father had been the one to bring their home crashing down around them, and both Katie and Tezra had felt it was their own fault for all those years. She couldn't believe it.

As for Daemon, this concern he had that other ancients might want her for their mate was utterly ridiculous. Hell, most of his people were furious with him for taking up with her. And now, no one wanted her as a mate, vampire, human or hunter. Well, Bernard maybe. And occasionally a desperate vampire who turned up at her door, expecting an audience.

Craving Daemon's touch, she shoved her wet hair out of her face, wishing she had a crystal ball that would reveal whether Katie would be all right if Tezra returned to him. She longed for his spine-tingling kisses and wished she could have everything else he dished out.

Walking back into the bathroom, she intended to get on with her day. Time to discover who was stealing financial files from police headquarters, then make plans for a night of margaritas with Mandy Salazar. She wondered then if Mandy had known anything about her father's work with the police. Nah. She didn't start working as a police dispatcher until a few years later.

After drying her hair, Tezra returned to the bedroom. When she reached for her lingerie drawer, Daemon said, "No need to dress."

Her heart racing and her head spinning, she whipped around. Lying in her bed under the pale blue sheet, Daemon rested his head in the crook of his arms. His black diamond eyes looked admiringly at her nude body. His obvious full-blown erection reached heavenward.

God, he was beautiful, but cold chills snaked down her skin, and her heart throbbed with a deep ache. She wanted him, lusted after him with such overwhelming need it scared her. "That sneaky little sister of mine! She invited you in when I was halfway down the hall!" she said, trying to get her emotions under control and distract herself from wanting to devour him whole.

He grinned satanically. "Katie got tired of my asking about you, *and* she says your mood has been out of sorts. She thought I might be able to...help. You know, you are the most stubborn woman I've ever met. I had intended to intervene several times over the last few days...well, in truth since the minute you left me, but I wanted to see how long you'd attempt to resist me." He raised a brow, his mouth lifting in a self-satisfied smile.

Conceited vampire.

"You shouldn't be here." Tezra jerked her panties and bra out of the drawer. She fought the tears that threatened to spill at the sight of him. "I have to be here for Katie." She choked on the words. She quickly brushed away tears, her heart sinking like an anchor into the darkest depths of the Mariana Trench.

In a flash, he stood behind her. His rough hands caressed her arms, sending a rush of warmth through her. "Tezra, love." He pulled her hair away from her neck, exposing the sensitive skin, then nuzzled her shoulder. "You haven't fed."

She *hmpfed*, trying to ignore the way his touch undid her. Even now the sound of his heart hammering made her own pick up its pace. The blood rushing through his veins called to her, pleaded with her to consume her fill. The friction of his warm skin rubbing against hers stoked a fire deep inside her. He smelled of Irish soap and pure musky Daemon.

"I'm all yours, Tezra." His fingers stroked her nipples, sending sparks of erotic sensations through every nerve ending.

She dropped her panties on the floor. His velvet lips mouthed her shoulder, distracting her, making her crave what she knew she shouldn't want. "But Katie—"

"She wants you to return to me. It's all she's told me the last few days, once she realized how attached you were to me. How you couldn't bear to be without me." He gave her another conceited smile.

She ground her teeth. The blood pulsing in his veins called to her, begging her for satisfaction. He rubbed his erection against her bottom, and her short curly hairs dampened.

"Why hasn't she told me?" But then again, she had. And Tezra hadn't believed her. Hadn't felt her sister would truly be all right without her guidance. If Tezra had only been there when their parents had faced Krustalus...

"Come to bed."

"I don't know that I can do this yet," she hissed, unable to keep her canines from extending. *Leave*, she silently pleaded, but he was a drug she couldn't resist, addictive as hell.

He chuckled against her ear and nibbled the lobe. "Come, use that pent-up frustration on me. You can give my people hell tonight at the bash I'm having."

"Not another—"

Licking her jaw, he wrapped his arms securely around her waist and pulled her against his hard body. "The last one, well, that was to bring Krustalus and Mustaphus to their just rewards."

She ran her hand over his arm in a loving caress. "And Lichorus." When he held her like this, he felt so right, and she never wanted to let him go.

He lifted her in his arms, and she dropped the bra on the floor. Carrying her to the bed, he said, "It'll be different this time."

She shook her head, not believing his words. "They hate me. Though all that really matters is my sister's emotional stability."

He raised his dark brows. "My people will love you, or else.

And your sister will be fine. You are my mate, for now and always. But I will give you more time to realize this."

"Your mate?" She socked him in the shoulder. "You sound like some bigheaded barbarian." But she couldn't believe he'd say she would be his mate. What if she turned out like the other women in his life? Rogue vampires he had to destroy?

He laid her on the bed, grabbed her ankles and shoved her legs apart. Grinning, he sank into her. "That's what you love about me, Tezra. I'm your barbarian. You wouldn't have it any other way."

"I'm your ward, you said," she reminded him. "You would never take a mate."

"The minute I saw you crouching at the police crime scene, I was compelled to make you mine, vixen."

His erection stretched her to the limit, and his hands massaged her swollen breasts. But it was his blood calling to her at a fevered pitch that distracted her most. When his neck was in reach, she didn't wait a minute longer to satisfy her bloodlust, the need as grave as if she'd crossed the desert without a drop of water to quench her thirst. Only this time, she used the utmost restraint—though it nearly killed her to show moderation—and bit into his skin more gently. His moan of pleasure filled her with orgasmic delight, and she sucked with enthusiasm. Her spirits lifted, and she knew then she couldn't resist him ever.

She raised her hips and met his plunges, concentrating on the feel of him bearing down deep inside her. She wanted him like this, forever, making love to her, sharing their blood, caring for one another like soul mates did. She knew then they were bound to each other in ways she couldn't fathom.

Another orgasm rippled through her, taking her to that higher plane as he came, his seed warming her, his hard body rocking her, his thoughts reaching out to her. *"I love you, Tezra, for all time."*

The second bash was as well represented as the first, but this time only vampires were in attendance. Katie had a date with a hunter in Portland while Patrico and Bernard watched over her there. And she'd convinced Tezra she wanted to live in the hunter's dorm, to be with hunters her own age. To enjoy life to its fullest. Tezra wouldn't deny her that chance to regain her life.

This time the amount of blood drinks being offered at the bash was in short supply. Several drank wine instead. Was this going to be a typical vampiric party then? Filled with debauchery?

Butterflies fluttered in Tezra's stomach at the sinful thought, though after the earlier love-fest with Daemon, she was prepared for anything. She stiffened her spine and moved away from Daemon, who greeted his guests with aplomb. Atreides, Voltan, Maison and ten other extremely loyal vampires Daemon had pointed out to her earlier stood nearby, watching for any signs of revolt or any threats to her safety.

Anatola was the first vampire to greet Tezra, bowing politely, her blonde hair piled on her head in swirling curls, a black satin dress clinging to her curves, her blood-stained lips turned up in a small smile, but her eyes held no warmth.

"Daemon has made you accept me," Tezra stated, trying to keep the anger out of her words.

The ancient vampiress's smile broadened. "As was necessary. You do not think any of us would easily bow to a fledgling vampiress, do you?"

"Because I'm an investigator with the SCU and before this trained as a hunter." Born as a hunter, first and foremost.

Anatola shrugged. "Because you are a fledgling. You have the power, being the one he loves and respects now above all others. Do you not see how we might feel petty about it? Either you accept your fate and grow with it or you give up our prince."

Daemon stood across the room, as formally dressed as before. Although his clothes were similar to most, he stood out as the prince of his people with his elegant posture and charming manner. Others spoke with him, but his dark brown eyes fixed on her and Anatola. She was sure he was trying to hear their conversation, but with all the telepathic and voiced communications swirling about them, she figured he couldn't make out what they said. She attempted to keep her expression neutral so he wouldn't feel obligated to leap in and protect her. If she were to win his people over, she'd have to stand up to them without his help.

Tezra squared her shoulders and raised a glass of wine. Before she spoke, all conversation ceased. She declared with heartfelt surety, "I am Daemon's lifemate."

Daemon lifted a brow, his dark countenance quickly turning light. Their gazes locked, and she blew him a kiss. "For all eternity."

The arrogant smile curving his mouth said he already knew.

Before she could end the conversation with Anatola, Daemon appeared at Tezra's side.

"To my lifemate, who all shall respect and protect always." Daemon raised his glass.

Everyone toasted to them, and Daemon and Tezra drank their wine. He slipped his arm around her waist, warming her to the marrow of her bones. How could she have stubbornly resisted him for so long?

"This calls for a celebration, love."

"We're already celebrating, Daemon." She knew full well what he was up to and was glad for it. "If you intend to whisk me away to someplace quiet…"

He leaned down and kissed her lips. "You have agreed to be my mate, which means we have to seal the bargain."

She laughed, loving the way he was so sexually attuned to her. "We have sealed the bargain many times already. Besides, what will your people think if you leave the party?"

His lips hiked up devilishly. "They will be most pleased. When the prince and his mate leave, the guests are free to do as they like."

"In other words, the sooner we vacate the premises, the happier your guests will be?"

"That's the gist of it."

"Well, hell, Daemon, whisk me away then. I'll do whatever it takes to please your people."

"*Our* people, and now that you're here to stay, they will find me a much more agreeable leader and will know the reason."

"Our people." Tezra's heart swelled with pride. She hadn't won them all over, but she was making headway. Most importantly, Katie was well on her way to having a good life and Tezra was too.

He kissed her hand and slipped a ring on her finger, a sparkling emerald and diamond-clustered beauty that stole her breath. "To replace the Mickey Mouse watch you got as a youngster when you wanted your birthstone ring like Katie's."

Tears filled her eyes, but before she could tell him how much she loved him, blackness surrounded her. She knew as soon as they "landed" she'd be soaring the galaxy in Daemon's arms again.

Only this time—as lifemates forever.

About the Author

To learn more about Terry Spear, please visit www.terryspear.com. Send an email to Terry at terryspear@ymail.com or join her newsletter to read free serialized stories and receive all her updates.

GREAT
CHEAP
FUN

Discover eBooks!

CPSIA information can be obtained at www.ICGtesting.com
Printed in the USA
LVOW131456190313

325017LV00002B/284/P